Praise

for The Dad Who Stayed

"New and full of surprises."
—2025 Utah Book Awards

"*The Dad Who Stayed* depicts with hilarity and deep compassion the inner world of a kindergarten-age boy beginning to navigate the outer world. Every emotional payoff, whether flash-of-lightning funny or tearfully joyful, is earned through a rich depth of honesty that is the polar opposite of sentimentalism."
—Darrin McGraw, co-author of *Animal Future*

"*The Dad Who Stayed* is a fun, nostalgic trip through childhood in the 1970s. It brought to my mind memories of my own experiences and things I'd never thought about them before."
—Reader L

"David Rodeback deals with difficult subjects with grace and humor. These stories of relationships across the lifespan will make you laugh, break your heart, and enrich your soul."
—Reader S

Also by David Rodeback

Poor As I Am and Other Stories at Christmas
Hearts Together (a novel)

The Dad Who Stayed
and other stories

David Rodeback

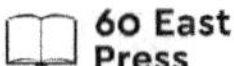

60 East Press — American Fork, Utah

60 East Press
867 N 60 E
American Fork, UT 84003
60eastpress.com

"Marie" first appeared in *Metamorphosis: A Collection of Poetry and Prose*, published in July 2019 by LUW Press.

"Her Voice" first appeared in *Shadowed Hourglass: A Collection of Poetry and Prose*, published in 2021 by LUW Press.

"There Might Be Another Way" first appeared in *Lost and Found: Second Chance Romance Stories*, published in 2022 by The Writers' Cache.

LCCN: 2023942099
Trade Paperback ISBN: 979-8-9883510-2-3
eBook ISBN: 979-8-9883510-3-0

Printed in the United States of America

No part of this book's text was written by or with the direct assistance of artificial intelligence (AI).

Book cover by BookCoverZone

Contents

Short Stories

For Mom and Dad

The Dad Who Stayed

60 East
Press

60 East Press — American Fork, Utah

Prologue

Some dads taught their boys to fish, play basketball, and fix cars. At worst, they taught them to curse when they are angry or to sit around watching television in the evening and on holidays, while the women work.

My dad taught me to run away.

I don't think he knew he was teaching me that, or cared. If it ever crossed his mind, he probably thought that, by leaving Mom two months before I was born, he had avoided affecting me at all.

He was wrong.

· · · · ● · ● · ● · · ·

My earliest memory of childhood is asking Mom, when I was three or four, where my daddy was. She shrugged, looked a little sad, and said softly, "You don't have a daddy, Joey."

"Oh," I said. I must have been concerned, because I remember asking, "Is that okay?"

"It's okay," she said.

We lived in a small two-story house on Sixth Street. Our apartment was the whole first floor. An overweight, bald man with a beard rented the second floor. He worked nights, so we tried to be quiet during the day. We must have been quiet enough, because I never heard him complain. I hardly ever even saw him.

It was the early 1970s, and the people in our neighborhood fell roughly into two groups. One was mostly university students. They were busy burning draft cards and women's underwear and experimenting with drugs and free love. I didn't know what "free love" meant, but it didn't sound like a bad thing.

This group spray-painted a word on stop signs around the city. Mom said the word was *war*, so the signs read, "STOP WAR." I didn't know it meant that the Vietnam War should be ended. I thought it meant, "Stop, there's a war ahead," which, for some reason, there never was.

The second group tried to ignore the first group and scrape out a living.

Mom called the first group "hippies." The second group she called "people like us."

Chapter One

Adam

THERE WERE HIPPIES ACROSS the back fence. They were hairy, colorful people who planted marijuana between the corn in their garden. One day I saw them sunbathing nude in their back yard, and they saw me, even though I was so short I wasn't even in kindergarten yet. The next week, they built a tall wooden fence with no knotholes.

One day that summer, an African-American couple (that's not what they called themselves then) moved into the house next door. They seemed friendly, but I took one look at their hair and clothes and decided they were hippies, not people like us. So I tried to avoid them.

They built a lot of small cages out of lumber and chicken wire in their back yard, and they started fixing up the house. I always made sure they weren't outside before I peeked through the chain-link fence to watch the little animals they put in the cages. Mom said they were prairie dogs, but they didn't look like dogs. They looked like rats.

One afternoon, the sky was full of dark clouds, and the prairie dogs weren't acting right. They were jumpy, and they made little yipping noises.

I heard a voice say, "The prairie dogs are afraid of the tornadoes. Aren't you?"

I was too startled to run away, so I made a friend.

"I'm Adam," he said. "What's your name?"

"Joey Robinson," I said. "Do you live here?"

"I do now. I get to live with my aunt and uncle this year, and all their animals."

"I don't have any animals," I said. "I have a mom, but I don't have any aunts and uncles."

"That's okay," he said. "You can use mine."

Adam said tornadoes were small, circular, very powerful winds that could rip houses apart and even blow drinking straws through fence posts. He said you could listen to the radio and find out when they were coming. He had just heard there might be some in our town that afternoon, and he planned to watch them.

"Do you think they will ruin my house?" I asked.

"No, they usually just hit a few houses and leave the others alone."

"Why?"

"Dunno." He shrugged. "Maybe God tells them to."

I had heard of God, and I was pretty sure he didn't like hippies, so I was worried. "Are your aunt and uncle hippies?" I asked. If they were, their house was in danger.

"No way, man. They're married. They're square."

"What's 'square'?"

"It means not hippies."

"I don't think God likes hippies," I declared. "So your house is safe, and my house is safe, but he'll probably have the tornadoes hit that house." I pointed to the one with the new fence.

"Cool. Let's watch."

I probably should have run into the house, interrupted Mom's work, and told her there were tornadoes coming to wreck the hippies' house, but I was afraid she wouldn't let me watch. I let her work.

Adam brought out a radio, and we turned it on, so we'd know exactly when the tornadoes were coming. He said the darkest clouds were the ones tornadoes came from, so we watched those, he from his side of the fence and I from mine.

While we watched for the tornadoes that never came, I learned that Adam was from Nebraska, but his mom was sick, so he came to live with my neighbors.

"What kind of sick?" I asked.

"Drugs. She takes drugs."

"Like marijuana?"

"And some other stuff," Adam said sadly.

"What about your dad?" I asked.

"Ain't seen him in a long time."

"Do your aunt and uncle take drugs?"

"No, man, they got too much religion for that. I don't take no drugs neither. Drugs is bad stuff. Drugs make you stupid."

"That's what my mom says. What about those animals?"

"Animals don't take no drugs."

"No, I mean, what kind are they?"

"Oh. They're prairie dogs. Uncle does science stuff with them for the university."

"They don't look like dogs."

"They're not. They're more like rats, I guess, but cute instead of gross."

"I like them. Can you get them out and play with them?"

"Nope. Uncle says if we take them out of their cages, they're not scientific."

That evening, while we ate our macaroni and cheese, I told Mom about Adam. He already felt like my best friend, and not just because I had never had a friend before. He was nice to me, even though he was a year older and about to start first grade, and he knew lots of amazing things.

I told Mom about watching for tornadoes that didn't come. I told her the people next door weren't really hippies. They were people like us.

Chapter Two

School

I STARTED KINDERGARTEN, AND Adam started first grade. I liked having a friend at school. I think if the kindergarten recess had been at the same time as the first grade recess, I wouldn't have had a bloody nose and gotten in trouble and missed two recesses in the same week. And if my dad hadn't run away before I was born, my mom and my teacher, Miss King, might have liked each other.

The time I got a bloody nose was my teacher's fault. We were learning our phone numbers, and one day, just before recess, she gathered all of us in the corner of the room. She sat in her favorite chair, like she always did when she read a book to us. We sat on the rug around her to listen.

She didn't read to us. Instead, she asked us to recite our phone numbers. I had a cold, and when it was my turn to say my phone number, I had to clear my throat first. She thought I had to stop and think, so she gave me an "S" for "Satisfactory" instead of an "O" for "Outstanding," because I wasn't fast enough.

It wasn't fair. I knew my phone number. The only thing I didn't know in kindergarten was how to tie my shoes right, but that wasn't the same as my phone number.

I was so angry I was afraid I would cry, so instead of playing at recess, I hid. It was raining outside, so recess was in the classroom. We had big rolling carts full of big cardboard blocks. When we weren't using the blocks, the carts rolled out of the way under a counter. When we were using the blocks and the carts were out, under the counter was a good place to hide.

Some kids who never let me play with them were building a castle with the blocks. When they rolled the empty carts back under the counter to get them out of the way, one cart hit me and gave me a bloody nose. They probably didn't know I was there, but they might have done it anyway, if they had known.

I only got a little blood on my shirt. Mostly I used my handkerchief.

The next day, the weather was nice. During our first recess, our student teacher, Miss Whitney, was sitting on a bench, watching us. I liked her a lot, so I went to talk to her. It was fun until I called her a steam shovel. I didn't mean anything bad. We were just joking around. But Miss King heard it, and she didn't like it. I missed the rest of that recess and the next one, because she made me sit in the classroom while the others played.

I didn't blame Adam. It wasn't his fault. But if we had been in the same class, I would have been playing with him, instead of hiding under the counter one time, and calling my student teacher a steam shovel the other time.

· · · ● · ● · ● · ·

MOM WAS ALWAYS WORKING, doing something with big books of numbers that she could usually do at home, instead of going to an office or a factory like most parents. She started very early in the morning. Before I was in school, I would sit with her and do my work, drawing pictures and practicing my letters and numbers.

In the afternoon I would play. After I started school in the morning, I couldn't work with her, but there was still time to play in the afternoon.

When dinner was done and the dishes were washed, she would be too tired to work anymore. She would sit in her favorite chair in the living room, and I would sit on her lap. We'd watch TV or have a talk, and then we had a story or two. Then she would hug me, and I would go get ready for bed and brush my teeth. She usually fell asleep while I was doing that, so I'd go back to the living room, wake her, and walk her to her bedroom. Then I went to my room, said my prayers, and got in bed.

Mom worked so hard in the morning that sometimes she didn't even look up when I said goodbye and walked out the door. I liked that, because I could wear whatever I wanted to school. Mostly I wore the same shirt and pants all week, but sometimes she noticed and made me change.

Two or three days after the nosebleed under the counter, I was still wearing the same shirt. During my bedtime story she noticed the little spot of blood, and I had to tell her about it. Then I told her about calling my student teacher a steam shovel and missing recess. I wasn't going to tell her that, but I did. She wasn't angry about the nosebleed or the steam shovel, but she made me promise to wear a different shirt tomorrow.

"Besides," she said, "you and I are going to a parent-teacher conference after school. You'll want to look your best."

"What's a parent-teacher conference?"

"That's where you and I go and talk with your teacher about how things are going for you at school."

"Am I in trouble?" I tried not to look worried.

"No, of course not. We're just going to talk to your teacher."

I thought that meant Miss King was in trouble for what had happened. That was okay with me, as long as Miss Whitney wasn't in trouble too.

When we went, Miss Whitney wasn't even there, and my trouble at recess never came up. Mom and Miss King talked about math, penmanship, and other stuff, and I mostly ignored them. Then Miss King asked if my father would be coming to any parent-teacher conferences during the year.

I knew the answer to that. "I don't have a father. Or a dad."

Mom corrected me. "Actually, you had one, but he's gone now."

"Gone to where?" I wondered.

"Just gone away," she said with a shrug.

"I see," said my teacher.

I saw too. I saw the same look on Miss King's face that I had seen when I called Miss Whitney a steam shovel. I was glad my mom didn't have any recesses to lose, because Miss King thought it was bad of her that I didn't have a dad.

I thought Mom saw it too, and it bothered her, because she didn't talk much after we got home. She just held me while we watched *Bonanza*. I didn't see her cry, but she looked like she wanted to.

I didn't ask her any more questions about my dad that night or even that whole week. But anything I couldn't ask Mom, I could ask Adam. The next time I saw him, I asked, "Adam, is it bad when you don't have a dad?"

He thought for a minute, then said, "I don't know. I sort of miss mine, but he's a bad man, so I guess it's okay that he's gone. When he was home, he and my mom always yelled at each other. That's when I was younger, so it usually made me cry."

"Aren't kids supposed to have a mom *and* a dad?" I asked.

"I don't know. You're okay with just a mom, right? I do okay with just an aunt and uncle, don't I?"

"I guess so."

"Anyway, there's weirder things than not having a dad," he said. "I heard it on the radio."

"What things?"

"There's this guy that wants to marry his horse. I told Aunt and Uncle about it, and they laughed. They didn't believe me, but I really heard it."

"That's dumb," I scoffed. "If they have kids, will the horse be the mom?"

"I don't know," said Adam. "But I bet the kids will look stupid."

I wanted to say something just as funny after that, but all I could do was laugh.

Chapter Three

Prowler

ON FRIDAY NIGHTS MOM and I went to a grocery store together. One time, we finished dinner late, and it was getting dark while I was still getting my shoes on. Mom went outside, and I heard her yell. I wasn't sure what she said, but it didn't sound like she was yelling at me.

When I had my shoes on, she was still standing on the doorstep.

"Did you yell at me?" I asked.

"No, Joey."

"Who were you yelling at?"

"It doesn't matter."

When we got out to our car, the little door to the gas tank was open, and the gas cap was missing.

"Stupid prowler," Mom grumbled as she closed the little door. "I guess we'll get a new gas cap tonight."

I worried that the gasoline would come out, if we drove the car without a gas cap, but she said it would be okay for a little while. After the grocery store we went to a store that had car stuff.

I asked Mom why a prowler would want our gas cap. She told me not to worry about it. Then she said we were stopping for ice cream cones on the way home, which we did.

The next day, I asked Adam what a prowler is and why it would want our gas cap.

"I could just tell you," he said, "but let's do what Aunt and Uncle make me do, when I ask them what a word means."

"What's that?"

"Look for it in the dictionary."

"You have a dictionary?"

"Yeah, a big one."

"I don't. What's a dictionary?"

"Duh! It's a big book that tells you what words mean."

"Does it have every word?"

"Sure. Let's go look for *prowler*."

That was when I learned that a dictionary is a big book that explains words you don't know by using other words you don't know. We found *prowler*, but when we were finished reading about it, we still didn't know what it meant. The only part we understood was the first three words, "a person who." That didn't help a lot.

"That's okay," Adam said. "Aunt will tell us, if we've tried the dictionary first."

"Let's go ask her," I said.

"Okay, but first, are there any other words you want to look for?"

There were some words I had learned at recess, then used at home—but only once. When Mom heard them, she got mad and told me never to use them again. She wouldn't tell me what they meant, but she said that, if she ever heard me say them again, she would wash my mouth out with soap. She even said I should be glad I didn't have a dad, because, if I did, he would probably have spanked me for saying those words. After that, I only used them at school, when a teacher wasn't there to hear.

We found all those words in the dictionary, but we didn't understand very much about them either. The explanations used the words *vulgar* and *obscene* a lot, so when we asked Adam's aunt about *prowler*, we asked about those too.

She shook her head and frowned. "If you insist on looking up naughty words in the dictionary, you can't use the dictionary anymore."

I didn't see how that would be a problem, since it wasn't very helpful anyway.

"Why are you curious about prowlers?" she asked.

"We had one at our house last night. It stole our gas cap. What's a prowler?"

"It's a person who sneaks around people's yards, looking for something to steal."

I was pretty worried. "Do they hurt people?"

"No," she said. "They run away when they see or hear you coming."

"That's good." I felt better. "Why would the prowler steal our gas cap?"

"He was probably trying to steal your gas, and he had the cap in his hand when your mom frightened him away."

Prowlers sounded pretty harmless, except that they steal your stuff, but just to be sure, I asked, "What should I do if I see a prowler? Yell at him?"

"Oh, no," she said. "You should tell your mom, so she can call the police."

Obviously, if we needed the police, prowlers were worse than she was saying. But I didn't tell her that. After that I was almost as afraid of prowlers as I was of fires.

Once, when I told Adam I was scared of fires, he told me there was nothing to worry about, because his uncle knew the fire chief, and he wouldn't let any fires burn down my house.

It would have been good if Adam's uncle knew the police chief. We never had another prowler, but I kept worrying. For a long time, whenever I went outside at night—because prowlers usually don't come when it's light—I carried an empty water pistol and pretended it was a real gun. I wasn't sure it would scare a prowler, but I felt better.

Sometimes when I watched *Bonanza* on television, I wished I had a dad and two big brothers who carried real guns, like Little Joe had.

• • • ● • ● • • •

ADAM HELPED ME NOT to be scared of some things, but he didn't help with bees. I had never had a bee sting, but I was scared of them anyway. When I saw a bee on a dandelion in the lawn, I stayed away from it. When Adam saw one, he stomped on it, even with bare feet. I knew that would make the bee angry, so I ran away. But Adam never ran away, and the bees never stung him.

I knew I would get older and be a first grader like he was, and I would know a lot more stuff. But I couldn't imagine ever getting old enough or knowing enough things that I wouldn't be afraid to stomp on bees with my bare feet.

Chapter Four
Potato Chips

MOM OFTEN SAID I was a very good boy, and most of the time she was right. But sometimes I was bad.

Once we had hot dogs, potato chips, and green beans for dinner. I loved potato chips, but we didn't have them very often. When I asked for seconds, Mom wouldn't give me any until I finished my green beans. I did not like green beans.

She had to go to the bathroom for a few minutes. I stayed at the table, and I probably would have taken more chips if she hadn't said, as she was leaving, "Don't touch the potato chips. If you've finished your beans when I get back in a minute, you can have some more. But don't touch them while I'm gone."

I knew better than to disobey, but I sat there thinking how unfair it was to have to eat beans before I could have more potato chips. The longer I thought about it, the madder I got. I went and stood outside the bathroom door and told Mom through the door that I wanted more chips, and I wasn't going to eat my beans.

She said no, if I was going to be like that, I couldn't have more chips, and I still had to eat my green beans.

I had an idea. "You know what, Mom? If I had a dad, he'd give me more potato chips."

She didn't say anything.

I stood there a little longer, getting even madder, until I finally kicked the bathroom door as hard as I could. It was a dumb thing to do. The door was hollow, and my toe went through the wood on my side of the door. It didn't go through her side of the door, but I knew I was in big trouble. I wanted to run and hide, but I was too scared to move.

The door opened. She looked at me, then the door, then back to me. She spoke so calmly it scared me even more. "What do you think a dad would do with you now?"

What Mom did was, that was the end of my dinner. She sent me to bed without our talk and with no story, and it was a long time before we had potato chips again.

She never said anything about the door, but she never fixed it either. That was probably on purpose, because every time I saw the hole, I remembered what I had done. After that, I tried not to get mad about stuff. I still did sometimes, but maybe less. I didn't kick holes in any more doors.

I was still angry at Mom a few days later. I tried to be angrier at her than I was ashamed of myself, and it seemed to work.

That same week, Adam got in trouble with his aunt and uncle for not doing his chores. He told them he didn't want to live there anymore. He wanted to go back to his mom. I knew that wouldn't work, because she took drugs, but I started to think that maybe I would rather live with my dad, whoever he was.

I didn't know his name or where he lived, so I couldn't really go live with him, but at least I could run away. That was what he did, Mom had said. I wondered if it was because of potato chips and green beans. I didn't ask.

For two days I thought about running away, until I had it all figured out. I couldn't go far, because I didn't have enough money for a bus ticket, and besides, I wanted to be close enough to play with Adam. The park two blocks away would be perfect.

We had explored every inch of the park. There was a shortcut through it on our way home from school. It went through some bushes and trees and over a little bridge, because there was a creek too.

Adam and I weren't supposed to take the shortcut, because my mom and his aunt thought there might be bad people hiding in the bushes. We almost always took it anyway. We were also supposed to stay away from the bushes when we played in the park, but we didn't. We never saw any bad people anywhere, so we didn't worry like the grownups did.

We knew a tiny clearing in the trees and bushes that was hard to get to. We never saw candy wrappers or cigarette butts there, like we saw everywhere else, so we didn't think anyone ever went there except us. That's why the park was a perfect place to run away.

Adam was sick on the day I planned to run away, so we couldn't play. Mom was hurrying to finish some work. She didn't notice when I left with a blanket for making a tent, a plastic cup for drinking water from the creek, my favorite book of Snoopy cartoons, my jacket, three peanut butter sandwiches, and an apple. I was mad at Mom, but I didn't want her to think I had been kidnapped, so I left her a note I had worked on for a long time the day before: "Dear Mom, I didn't get kidnapped. I ran away. Love, Joey."

I got to the park, squeezed my way through the bushes to our secret clearing, and built a little tent with my blanket and a couple of sticks. Then I sat down by my tent to read my book, eat my sandwiches, and drink some water I got in my cup from the creek. That was when I discovered I had made a really dumb mistake.

Piggy banks were for little kids, so I kept my money in a jar. I had more than two dollars. As I was getting ready to run away, I saw the jar and thought I should take it with me and buy potato chips. I could have done it. A grocery store was only two blocks from home, in the other direction from the park. But I forgot until I was eating my first sandwich. By then it was too late. I couldn't go back.

It was November and not very warm outside. That's why I took my jacket. But it was warm in my tent, especially when the sun came out. That was probably what made me fall asleep after I crawled into it, which was after I finished my first sandwich.

Chapter Five

Found

WHEN I WOKE UP it was dark. I heard voices, then someone rustling through the bushes. That's when I realized why Adam and I had never seen the bad people Mom said went to the park. We were always there in the day, and the bad people went there at night.

I wasn't very worried, because I knew our clearing was a secret. Besides never seeing any trash there, we were pretty sure adults were too big to get through the bushes. If I was quiet, no one would ever know I was there. Even if I sneezed or something, the only way the bad people could get to me was if they cut down the bushes, and not even bad people would do that in the dark.

I was a little more scared when I realized the sounds were getting close to me and I saw the light of a flashlight waving around in the bushes. I wanted to yell for help, but I had to be quiet.

I thought I might be less scared if I closed my eyes, so I did. It helped. Then the rustling stopped. Right before I heard the voice, I knew that, if I opened my eyes, I would see someone in front of me.

I must have looked scared, because what the voice whispered was, "Joey, don't be scared. It's me, Adam." I opened my eyes, and it really was Adam, carrying his uncle's flashlight.

"I thought you were sick."

"I am," he said.

"They let you come to the park when it's dark and you're sick?" I couldn't imagine that.

"Uncle brought me here to look for you."

"Oh. Why are we whispering?"

"Because if you don't want to leave, I won't tell him I found you."

I didn't know what else to say, so I said, "That was good thinking." Adam was a real friend.

I offered him one of my sandwiches. He ate it while he told me, between bites, what had happened at our houses after I ran away. Mom found my note, then looked all over our house and yard. Then she went next door to see if I was there or if Adam had run away too, which he hadn't. The grownups asked Adam where he thought I might go. He said they should look in his yard. He thought about the clearing, but that was our secret, so he didn't tell them right away.

They didn't find me in Adam's yard, because I wasn't there. Mom was about to go home and call the police, so Adam pretended he had just thought of the clearing. His aunt stayed with Mom, and his uncle brought him to find me.

On the way to the park, Adam came up with a plan. First, he told his uncle that, if they yelled my name, I would probably be scared and just hide. Then he said there were two ways to get to the clearing, even though there was only one, unless you had a helicopter. He would take the long way, because it would be quieter and he wouldn't scare me and make me hide. What he was really thinking was, if I didn't want to go home, he could say I wasn't there, and his uncle would never know I was.

"You're really smart to think of all that," I whispered. "If I was smart, I would have bought potato chips."

"Peanut butter sandwiches are good, too," he said. "Did you bring anything to drink?"

"I drank out of the creek with my cup."

"Uncle says that makes you sick."

I did get sick, but not until the next day.

"So do you want me to tell him I found you or not?" he asked.

I thought about it. "I guess so."

"Are you sure?"

I said I was sure, but I was lying.

"I found him!" he yelled to his uncle. "We're coming."

I thought Mom would be really angry when I got home, but she mostly seemed happy and sad at the same time. She hugged Adam and his uncle and thanked them for finding me and bringing me home. Then she hugged Adam's aunt for staying with her. Then everybody left.

She sat me on her lap in the chair and turned my head so she could look me in the eye. "Don't ever run away again."

"Okay," I said.

She looked at me for a minute or two, and she was crying a little. Finally she asked, "Why did you run away, Joey?"

I just shrugged. I knew she would ask again, but I needed a minute to think. Potato chips sounded like a stupid reason to run away, so I couldn't tell her that. I didn't want to just make up a reason either, because that would be lying. I needed to tell her something true—just not about potato chips.

She had another question. "Did I do something to hurt you, Joey? Something to make you want to run away?"

I shrugged.

"Was it that thing with the potato chips the other day?"

I shrugged again.

She was silent for a minute. Then she said, "Joey, please tell me. Why did you run away?"

This time, what I said was, "I ran away because I wanted to be like my dad."

She looked surprised. "You're better than your dad. You don't have to be like him."

Later, when I remembered that night, I thought that was probably when she decided it was time to get me a new dad.

Chapter Six

Jack

WE STARTED GOING TO church on Sundays. On some of the Saturdays there were dinners and bazaars. When I asked Mom why we suddenly started going, she said it was because we were supposed to. But I knew that, if we were supposed to go to church then, we should have been going before. So I thought to myself that she was looking for a husband for her and a new dad for me, and the best place to find one must be at church.

The first few times, we went in our car. Then one Saturday our car broke. On Sunday Mom told me a man was coming to take us to church, and I should go outside and tell him she would be out in minute or two, if he came before she was ready. When a man in a car stopped in front of our house, I hardly even looked at him. I hopped in the back seat and told him Mom would be right out.

"Young man, do I know you?" he asked. "I think you must have mistaken me for someone else."

I froze, and I felt my face turn red. I tried to say I was sorry, but I couldn't make a sound. I got out of his car and went and sat on our front step.

He didn't try to stop me, so he probably wasn't a kidnapper. But I might have died of embarrassment, or Mom might have killed me herself, if she found out I got into a stranger's car. Never get in a stranger's car was pretty close to her biggest rule for me.

A minute later, a woman from the house across the street came outside and got into the man's car, and they drove away.

My face was still red when Mom came out, and she asked if I was feeling okay. I couldn't tell her I had broken a really big rule. I said I was tired from running around. She frowned, because I wasn't supposed to run around in my church clothes, but she didn't say anything.

The man who was coming to take us to church showed up just then. Mom called him Brother Langer. He seemed nice, but he was weird. He stood up in church that day and sang a song all by himself.

He came back to our house on Monday, on his way home from work, and fixed our car. He called me his supervisor, and he let me watch the whole thing. It took a whole hour. It was a good thing we started going to church before the car broke.

Two or three days later, he called to see if the car was still working okay. At first I didn't know who he was, because he said his name was Henry, but then he said he was Brother Langer and I knew.

I told him Mom was in the bathroom, but the car was working fine. He asked me how Mom was doing. That made me think he was probably helping us because he liked Mom, and Mom was probably letting him help because she liked him and thought maybe he would be a good dad for me.

When she got out of the bathroom and I told her he called, she said I shouldn't have told him she was in the bathroom, because it was embarrassing. I was about to ask her if he would be a good dad for me, but she was already upset, so I didn't. Besides, she'd probably just say she'd tell me when she was ready, or when I was ready, like she did with other things.

· · · ● · ● ● · ● ● · ·

ONE DAY, WHEN I got home from school, Mom was dressed up almost like it was Sunday, so I asked if we were going to church. She said we were going to dinner at Brother Langer's home, and I should dress nice too.

When we got there, he answered the door and told us to come in. A woman came out of the kitchen to meet us, and he said she was Sister Langer, his wife. I must have looked confused, because he asked me if something was wrong. I said, "I didn't know you have a wife."

She smiled, and he laughed, and I quit thinking Mom wanted him to be my dad.

He said she'd been sick, but she was better now. She said her doctor told her to stay away from places with lots of people for a while, or she might get sick again. I sometimes stayed home from school when I was sick, but I had never heard of people staying home when they weren't sick anymore.

The doorbell rang. "That must be Jack," said Sister Langer.

They called Jack "little brother," but he wasn't little. He was taller than Brother Langer. He smiled at Mom when he shook her hand.

When Mom introduced me, he didn't just reach down to shake my hand like most people did. He knelt down and looked me in the eye. We shook hands firmly—he complimented me on that—and then he said, "Now that we got that out of the way, gimme five." He said "five" in a cool way, like "fiiiiiiive." After that, it was dinnertime.

During dinner I asked Jack if he had a wife too.

Before he could answer, Mom said, "Joey." I looked at her, and her face was red. But she didn't sound angry.

Then I looked at Jack, because he laughed. "No, I don't," he said. I thought he looked at Mom for a second and smiled before he looked back at me.

After dinner, Brother and Sister Langer—Mom called them Rob and Susan when she talked to them—insisted that Mom and Jack go to the living room while they cleaned up. I was about to go with them, but they asked me to stay and carry the dishes to the sink. When that was done, they gave me a rag that was sort of wet and asked me to wipe off the table.

I did it, but I didn't want to. I wanted to be where Mom was. I was her boy. Instead, I was in the kitchen helping other people with the dishes and the table, while Jack was with her in the living room.

Chapter Seven

Mom and Jack

AFTER THAT NIGHT WE mostly saw Brother Langer at church, and Jack started coming over a lot. He told me to call him Jack so there wouldn't be two Brother Langers.

He came to our house two or three times a week, sometimes for dinner. I wasn't sure I liked him as much as Mom did, but he was okay. They never left me to clear the table while they went to the living room without me.

Sometimes we all watched *Bonanza* or *Adam-12* together after dinner, like Mom and I did when it was just us. But when Jack was there, sometimes we watched *Monday Night Football* instead. At halftime I had to go to bed. On other nights Jack taught me to play checkers, which is a very cool game, except that nobody at school wanted to play it with me. Adam wanted to learn, so I taught him. It was the first thing I ever knew that he didn't.

When it was my bedtime, on the nights when Jack visited, he and Mom would read me my story together. They used different voices for different people or animals. After I went to bed, they would sit up talking to each other for a long time in their regular voices. Sometimes I would wake up when I heard the front door close. Before I fell asleep again, I would hear Mom getting ready for bed.

If I went to bed first, she always came to give me a kiss before she went to bed, even if I was already asleep. She said it was because I was her favorite boy in all the world. She had called me that for as long as I could remember, but with Jack coming over all the time, I started to wonder.

· · · • · • • · • · ·

I NOTICED RIGHT AWAY that, when Jack came over, Mom didn't sit in her favorite chair anymore, with me on her lap. It was mostly okay though, because, when she sat really close to Jack on the couch, I could still sit on her lap.

One time I left to go to the bathroom, and it took longer than usual. When I got back to the living room I went to sit on Mom's lap again, but I couldn't. She kind of didn't have a lap, because she wasn't sitting. She was taking up the whole couch, except for Jack sitting at one end. Her head was on his lap, her eyes were closed, and he was rubbing her cheek with the backs of his fingers. She was making little sounds like she liked it.

I stood in front of the couch and tried to figure out where to sit.

"Kris," Jack said very softly. Mom's name was Kristin.

She opened her eyes and saw me. "Hi, Joey. Give me a second. I'll make a place for you to sit."

"I think I'll just go to bed," I said.

"Sure, if you want. It's almost time anyway. We'll be in to say good night soon."

I turned and walked toward my bedroom. I felt really sad, and I walked slowly. I was almost to the hall when I heard the couch creak, and Mom said, "Joey, could you come back for a minute, please?" Her voice was soft.

I stopped but didn't turn around.

"Would you come sit a little longer? Please?"

I didn't move, and I didn't say anything.

"Little Joe asked that pretty girl to marry him, while you were in the bathroom. Don't you want to see how it ends? It's almost over."

I really didn't, but I turned around anyway. Mom was sitting up again, next to Jack. He had a little smile on his face, but she looked sad or maybe worried.

"I like it when you sit on my lap," she said. "It won't be very many years before you're too big for that, or you stop wanting to. Please?"

I figured she was right about me getting too big, but I wouldn't stop wanting to.

I walked back to the couch and climbed onto her lap. She held me more tightly than usual.

Little Joe didn't marry the pretty girl. Instead, he shot her dad, who was a bad man. She left Virginia City on the stagecoach to go live with her aunt in some city back east. She looked sad, and Little Joe looked sad, and I was glad.

• • • ● • ● • • • •

ONE NIGHT I WAS awake when Mom came to give me my kiss. She stood by my bed, just looking at me.

"Hi, mom."

She kissed my forehead. "You should sleep. Tomorrow we need to talk about something."

It sounded important. I could think of only one thing it could be. "Mom, am I still you favorite boy in all the world?"

"Yes, honey. Why do you ask?"

"What about when you marry Jack?"

"The answer will always be yes. I want you never to worry about that."

"Will Jack be my new dad?"

She gave me my kiss and smiled, but she didn't answer my question. "Would you like that?"

I'd sort of wanted a dad for a long time, if I would still be her favorite boy. And Jack was okay. But I wanted to sound grown up, so I used different words. "I guess that wouldn't be too bad."

"It'll be better than that," she said. "We'll talk more tomorrow."

After she left, I started to wonder. Jack was nice when he just came to visit. Would he be nice all the time, if he lived with us? Some kids at school talked like their dads were mostly mean. And Mom was spending more and more time with him already, which made my stomach ache, but I didn't tell her.

Chapter Eight

Okay

T HE NEXT DAY M OM made me pancakes instead of working. While we ate, she said, "Joey, we need to talk."

I just nodded. I wasn't supposed to talk with my mouth full.

"Were you listening to Jack and me talk last night, when we thought you were sleeping?" She sounded like I might be in trouble.

I swallowed. "No, I was asleep."

"Honest?"

"Honest."

"Are you sure?"

"I was asleep. I think I woke up when he closed the front door, because then I heard his car start."

"Then why did you ask if he's going to be your new dad?"

"I know I'm just a kid," I said. "But why did you think he's been coming over so much? I thought he already asked you to marry him, and you were waiting to surprise me or something."

Her cheeks turned a little red, but not like they did when I was in trouble. "So you didn't know that last night, after you went to bed, he asked me to marry him?"

"Did you say you would?"

"You didn't hear?"

"I already said that. What did you tell him?"

Now she smiled. "I said I would. And I said you'd be as happy about it as I am. Are you happy? About getting Jack for a dad?"

I wasn't smiling, but I tried not to frown. "Do I really need a dad?"

"Don't you want one?"

"Maybe. I don't know."

"A dad is a really good thing for a boy to have. Especially when he makes the boy's mom happy too."

"Does he do that?" I was pretty sure I knew the answer.

Her smile got really big. "Yes, he does."

I felt like crying, but I tried really hard not to. "I thought you were happy with just me."

She grabbed my hand and squeezed it. "I have always been happy with just you, Joey. How could I not be? I'll be even happier with three of us, and I think you will too. I could never love him more than I love you. But I love him almost as much. And he doesn't just love me. He loves you too."

She let go and smiled again. "What do you think?"

"Is he coming to live with us?"

"We'll all live together," she said, "but we haven't decided where."

"Will he have his own room?" I didn't see how that could work, if he moved in with us. We had only three bedrooms: mine, Mom's, and the one she used for her office.

"No. He and I will share a room, and you'll still have your own."

I thought for a minute. "Okay."

"Okay what?"

I had to think a little more. "I guess it's okay if you marry him."

"Just okay? You guess?"

I shrugged. "I don't know. Being happy is nice."

"Joey, getting a dad doesn't mean losing your mom. I want you to remember that."

"Okay." I felt a little better.

She smiled and squeezed me again. "You were right. We were going to surprise you with the news. I guess you're too smart for that."

I said it the way Adam might have. "It looked pretty obvious to me."

Mom said the wedding would be in a couple of months, at the beginning of my spring break from school, and there were lots of important things to do before then.

I knew one of them. "Does Jack have a nice apartment?" I asked.

"He does, but it might be a little small for three of us. I've been there a couple of times, when we left you with someone and went out."

"Do I get to see it sometime?"

"Sure," she said.

"Okay," I said.

Chapter Nine

Decision

O NE SATURDAY MOM WOKE me early and told me to get dressed, because we had big day ahead of us. At breakfast she said, "Today Jack and I are deciding where to live after the wedding. We're all going to be a family, just like you and I already are, and before we decide, we want to know what you like and what you don't."

On the way to Jack's apartment, Mom said we could live there or in the house we were already renting most of, or in some other house or apartment that we would have to find. They said they wanted me to think carefully about what was good and bad about each apartment, the way a boy saw it.

"You don't get to make the final decision about where we live," she said, "but we want to know what you think. We both do."

Jack's apartment felt almost as big as ours. I could have my own bedroom there too, and it had a bus stop right in front. That was good. But Jack said the nearest park that was good for kids was half a mile away, across a wide, busy street. That was bad. I looked around the apartment, then walked around outside, then inspected the apartment again.

Finally they asked, "What do you think?"

I said, "It's nice, and the bus stop is close. That's good. But I really like having a park, and I like living next to Adam."

"Honey," Mom said, "friends are important. Neighbors too. But Adam probably won't live there forever."

I didn't want to think about that.

"So what do you think?" asked Jack. "All things considered, what's the boy's-eye view? We'll consider what every member of the family thinks when we decide," said Jack. "If you want to think about it until after lunch, that's okay too."

I already knew what I thought, and I tried to say it like a grownup. "The apartment would be fun, but our house is a better place for a kid like me."

"What if Adam wasn't there?" Mom asked.

I still didn't want to think about that, but I nodded. "Yeah. The same."

"Thanks for thinking about it and telling us," Jack said. "How about lunch at McDonald's?"

McDonald's was my favorite, but what we did after that wasn't. We went to a really big store to buy me a suit for the wedding. I had never had a suit before, just some nice pants and a good shirt. I also got a new tie, a tie clip with an airplane on it, and some new shoes that Mom and Jack said would stop pinching soon. It was all okay, except the shoes. Or it would have been, if it hadn't taken about a year.

We finally drove home with all the clothes they bought me. Before we got out of the car, Mom and Jack turned around in their seats and looked at me. "Would you like to know what we decided?" Mom asked. "About where to live?"

It was a little scary, but I nodded. I looked at Mom, then Jack, then Mom, then Jack again, wondering who was going to tell me.

Jack finally smiled. "We've decided to live here."

I smiled really big.

"I'm glad you're happy," Mom said.

"It's really cool," I said. But that wasn't enough, and I still wanted to sound grown up, so I said, "It's utterly groovy."

Jack laughed, and I thought Mom was going to laugh too, but she asked me a question instead. "Where did you learn the word *utterly*?"

"On TV, I think."

"Where did you learn the word *groovy*?" Jack wondered.

"I don't think I should tell you. Is it a bad word?"

"No," Mom said. "But I've never heard anybody use it with *utterly*."

It didn't look like I was in trouble, so I said, "Sunday School."

This time Mom laughed too. "Really?"

"That mean teacher says it's an evil hippie word, and we should never use it. Am I in trouble?" I still didn't think I was.

"No, Joey," Mom said.

Jack was still laughing. "You shouldn't necessarily believe everything you hear in Sunday School."

"Are there other important things today?" I asked.

"I don't think so," said Mom. "Can you think of any?"

"Yes," I said.

"What did we miss?" asked Jack.

I looked at him and sort of wished Mom and I had gone shopping and eaten at McDonald's by ourselves. Or that I hadn't said anything until it was just Mom and me. I'd been wondering something all day.

I looked at her, not Jack. "After the wedding, do I keep calling him Jack, or do I have to call him Dad?"

They looked at each other, and something in their faces made me wonder if they were thinking the same sad thought or different ones.

"Well," said Jack, "I like my name, and you could keep using it. But if you ever want to call me Dad, that would be nice. It's up to you, and you don't have to decide right away."

"I'll think about it," I said.

Mom smiled a little, but there were tears in her eyes. I had asked her before, and she always said to believe the smile, not the tears. This time I kind of believed the tears.

Chapter Ten

Don't Ask Juan

I BORROWED A PICTURE of Jack from Mom and took it to school for show-and-tell. I told my class that Mom was getting married to Jack, and I showed them the picture.

Some kids cheered, and Miss King said it was very nice. "You're getting a new dad," she said. "That's happy news."

"I don't know if he's going to be my dad yet," I said.

One girl asked what happened to my old dad. I said he was a bad man who ran away a long time ago. Then a boy asked if was he a robber or some other kind of crook, and were the police looking for him? I said I didn't think so.

At recess Juan, a big kid from Mexico—that meant it was okay to call him a Chicano, but not some other words—came up to me and asked, "When is the wedding?"

"During spring break."

"You should ask if you can watch the honeymoon," he said.

"What's that?"

"Stuff the bride and groom do after the wedding. You should see it and tell us about it."

"Have you seen it?"

"No, but I heard about it."

Juan knew lots of things the rest of us didn't know, and he was a good storyteller. Sometimes, when we were tired of playing football, we would spend recess listening to him. I liked those times, mostly because I wasn't very good at football, but I was good at listening. He told us jokes and stories he learned from his brothers and uncles. I pretended to understand, and I laughed when he and the other boys did.

One time, after a long story with lots of details and some new words for body parts I'd never seen, I went to talk to Juan in private. I asked him, "What did you call these things?" I made a motion with my hands.

"What things?"

"The two things on the front of a woman," I said. "What did you call them?" I already knew some words I wasn't allowed to use, which some of the other boys used at recess. But I wanted to know the right word.

"In my story?" he asked. "Headlights."

"Headlights?"

"That's what I said."

"Okay, thanks." I knew that wasn't the right word either. Headlights are on cars, not women.

The next time Jack was at our house for dinner, I asked him and Mom, "How long is the honeymoon? Is it like part of a day or a lot of days?"

"What do you know about honeymoons?" she asked.

"Nothing. Is it fun? Can I go with you?"

"Why do you ask?"

I knew from her tone that this wasn't good. "Juan told me to."

"Who's Juan?"

"He's in my class at school. He said I should ask if I can watch the honeymoon."

Jack laughed so hard that milk came out of his nose, but Mom didn't. She sent me to my room. She said we would have a serious talk later, and until we did, I couldn't leave my room except to go to the bathroom.

When she came to my room after Jack left, she didn't yell, but she was still angry. "Do you have anything to say to me?" she asked.

I knew what that meant. "I'm sorry?"

"Thank you. You owe Jack an apology too, next time you see him."

"Okay. No, wait. He thought it was funny."

"He was wrong, and you owe him an apology. This boy named Juan, he's your age? And he talks about honeymoons?"

"Sometimes at recess. He tells us stories and jokes."

She relaxed a little. "That's what Jack said you'd say. He said recess was like that when he was a boy. So what is recess like? I was never a boy."

"Usually we play football," I explained. "But sometimes we listen to Juan tell jokes or stories." I could see she was about to ask me something. "He's a Chicano."

"What kind of jokes and stories does he tell? Dirty ones?"

"I don't really understand them. Sometimes they're about women's bodies."

"About sex?"

"I don't know what that is. But yeah, Juan says that word sometimes."

"Joey, when your friends are telling stories about women's bodies or even about men's bodies, or sex, those are usually dirty stories, and you shouldn't listen to them."

"Okay," I said. "I can shoot baskets or something."

"I would be very glad if you did."

"Okay."

I thought we were done talking, but we weren't. "After the wedding, the bride and groom—that's me and Jack in this case—usually go on a trip together for a few days. That's so they can spend a lot of time alone together and get to know each other better and get used to being together. So no, you can't watch the honeymoon, and if you ask again, that will be very rude, not just ignorant."

"I'm sorry," I repeated.

"Do you think Juan was trying to get you in trouble, when he told you to ask?"

"I don't know. Is the honeymoon sex?"

"That's part of it. Sex is a good thing, but you're only supposed to do it when you're married. I can explain how it works right now, if you want."

I was pretty sure I didn't. "Maybe later," I said.

"I want you to promise me something," she said.

"Okay."

"When you want to know about these things, ask me or Jack, not Juan, okay?"

I promised. But the truth was, I wanted to go on a fun trip with Mom, and with Jack if he had to go too. I didn't want to stay home while they went without me.

I wanted to tell Jack she was my mom too. But that wasn't exactly right. She wasn't his mom.

She was mine, not his. That's what I wanted to tell him.

Chapter Eleven

Churches

I N MY BACK YARD one day, Adam asked me, "Are they getting married in a church?"

"Yes," I said.

"Do you think it's a true church?" he asked.

I said, "Huh?"

"Everybody at my church always says how they know it's a true church, and sometimes they say all the other churches are wrong."

"Wrong about what?"

"God, I guess."

"Doesn't every church believe in God?" I didn't know a lot of churches, but that much had to be true.

"I guess so," he said. "Maybe they have different ideas."

I thought about that for a while. "Doesn't everybody get their ideas about God from reading the Bible?"

"I think so, but in my church they talk about other books too."

The Bible was hard enough to understand. I didn't need to hear about any other books. So I asked Adam, "If your church is right, and mine says different things, does that mean mine is wrong?"

"I guess so."

Part of me was glad to hear it, because I didn't like my Sunday school teacher, and the pastor was boring. But it could still be a problem. "Do you think it's okay for Mom and Jack to get married in my church anyway?"

"Probably. If God was angry about all the different churches, he could just blow them up, I guess."

"I think I'll ask them anyway."

"I'll ask Aunt and Uncle too," he said.

When I asked Mom and Jack, it wasn't like the time I asked about the honeymoon. But just in case, I didn't tell them the question came from Adam.

They said there were good people in a lot of churches, and most churches believed pretty much the same things about Jesus and about what it meant to live a good life, and the differences were just details.

Adam's aunt and uncle said the same thing. When he asked them what "true church" meant, they said they thought their church was a little truer than the others. But if we thought ours was a little truer, it was okay, because we were nice people.

Adam's Sunday school teacher was a lot like mine, and he didn't like her. Sometimes he hid when he got to the room before the teacher, just like I did, and it was always under the table, and she always caught him and was angry. She wouldn't let kids say *groovy* in her class either.

We thought our Sunday school teachers would have been even meaner about those things, but they were probably afraid to be as mean as they wanted at church.

"Do hippies have churches?" I wondered.

"Weird churches. Remember that time we had to boil our water at home, or it would make us sick?"

I remembered that, and I remembered how sick the water from the park had made me after I ran away.

"The reason," said Adam, "is a bunch of hippies were up at the lake where our drinking water comes from. They camped there for a long time and did their church things outside. They went skinny-dipping in the lake, and they peed in it, too."

"What's skinny-dipping?" I asked.

"Swimming without a swimming suit."

"You mean naked? People do that?"

"Hippies do. That's how they got germs in the water, so we had to boil it before we could drink it."

"Gross! We were drinking water that was peed in?"

"Yup." Adam always smiled really big when he grossed me out.

"Yuck! Can't they clean it before it goes in our water pipes?"

"I think they always clean it some," he said. "But when the hippies were up there, it got so dirty that they couldn't clean it all the way. I think the police made them camp somewhere else, so the water's okay now."

"Are you sure?"

"Uncle says they do tests to check for germs in the water, and they would tell everybody if it was bad."

It made sense, and I mostly believed it, but I still drank milk or juice instead of water for the next few days. I didn't even drink Kool-Aid, because everybody knows you make that by putting the powder and sugar in water.

Then I found a black widow spider in Mom's tomato patch. I quit worrying about drinking hippies' pee and started worrying about poisonous spiders instead.

Chapter Twelve

Hippies or Not

Two weeks before the wedding, Adam came over and told me he was moving with his uncle and aunt to a place called Schenectady, because his uncle had a new job at a university there. They were leaving after Mom and Jack's wedding.

We were both really sad, and we tried to think of ways to stop them from moving. Adam said they hadn't even asked him where he wanted to live. We decided to talk to his aunt about that.

She was in their living room, talking to a man with very long hair and a fuzzy beard, and a woman with even longer, straight hair and very plain clothes. Adam's aunt stopped talking to them for a minute and asked us what we wanted. She was almost always nice to us.

"I'm sorry, Adam," she said, when we explained. "And Joey. But I'm sure you'll learn to like New York, and you two can write each other letters."

Then it got even worse. His aunt introduced us to the people she was talking to, Barry and Autumn. They were buying the house, she said, and they would move in very soon.

I was so sad I forgot my manners. I turned to them, and I might have sounded a little bit mean. "Are you hippies? You look like hippies."

"Young man," said Adam's aunt in a tone I knew meant trouble. "That's not very kind."

"No," said Barry. "It's okay." He turned to me. "We look like hippies, and some people think we are, but we're not as bad as a lot of hippies."

I needed to know more. "Do you grow marijuana?"

Adam's aunt made a weird noise and put her hand to her mouth.

Autumn laughed. "No, we don't. We don't smoke it either, and we don't put it in brownies. And we don't let anyone else use it at our house."

"Do you use heroin or LSD or hashish?" I asked next.

"No, of course not," Autumn said. "You know about those?"

"Mom lets me watch the news."

"That would do it," Barry said.

I had more questions. "Do you run around outside with no clothes on, or forget to put on your underwear when you get dressed?"

Adam's aunt tried to end my questions then, but Barry raised his hand a little. He was smiling. "It's okay. No, Joey, we don't do any of that, either."

Maybe they weren't so bad. "Do you have prairie dogs?"

"No, but we have a big, black dog named Boris. He's friendly. What's your next question?" Barry and Autumn smiled a little and looked at each other.

"Is Autumn a hippie name?"

"It could be," she said. "My parents named me Jane, but I changed it to Autumn."

"You can do that?"

"You pay some money, fill out some papers, and talk to a judge about it."

Adam's aunt said there would be only one more question, so I'd better make it a good one.

I did. "Are you married?"

"No," said Autumn. "We don't believe in marriage. But we do love each other." I saw how they looked at each other, and I thought it must be true. "We're having a baby in a few months. Do you like babies?"

"I don't know whether I like them or not. I don't know any babies."

"I guess we'll find out soon enough," said Autumn. "I hear you're getting a new dad soon."

"Maybe," I said. "My mom's getting a new husband. I don't know if I want him to be my dad yet."

"Don't you like him?" she asked.

"Yeah, I guess. He's nice to me. He's nice to Mom too."

"That's important," she said. "I'll bet you'll like having him around."

"Maybe."

"I think you're going to be a nice neighbor."

That surprised me and embarrassed me a little. Adam's aunt said she doubted such a nosy, impolite boy could be a good neighbor. It was the only time I ever heard her say anything bad about me to anybody. But I think she still liked me, because she invited me to go with her, Adam, and his uncle the next day, to turn all the prairie dogs loose outside of town.

Chapter Thirteen

Invitation

I TOLD MOM ABOUT the new neighbors who looked like hippies, but maybe they weren't. She didn't seem very worried. Before I could tell her about the prairie dog trip the next day, it was bedtime, and I forgot.

When I got home from school the next day, she wasn't there. There was a note saying she was out getting the wedding dress, and I could go to Adam's to play, if I wanted.

I wasn't supposed to go anywhere else without her permission, but I couldn't miss the prairie dogs. Besides, it was almost like being at Adam's house, because I'd be with the same people. I asked his aunt to write a note for me, and I told her what to say.

"Dear Mom, I'm not running away. I'm going with Adam and his aunt and uncle and the prairie dogs, to set them free. I'll come back."

The reason I said I'd come back was to help her not to worry. To help her not be mad at me anyway, if she was, I said, "I bet you are really pretty in your wedding dress."

I wrote the last part myself, "Love, Joey." I raced home to leave it on the kitchen table and hurried back to Adam's. The four of us climbed into their pickup and drove to the prairie. We drove until we couldn't see a single house, and then we took a narrow, bumpy trail off the main road for a while, and then we just stopped.

Adam's aunt and uncle unloaded the first cage and showed us how to open it and let the prairie dog out. Then they put us in charge of opening the rest of the cages. We had to poke some of the prairie dogs with sticks to get them to leave. We watched them run back and forth, then stand up and look all around, then run around some more, and then we drove away.

We stopped for hamburgers and ice cream. While we ate, Adam's aunt and uncle talked about how moving to New York was a big adventure for him, and getting a new dad was a big adventure for me. I was about to say I wasn't sure he'd be my dad, but I remembered I'd told them already.

They said that, when they found a new home in Schenectady, Adam could call me long distance and give me their new address, so I could write to him. Adam promised to send me some post-cards before that, from fun places on the way to New York.

Mom always made me thank people who were nice to me, so I thanked Adam's uncle and aunt for the hamburger and ice cream. I didn't want to. I didn't really like them anymore. They were taking Adam away, and they talked like I should be happy about it.

When I got home, I asked mom if they were all coming to the wedding before they moved away.

"Of course they are," she said. "Why do you ask?"

"I still like Adam, but I don't like his aunt and uncle anymore." I told her why, and I cried a little, but only for a minute.

"I understand," she said. "But you know that sometimes we act happy about things that make us sad, so we don't make other people sad too."

"Are they doing that?"

She smiled. "I think they are. Moving is sad for everybody. You leave your house, your neighborhood, your friends. It helps to think happy thoughts about it when you can. Does that make sense?"

"I don't know. Should I act happy that he's leaving?"

"It might be easier for him if you don't act as sad as you are, but no, you don't have to pretend to be happy."

"Am I supposed to act happy that Jack is coming to live with us?"

"You don't have to pretend that either, but I want you to try to be happy about that. I'm happy about it, and I'm not pretending."

"Okay. I can try," I said. "He is nice."

"He really is. Are you excited to see what a wedding is like?"

"I guess so."

"Is there anything we could do to make you more excited about it?"

I had a weird idea. "Can we invite Barry and Autumn, too? Are they on the guest list?"

"They're not. Do you want to invite them?"

"Are they the bad kind of hippie?" I asked.

"I don't think so. We're going to be neighbors, and if you want to invite them, we can invite them."

"Would it be okay if they brought Boris?"

"Who's Boris?"

"Their big, black dog. They say he's really nice."

"Weddings aren't really for dogs," she said.

"Okay," I said.

"Do you like Barry and Autumn?" she asked.

"Maybe. They were nice to me, even though I asked them a lot of questions. Is it okay to like them, if they're not people like us?"

She laughed. "As long as they're not the bad kind of hippie, and as long as they don't use drugs."

"What if they don't believe in marriage? They said they don't."

"Well, it's wrong to live together like that if you're not married, but we don't have to tell them that, especially if they don't believe in it."

"If it's wrong, won't God be angry?" I saw tornadoes in my mind.

"I don't think God gets angry that much," she said. "I do think that sort of thing makes him a little sad."

Usually, when I was really naughty, Mom was sad too, instead of angry.

"When you talked to them, did they seem like good people?" she asked.

"Yes."

"Do you think they'll be nice neighbors?"

"Yes."

"Tell you what. Tomorrow we'll take an invitation next door. If Adam's aunt and uncle don't know Barry and Autumn's address, we'll leave it there for them to pick up next time they come."

· · · · ● · ● · · ·

WHAT ACTUALLY HAPPENED WAS that Mom was busy on the phone, doing something about the wedding, so Jack went next door with me. They had Barry and Autumn's address, so we wrote it on the envelope, and Jack went to the post office with me to mail it.

I was worried that he'd want to talk about being my dad, while we walked, but he didn't say anything about that. He told me what it was like when he played on the baseball team in college.

"I'm bad at baseball," I said.

"Would you like me to teach you?"

I thought about it. "Okay."

"Do you have a baseball glove?"

"No."

"We'll go shopping for a good one, but probably not until after the wedding."

I said thanks, even though we hadn't actually done it yet.

Chapter Fourteen

Nightmares

Most nights, I didn't have bad dreams, which Mom called nightmares. When I did, they had snakes in them. At first, when I woke up, I would be so scared I couldn't move, because the snakes might be in my bed. After a couple of minutes, I would be almost as scared, but I could sit up, because they weren't in my bed, even if they were under my bed. After a while, when they probably weren't under there either, I could go to Mom's room and get in bed with her.

She usually didn't wake up. If she did, it was only long enough to put her arm over me and hug me. Either way, I would fall asleep and not wake up again until morning. Sometimes when I didn't have bad dreams, I woke up in her bed anyway.

That Friday night, I had my bad dream and went to her bed. In the morning I woke up before she did, and I started to think. There wasn't room in Mom's bedroom for two beds, unless it was two small beds like mine instead of two big beds like hers. I thought about that for a while. Then I had an idea. Maybe there were bunk beds made out of beds as big as Mom's.

She said I should say "good morning" when I saw her for the first time after we both woke up, and she always said it to me. So when she woke up, I said, "Good morning. Are you getting bunk beds after the wedding?"

She turned a little bit red. "I suppose we might eventually, if a little brother or sister comes along. Your room would seem really small if we put two beds side by side. But we'd probably keep the baby in here for a while, in a bassinet."

"I meant bunk beds in here," I said.

She rubbed her eyes. "Why would we put bunk beds in here?"

"You said that, when Jack moves in after the wedding, he'll sleep in here with you."

She smiled. "You're right. I did say that. Can you think of some way that would work besides bunk beds?"

I looked around. "I don't think another bed this big would fit in here."

"It probably wouldn't," she said. "What's your next idea?"

When she asked me that, I got another idea, and I didn't like it. "I don't know," I lied.

She gave me a squeeze. "As you know from experience, this bed is just big enough for two."

I also knew that two was less than three. This was bad. After the wedding, Mom and Jack would be two, and there would be no room for me.

I must have looked sad, because she squeezed me again and said, "I know it's a lot of changes for both of us, some little changes and some big ones. It'll be a lot of changes for Jack too. But we both love him, and he loves both of us, and he and I both love you. We'll all be okay. We'll be better than we've ever been."

"Okay," I said, even though it wasn't, and I wasn't sure I loved Jack. "Will you cuddle with him, when he's in your bed?"

She turned a little bit redder. "I think I'll cuddle him a lot. But I won't stop cuddling you."

Maybe she would cuddle me if Jack was on a trip one night, but on other nights there wouldn't be room for me. I didn't tell her that. But I knew the word for what I would be and she wouldn't, after the wedding.

I knew because one time she was sitting in her chair and looking sad and crying a little. When I asked what was wrong, she said sometimes she was lonely.

"What's lonely?" I asked. That was a long time before we met Jack or even Adam, and I didn't know as many words.

"Lonely is what you feel when I go out somewhere, and you stay home with a babysitter, and you miss me. Lonely is what I feel when you're not here with me."

"But I am here," I said. "Why are you lonely?"

She reached for me, and I climbed up on her lap, and she held me tight and said she wasn't lonely when I was with her. "But sometimes I'm lonely for somebody else too. Sometimes a mom wants there to be a dad. That's one of the reasons why people get married. In some ways it's harder to be lonely when you're married."

So I knew Mom wouldn't be lonely after the wedding, because Jack would be with her. But I would be lonely sometimes, starting with the honeymoon, when they would leave me with someone and go far away by themselves.

I had been a little bit excited for the wedding sometimes, but that kind of stopped when I thought about how lonely I would be as soon as it was over.

· · • · • · • · · ·

I DIDN'T HAVE THE bad snakes dream very often, but I had it again the next night. When I sat up in my bed for a while, I decided I should be a big boy now, not a little one. The way to do that was not to go to Mom's room and get in bed with her, because pretty soon I wouldn't be able to do that.

I had to get out of my room, though. In the morning, when Mom found me sleeping in the hallway with my pillow, she woke me up.

"What's wrong, Joey? Why are you out here?"

"I had the snakes dream again," I said, after I sat up.

"I'm sorry. Why didn't you come to my bed?"

I looked away. "I was practicing."

"Practicing what?"

"Being a big boy."

She sat on the floor beside me. "Tell me how sleeping in the hall is being a big boy."

"After the wedding, when Jack is in your bed and you're not lonely anymore, and I have the snakes dream, there won't be room for me. It's only big enough for two people."

She tilted her head and her face changed a little, but not in a way that made me think I was already in trouble and it wasn't even breakfast yet. "You were sad last night, when Jack was here, weren't you? I'm sorry I didn't ask you about it then."

I shrugged.

"Changes can be a little scary," she said.

"Are you scared too?" I asked.

"I wouldn't say scared, exactly. I'm nervous about some things, and that's part of the way to scared. But he's a good man, and you're a good boy, and I'll still be your mom. We'll figure everything out."

"Okay," I said, but it was still sort of a lie.

"I really love him, Joey."

"I know."

"He makes me happy."

"I know."

"But I love you even more."

I just looked at her for a second. "I know."

"He'll be a great dad."

I shrugged.

"With a mom and a dad, you'll be less lonely than with just a mom."

I hadn't told her I would be lonely. And I didn't think it worked that way.

"I'm your mom. I know these things," she said, like she knew what I was thinking. "Let's go make breakfast. How about pancakes in our jammies?"

I was a big boy now, so they were pajamas, not jammies. But pancakes were my favorite.

Then she said something really cool. "You know what? I think I'll get a bigger bed."

Chapter Fifteen
Wedding

A FEW DAYS BEFORE the wedding, Mom and Jack sat me down in the living room for a talk. I was afraid they'd caught me doing something bad again—not very bad, but bad enough to get me in trouble. I wondered what they had found out.

It wasn't that.

"We've been talking about it," Jack said, "and we'd like you to go with us on our honeymoon."

After we talked about honeymoons before, and after some more talking with the boys at school, I thought this was a pretty bad idea. I must have looked shocked or something, because Jack hurried to explain. He said we would go to California, eat in restaurants, do lots of fun things together, and even visit Disneyland and Sea World. I'd have my own hotel room right next to theirs, with my own TV and a door between our rooms. There would be a swimming pool too, but I should always have at least one of them with me when I used it. And we would go for ten days, not just a week.

Mom wanted to talk about how much fun Disneyland would be, but I was more interested in something else Jack mentioned: visiting a Navy base, where we could watch the airplanes and helicopters land and take off, and also tour a huge aircraft carrier. Maybe we would even go fishing in the ocean, he said.

That didn't sound too gross, so I asked, "Why?"

"Why what, son?" asked Jack. It was the first time he ever called me "son," and I sort of liked it a little. But I sort of didn't like it too. I didn't know what I should say or do about that, so I just asked my question.

"Why do you want me to go on your honeymoon? I thought you were supposed to do that without me."

"Well," said Jack, "to tell you the truth, there are four reasons. One, we like you. Two, we think you'll have fun. Three, we think we'll have fun having you along. And four, we know Adam's moving away, and we don't want to leave you here for a week all alone, without a mother or a best friend."

They wouldn't have left me alone. I would have gone to live with someone from church for a week, probably Jack's brother and his wife, or maybe my Sunday School teacher, which would not be groovy. But sometimes Jack talked to me like I was older. I liked that.

"I also have something I hope you'll do for me at the wedding," Jack said. "The bride, who is your Mom, will have what's called a maid of honor standing with her at the wedding. Have you ever heard of a maid of honor?"

"No."

"She's a good friend of mine from college," Mom said. "She's coming to town for the wedding."

"Okay," I said. I didn't see how that was about me.

"The groom, which is me," Jack said, "has what we call a best man standing with him at the wedding."

"Do you have a friend from college?" I asked.

"Yes, but one of my best men will be my brother. You know him already. I want you to be my other best man. What do you think?"

This was pretty weird. And I wasn't a man. I was a boy. "They let you have two?"

"It's unusual, but yeah, they'll let me. You don't have to say anything, just be there with us, looking handsome in your suit. This way, you get to participate, not just sit and watch like everybody else. What do you say?"

I looked at Mom. She smiled and nodded, so I looked at Jack and nodded too.

"Thank you, Joey," he said.

Mom and Jack told me how the wedding would go, and some of the things they and the pastor would say, but they said it might be hard to understand. Jack said, "Just listen for us both to say, 'I do.' That's the best part. Then I'm going to kiss her in front of everybody. Actually, that's probably the best part."

"I've seen you kiss her before," I said.

"True," he said with a big smile. "I mean the best part for me. I like kissing your mom."

"Jack," said Mom, like she wished he hadn't said that in front of me. But I was a big boy.

I turned to her. "Do you like kissing him?"

"Yes. Very much." Her face turned really red. Jack was watching her too, and he still had the big smile.

"Okay," I said. "I'll try to listen for when you say 'I do.'"

• • • • ● • ● • • • •

THE WEDDING WAS NICE. Adam and his uncle and aunt came, and so did Barry and Autumn and a lot of other people. They all said it was good. I mostly liked it, except for my shoes, but I didn't know if it was better or worse than other weddings, or the same.

I was a best man, like Jack wanted. Mom was dressed all in white, except for the flowers in her hair, and she looked really happy. Jack was happy too. He was dressed in a black suit. I didn't understand very much of what they said, but I heard, "May we have the rings?" and I heard Mom and Jack say, "I do." Then the pastor said, "You may kiss the bride," and Jack kissed her in front of everybody, like he said he would. The other people clapped, and I didn't feel as bad as I usually did, when I saw them kissing.

Chapter Sixteen

Honeymoon

AFTER THE WEDDING WAS a fancy party with food and music. They called it a reception. Some of the food was good, but the reception was so long it made my feet hurt, because I mostly had to stand with Mom and Jack while lots of people said congratulations. Then Mom and Jack cut the wedding cake, and they were really messy, which everybody thought was funny, except for Adam and me. We thought it was weird.

Mom threw a bunch of flowers at some women, and one of them caught it, and Jack threw a little piece of Mom's underwear at some men, and one of them caught it. Everybody laughed and cheered. Mom and Jack promised to explain later. All they would say right then was, "It's tradition."

At the end of the reception, Adam and his uncle and aunt walked up to us, and I felt really bad, because I knew they were there to say goodbye. I tried to think about my first trip on an airplane, and also about having a dad, which might be okay after all, if we visited an aircraft carrier.

But they didn't say goodbye. Adam's uncle said he had an idea. The airport was on their way, so I could ride most of the way there with Adam in their moving truck, and Mom and Jack could follow in Jack's car. I knew Schenectady was a long way to the east, and we drove west to the airport, so I wasn't sure it was really on their way. I thought they were just being nice, to help me not be sad. That made me feel like a little boy again, but riding in the big truck was fun.

We stopped at a gas station, so I could get out of the truck and into the car. Before I got out, they gave me two books to read. Adam's uncle told me to be sure to read what they wrote inside the cover of each book.

"I'm not allowed to write in books," I said.

"People at the university do it all the time," Adam said. "The first book is to read on the airplane. It's all about airplanes and airports and how they work. The other book is to read in your hotel room at night, when everything on TV is boring or stupid."

"Thank you," I said. The airplane book looked fun. The other one was thick and heavy.

Then we really did say goodbye, although if anybody said anything else, I was too sad to remember it later. Adam and his uncle shook my hand, and Adam looked sadder than I thought he would, because he was older. His aunt hugged me. I might have cried a little.

They stood next to the moving truck and waved, when we left for the airport in the car. I waved back, and I definitely cried a little then.

When I couldn't see Adam anymore, I thought about the postcards he would send me from their trip, and the postcards I would send him from the honeymoon. Then I wondered if I would ever see him again. I was glad it was dark in the car.

· · · ● · ● · ● · ● · ·

THE AIRPORT WAS INTERESTING, and the airplane ride was really fun. I was a little scared when we took off, but after that it wasn't very exciting, except dinner. The mac and cheese was good, and the airplane people kept asking if I'd like another soda or maybe some juice. I always said soda, until I got the hiccups.

I opened the airplane book and looked to see what was written inside. I could read it okay. I was the best reader in my kindergarten class, and Mom said I'd been practicing with the newspaper and my old books since I was three.

"Joey, you have been a very good neighbor, and we'll miss you. We hope you have a lot of fun on your honeymoon, and we hope you like flying on airplanes and reading this book. Thanks for not caring that our skin is a different color"—which was the first I ever heard of people caring about that. It seemed like a stupid thing to care about. They had signed their names at the bottom.

I got out the other book. It was called "Little Britches," which was a word I didn't know. Jack said it meant pants. So . . . little pants. I looked to see what Adam had written.

"Joey," he began, "you're my best friend, and I wish I didn't have to move away. Uncle says the boy in this book is a cowboy, but also a city kid like us. He says you're a good boy like the one in the book. You're a good reader too, so maybe you can read it yourself, or you can get your mom or your new dad to read it to you. I hope you like it."

At the end he wrote, "Your friend, Adam," and I had to try pretty hard not to cry a little more right there on the airplane. Mom always said it was okay to cry, but I didn't want her and Jack to think I was afraid of riding on an airplane or something dumb like that.

• • • • • • • • • •

T HE HONEYMOON WAS FUN. We went to all the places Mom and Jack said we would, plus some movies in the afternoons. Mom and Jack kept falling asleep in the movies, even though both hotels had big beds and plenty of pillows.

I went right to sleep the first night, after our flight. The second night I didn't, and I was a little scared in my room alone, but I didn't bother Mom and Jack. There was a door between our rooms, two doors, actually, and they said if I really needed to, I could open mine and knock on theirs. But I never did. I had treats, drinks, my own TV, my books, and lots of pillows.

The food at the restaurants was really good. I mostly had a hamburger and fries, except when I had a cheeseburger and fries, or when it was breakfast.

I liked the new books a lot. Jack read me and Mom the first chapter of the book about little pants, which didn't explain about the pants at all, and then I read it to myself again later, which took a lot longer. We did the same thing with the second chapter. After that I tried reading the third chapter on my own, which was really hard, but I mostly figured it out, and the next day, Jack helped with the parts I didn't understand.

I could tell Mom was really happy, and so was Jack.

I still called him Jack, but I was okay so far, except for missing Adam.

Chapter Seventeen

Fire

MOM SAID WE HAD more money after she and Jack got married. It seemed like we had enough before, except for two times when I wondered about that.

One day, after listening to Juan at recess, I came home and asked Mom, "What's the difference between alimony and child support?" She told me, but I didn't understand. They were both money, she said, but we didn't have either one, so it didn't matter.

The other time was after Mom agreed to marry Jack, but before the wedding. I didn't hear what it was about, but I heard Jack saying, "Honey, I can afford it. I want to help. This time next month, it'll be your money anyway, as much as it will be mine."

Mom said, "This time next month, I'll be glad for the help. But Joey and I have made ends meet all these years. We can handle a few more weeks."

Even if I didn't know what they were talking about, I was happy when she said, "Joey and I."

· · · · **·** · **·** · **·** · ·

I GOT A POSTCARD from Adam with a picture of Niagara Falls, and I sent him one of some dolphins from Sea World. Then he sent me one with a picture of his new city, and I sent him one of the huge aircraft carrier.

• • • ● • ● • ● • • •

O NE NIGHT AT HOME, after we got back from the honeymoon, I couldn't sleep. I got up and went to the living room. Only one light was still on. Mom and Jack were on the couch, kissing or something. They seemed embarrassed, and I think they were about to scold me, but then we heard the sirens.

When I heard sirens in the daytime, I always ran outside to see if I could see the fire truck, police car, or ambulance. This time I ran to the front window, and what I saw scared me so badly I couldn't talk.

There was a big, new building three blocks away. It was seven stories tall, which I knew because we had gone there sometimes to watch the construction. The whole thing was on fire.

"Two men don't get to see something like this very often," Jack told Mom. "We'd better take advantage of the opportunity." Mom looked unhappy, and I was still scared, but I went outside with Jack.

I had always been afraid of fires, but I had never imagined a fire this big. I was afraid there might be people in the building, but Jack said there probably weren't at night, since it wasn't finished yet. Even if there were, he said, usually people can get out of a building when it catches fire, and they're okay.

Then I started to wonder what made the fire happen. Jack said he thought someone from the union might have started it on purpose, because they were using non-union construction workers, and the union didn't like that. He said the same thing had happened in some other cities near us.

I asked him what a union was, but I didn't understand his answer.

I was still scared, but I couldn't stop looking. We watched for a long time, and I saw Mom watching from inside. Then everything got a lot worse. Little pieces of the fire started falling on our lawn and our roof. Jack called them embers. He said they weren't enough to set our grass or bushes or roof on fire, but we got out the hose anyway, and every time an ember fell on the roof or the lawn, we sprayed water on it.

Jack was right. Embers fell on all the houses, cars, and yards on our street, and some of the houses didn't have people on the lawn with hoses, but nothing else caught fire.

It was really late when the fire died down, the embers stopped falling, and we stopped being firemen and went inside. Jack made me bring my sleeping bag and sleep in his and Mom's bedroom, so I wouldn't be scared. That was probably good, because I had dreams about fires that night. One was about embers landing in our living room and burning holes in the carpet, and we didn't have a hose inside to put them out.

After that night, my bedtime prayer got longer.

Later we read in the newspaper that Jack was right about what caused the fire too. Somebody from the union had started it, and the police had caught him, and he was going to jail for a long time. Jack was also right when he said there was no one in the building that night—except the person who set the fire, I thought. But he got out, or they couldn't have sent him to jail.

Jack said no one would ever set our house on fire, so I shouldn't worry about that. I said, "What if we told the police about the hippies growing marijuana, and they found out we were the ones who told, and they got angry?"

"Well, they'd probably be angry," he said, "but I don't think they'd set our house on fire. They'd be afraid to get caught."

"I don't think we should tell the police," I said. "Just in case."

It was the next day before I thought about how Adam wasn't there to watch the fire with us, and I was sad.

Then I thought that being a fireman with Jack was pretty good, even though I was scared. I was lot less scared because Jack was there.

Then some boys at school told me their dads hadn't even told them there was a big fire, so they could watch. Or if they saw it, their dads made them stay inside and go to bed.

"Your dad is cool," said Juan.

"I'm not sure he's going to be my dad," I said.

• • • ● • ● • ● • •

J ACK FOUND ME A postcard with a fire station on it, and I used it to tell Adam about the fire. I knew he'd want to know about something like that. But I never heard back from him, so I never sent him another postcard.

Chapter Eighteen

Sick

On Mother's Day morning Mom got sick, and Jack said he needed to take her to the hospital. That scared me a lot at first, but Mom said she'd be okay, and I shouldn't worry, so I mostly didn't.

My new aunt and uncle were gone somewhere, so Jack took me next door to Barry and Autumn's home, where Adam used to live. He said he'd see me later, or at least call, and he would leave a key to our house with Barry and Autumn.

Barry wasn't home, but Autumn was. She tried to take good care of me, even though she was really big, because she was going to have the baby soon. She fed me a weird cereal called granola for breakfast. It wasn't as good as my regular cereal, but it was okay, and I was hungry. Then she asked if I wanted her to take me to church, because she knew I went to church on Sundays. I said okay.

I thought she would just give me a ride in their yellow Volkswagen, then pick me up when it was over, because I knew she didn't go to our church. But she walked right in with me and sat down, and she stayed for the whole service. Then she asked if I wanted to stay for Sunday school. She said I should, because they'd said something in the service about kids making things for our moms in Sunday school. So I stayed.

Before my class started, a boy whispered to me, "My mom says that lady you came to church with is a hippie. Who is she?"

"She's my neighbor," I said. "Her name is Autumn."

"Where's your mom?"

"At the hospital. Jack went with her, so I'm staying with Autumn today."

"Is she a hippie? Did you do drugs for breakfast?"

"We did granola."

"What's that?"

"It's not drugs. It's a weird kind of cereal."

"Groovy, man! I can't wait to tell my mom. She'll freak out."

Autumn was right about us making nice paper flowers. The other kids gave theirs to their moms after Sunday school, but I kept mine for later.

On the way home I asked Autumn if she went to the Sunday school class for grownups. She said yes, so I asked if people were nice to her.

"That's a strange question," she said. "Why wouldn't they be nice to me?"

"Because some people at church didn't like hippies, and they thought you looked like one," I said.

She smiled. "I do look like one, but they were very nice to me."

I was glad.

That evening, Jack came to get me and take me to the hospital for a visit. I took Mom my paper flower. She liked it. When I asked what sickness she had, Jack said there were a couple of things, and one of them was probably the flu. I asked when she was coming home, and they said tomorrow.

She did come home the next day, but she had to stay in bed almost all the time after that. Jack took some time off his job to take care of her. By the time school was out, she wasn't any better, and Jack had to go back to work. He even got a second job, because there were doctor bills to pay. He told me I was in charge of taking care of Mom while he was working, and Autumn and Barry and my new aunt and uncle would be happy to help if I needed them.

Jack was so tired after work that sometimes I took care of him too. I even made sandwiches. He and Mom said they were very proud of me, and I was a very good boy, and they couldn't get by without me.

It was like that the whole summer, so I didn't get to play with friends. That was okay, because Adam was gone, and I didn't have any other good friends. I played a lot at home by myself, and I watched TV with Mom and answered the door when people from church brought us food. Sometimes the doorbell would ring, and I answered it, and there would be no one there, just an envelope with money in it. It was usually one or two twenty-dollar bills. Mom always cried a little and said she wished she knew who was doing it, so she could thank them properly.

Sometimes I watched out the window, in case they came to leave money at our door again, but I never saw anyone, and we never found out who did it.

Chapter Nineteen

Sicker

ONE DAY IN AUGUST Mom was a lot sicker, and I was scared. Mom was scared too, so I knew it was bad.

Jack was at work, and we tried to call him. I dialed the number Mom told me and handed her the phone, but all she could do was leave a message. So she sent me to get Barry and Autumn. They came and talked to Mom for a minute, then called her doctor. He wanted to send an ambulance, but Mom said that was too expensive, so Barry took her to the hospital in their car. They sent me home with Autumn. Barry said I should take good care of her for him, and I tried, but I still had lots of time to worry and try not to be scared.

Jack must have gone straight from work to the hospital when he got the message, because later he called Autumn's house from there. He told me he was coming to get me, because Mom wanted to see me.

"Is she okay?"

"You can see for yourself in a few minutes." He sounded tired.

What I saw for myself, when I got there, was that she was weak and very pale, and she talked even more softly than usual. She took my hand, pulled me close, and gave me a kiss on the forehead. I noticed her cheeks were wet.

"I have sad news," she said.

That's when I knew she was dying. She looked like she was dying, and she was weak and shaky when she hugged me.

"Joey," she said, "we didn't tell you this before, but I was going to have a baby, and that's mostly why I was sick and had to stay in bed all summer. But then I got sicker, and now I'm not going to have a baby anymore, at least not for a while."

"Oh," I said. "I thought you were going to die."

"I'm not, but I am sad. Partly I'm sad because you were going to be such a wonderful big brother."

"Will you have a baby later?"

"I don't know. I hope so. In the meantime, I'll bet Autumn and Barry will be glad to let you practice being a big brother to their new baby. It's coming soon."

Now I was worried about Autumn. "Do you think she'll get sick like you?"

"Oh, no, I think she's quite healthy."

"Okay," I said.

Jack took me to the hospital cafeteria for an ice cream sandwich before we went home. Mom came home two days later, and she was a lot better after that, but she was still sad sometimes, and she hugged me a lot.

• • • ● • ● • ● • • •

J ACK KEPT WORKING TWO jobs. He got more and more tired, and then he got sick and coughed a lot. But he kept working. Some days I didn't see him at all, because he was gone before I woke up, and he was still gone when I went to bed. Mom said she saw him more than I did.

One evening she looked worried, and she kept staring out the window.

"Are you watching to see who brings us money?" I asked.

"No," she said. "I don't need to know that, and besides, they already left some today. They wouldn't come again tonight. In fact, I think we'll be okay, and we won't need their help anymore, so they'll probably stop bringing it soon."

"Are you watching for Jack?" I asked.

"I guess so," she said.

"Is he okay?"

"I hope so."

"I heard him coughing last night, when I woke up," I said. "It sounded bad."

She reached out and pulled me to her, but she didn't say anything about Jack's cough.

"Will he have to do two jobs forever?" I asked.

"Not for very much longer."

"Good," I said.

"Yes," she said, and kept watching out the window.

"Why does he have to work so much?" I asked.

"He wants to take good care of you and me, and my being in the hospital was expensive."

I stood there next to Mom and tried to think of things good dads did that Jack wasn't doing. I couldn't think of anything. Finally I asked, "We already had Father's Day, right?" I knew because Mom and I had taken Jack to dinner at a nice restaurant, with cloth napkins and extra spoons and forks. Mom called it his first Father's Day as a father. I didn't agree, mostly, but I didn't say anything.

"It was in June," she said. "Seems like a long time ago."

We watched some more.

"Mom?"

"Yes?"

"Could we have Father's Day again soon?"

"There's one every year. It's always the third Sunday in June."

"Could we have Father's Day again this Sunday?"

"Sure, if you like."

I knew she was really worried, because she didn't ask me why. She just kept watching and waiting. She was still there when I went to bed.

Chapter Twenty

Rewards

MOM PROBABLY FORGOT ABOUT our extra Father's Day after that, and she probably didn't tell Jack, but I remembered.

He had to work on Sunday, but Mom said he'd be on time for dinner. After church, she cooked all afternoon, and she let me help her some. We made garlic bread, apple pie, and chicken with noodles. Everything was ready when he got home.

The garlic bread was the best, but Jack said nice things about the chicken. When I thought it was time for pie, he tapped his glass with his spoon and said, "Could I have your attention, please?" He already had our attention, but he was in a good mood, and he was having fun, I thought.

"This is not just an ordinary dinner," he announced. "It's a celebration."

I wasn't sure what we were celebrating, except maybe that he was home in time for dinner. Unless he really did know we were having Father's Day again. But he didn't say anything about that.

"This has been a long, hard summer for all of us. But the three of us are alive and healthy, and after today I'm only working one job, and here we are together. That's reason enough to celebrate."

It sounded like enough to me, even without an extra Father's Day.

"But there's more," he said. "There happens to be a young man in the family who has worked harder this summer than anyone had a right to expect of him."

Now I understood. "Jack, I'm really glad you don't have to work that hard anymore," I said. "Mom and I were worried."

He and Mom laughed, and I didn't know why. Then Jack said, "That's very kind of you, but the young man I was talking about is you. You've taken such good care of your mom, among others, that we have two rewards for you."

I didn't say anything, but I felt my eyes get big. On *Bonanza*, when there was a reward, it was always money.

A twenty-dollar bill appeared in Mom's hand, and my eyes got even bigger. "This is for you, Joey, but I don't want you to spend it. It's one of the last twenty-dollar bills the stranger left for us. I want you to keep it always, to remind you that there are good and generous people in the world—always at least one more than you know." She handed me the money.

"Are you ready for the second reward?" Jack asked.

I nodded eagerly. Another twenty-dollar bill appeared in Jack's hand, and I knew I was rich, even if I couldn't spend it.

"This is the other twenty-dollar bill the stranger brought us last time," he explained. "This is for you to save or to spend any way you want. You are a fine young man, and I am proud to know you."

He reached over and shook my hand. Then there was apple pie and ice cream for dessert. Mom wouldn't let me have thirds.

After I helped clean up the dinner dishes, I went to my room and closed the door. I was there a long time, writing in my notebook. Mom came and checked on me, to see if I was asleep, which I wasn't. I was very busy.

"Are you deciding how to spend your money?" she asked with a smile.

"No," I said.

"Have you already decided?"

"I think so. Do I have to tell you?"

"No, not now," she said, which meant yes, I would have to tell her later. "As long as it's a good thing, not a bad thing. Or a foolish thing."

"Okay."

"Do you want to watch TV with us for a few minutes before bedtime?" she asked.

"Would it be okay if we did something else?"

"What do you want to do?"

"I want to have an interview."

"What would you like us to ask you?"

"I want to ask the questions."

Her eyebrows went higher. "Okay. Where did you get the idea of having an interview?"

It was kind of a stupid question for a mom, but I didn't say that. "They do it on TV all the time."

"I guess you're right. Who will you be interviewing?"

"Jack."

"Are those your questions?" She pointed to my notebook.

"Yes."

"Then let's do it now. It's almost bedtime."

Before we went to the living room, I asked, "Mom, do Barry and Autumn have very much money?"

"I don't think so," she said. "Things will be pretty tight for them when the baby comes. But they'll be all right."

Chapter Twenty-One

Interview

"**A**SK ME ANY QUESTIONS you want," Jack said. "If I don't know the answers, do you want me to make something up?"

"No," I said seriously. "I want you to tell me the truth."

"You got it."

I opened my notebook and looked through the questions again, to make sure I had written them in the right order.

"That's a lot of questions. Are they all for me?" Jack asked.

"Yes."

"Then we better get started, so we can finish before your bedtime."

"Okay. Do you like roly-poly bugs?"

"Yes, but your mom doesn't." He didn't smile, so he was taking me seriously.

"I know. Do you like airplanes?"

"You know I like airplanes."

"What about prairie dogs?"

"I don't know any prairie dogs personally, but they seem okay."

"Do you like *Bonanza*?"

"Yes." Now he was smiling, and so was Mom.

"Do you like mountains?"

"Yes."

"Do you like fishing?"

"Yes."

"Do you like *Monday Night Football*?"

"As long as the Cowboys aren't winning."

"Are you afraid of fires?"

"A little bit."

"What about snakes?"

"Only the poisonous ones."

"Do you think people should get married before they have babies?"

"Yes, I do."

"Are you mean to them if they don't get married, but they have a baby anyway?" This was important. I liked Barry and Autumn, and they were nice to me.

"No. I try to be kind to them."

"Are you mean to hippies?"

"No."

"If I got in trouble at school for rolling down the ramp to the open space and running into my teacher and got sent to the office, would you be mad at me?"

"Probably a little."

"Would you yell at me?"

"No. Have I ever yelled at you?"

"No. Would you hit me?"

"No."

"Would you tell my mom?"

He smiled. "I think you should tell her."

Mom wasn't smiling anymore, but there was a light in her eyes, plus some tears that hadn't fallen yet. "Joey, did you roll down the ramp at school and run into your teacher and get sent to the office and not tell me about it?"

"Yes," I said, but she might not have heard me, because Jack interrupted. "Honey, this is Joey's interview. Let him ask the questions."

I looked at my list. "If you get mad at me, will you go away?"

"Never." He and Mom shared a look. They didn't look angry.

"If you get mad at Mom, will you go away?"

"Never."

"If I ran away, what would you do?"

"I would be sad, and I wouldn't stop looking until I found you. But I'm not worried about that, because your mom told me you promised not to run away."

I thought he was going to say, "run away again," but he only said "run away." I liked that.

I checked my list. "If we don't have enough money, or you have to work really, really hard, because one of us is sick and we have to pay the doctor and buy medicines, would you ever want to go away?"

"Never. Did I go away this summer, when we didn't have enough money, and your Mom was sick, and I had to work two jobs?"

"Jack, he'll ask the questions," Mom said. "But it's bedtime, Joey. Are you almost done?"

"I have two more questions, or maybe three."

"Okay," she said.

"What would you do if a prowler came and tried to steal gas out of our car?"

"I would make sure you and your mom were safe, and then I would call the police, so they could catch him."

"Okay." I got ready to say what came next.

"What's your next question, kiddo?" Jack asked.

I took a deep breath. "Mom said today could be Father's Day again, even if it isn't the third Sunday in June. Is that okay?"

"Sure."

"I have a Father's Day gift for you."

Mom smiled a very big smile.

"Did you spend some of that money already?" Jack asked. He knew I hadn't, because we hadn't gone anywhere since they gave it to me.

"I thought about it, but I couldn't think of anything good enough."

I had to stop again, to get ready for my next question.

"So what is this Father's Day gift?" he wondered. "Do I get to see it before you go to bed, which is very soon?"

"It's not something you can see," I said.

"Oh," he said.

I looked at Mom. She wasn't smiling anymore, exactly. There were tears on her cheeks, but they looked like the happy kind. Maybe she knew what I was going to say.

"Do you promise you're going to stay? Because if you promise, I'm going to start calling you Dad."

He smiled a different sort of smile, and I was afraid he would cry a little too, but he didn't. "Remember when I said 'I do' at the wedding?" he asked. "You were listening for that, I think."

"I remember."

"That was me promising Mom and God that I would stay. Now let's shake hands like men." He reached out his hand and I took it.

His hand was strong, and he didn't let go right away. He looked me in the eye and said, "I promise to stay. And you calling me Dad is the best Father's Day gift I can imagine. If it's okay, I'll keep calling you son."

I nodded.

Then he let go, and there was hugging and other stuff, mostly from Mom, and I went to bed.

Epilogue

THE NEXT TIME WE visited my new uncle, I made him promise not to tell, and I had him write "For the Baby" on an envelope, so it wouldn't look like a kid wrote it. I learned that trick from TV.

I got up early the next morning, put one of my twenty-dollar bills in the envelope, and sneaked out and slipped it under Barry and Autumn's front door. Nobody ever said anything about it after that, but Barry and Autumn must have told Mom and Dad, and they must have figured out who did it, because after that they never asked me how I wanted to spend the money.

. . . . . ● . ● . . . .

I BELIEVED DAD WHEN he said he would stay, and he did. He was nice to Mom. He taught me to fish and play basketball and fix cars. He taught me not to sit around watching football on holidays "while the women worked," he said, even when the woman was Mom.

Also, he taught me never to run away.

From the Author

THIS NOVELLA IS A work of fiction. I have woven scattered threads of memory into the fictional cloth, after dyeing most of them different colors, but Joey, Adam, and their adventures are largely the products of imagination. Joey's mom and Jack are even more so.

Yet my aim was historical in a sense. I wanted to recreate how the world looked and felt to a shy kindergarten boy, growing up in a progressive American university town in the early 1970s.

Childhood was childhood then, but it could scarcely remain untouched by the serious issues of the time. Then again, there are serious issues in every time.

What I have written, as you now see, is not a children's book, but a book about childhood which I hope adults can enjoy, as they remember their own childhood.

Short Stories

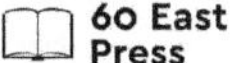

60 East Press — American Fork, Utah

Her Voice

THERE'S NOTHING LIKE THE sound of a mom reading to her children, when they're your children too. It's the exact opposite of their nightmares, the universal antidote to whatever imagined horrors the darkness may conceal. It works on me too, easing me away from today's and tomorrow's cares. And everything sounds better in Ann's British accent.

"*The Tale of Peter Rabbit*, by Beatrix Potter. Read by Mum, for Jake and Amber.

"Once upon a time, there were four little Rabbits, and their names were . . ."

Jake and Amber are still young enough to enjoy snuggling in our bed for their bedtime stories, and they're small enough to fit there between Ann and me. I'm in my pajamas because my bedtime is early too; I have to be on station by 5:00 a.m., almost an hour away. On work nights I hardly ever hear the end of the first story. I love falling asleep to Ann's voice.

When it's not a work night, I'm there for stories anyway. I love staying awake to her voice.

Sometimes in the middle of the night, half-awake for a fleeting moment, I'll put my arm around the warm body beside me, and she'll snuggle against me in her sleep and purr. At 3:45 a.m., when it's time for me to get up, I try not to wake her, but she drowsily welcomes and sometimes returns a hug and kiss before falling back into sleep for a couple more hours.

I shower, dress, and pause for a moment in each child's door-way, gazing happily on small, quietly slumbering forms in the pale white glow of the moon. Then it's off to work.

That's how things are for me at home, how they're supposed to be. I'm not content with everything in my life, and I don't always love a routine, but I love this one.

That is, I loved it until the storm came.

This morning, it's harder to wake up than it used to be, and it takes longer. Even as I fumble for my phone to turn off the alarm, I'm not certain I'm awake.

The moon's up, shining faintly through the bedroom window, but the color's wrong—brown, yellow, weak, eerie. The light is like sludge; it should probably smell bad. The alarm's cruel beep-ing is off a bit too. I must be more tired than usual, or maybe I'm coming down with something. I turn it off before it wakes Ann.

I roll over to put my arm around her and give her a squeeze and a kiss.

My arm falls onto the cool sheet. The wrongness of that shocks me fully awake.

The sheet feels crisp and clean on her side of the bed. No one has slept there since laundry day, at least.

Her walk-in closet is next to my not-walk-in closet. I quietly open its doors, because I love that it smells like her. This morning, it smells like dust and smoke.

The air in the rest of the house smells like smoke too. It seems like that's not new, but it hasn't always been that way.

Just past the closets is the master bathroom. The moonlight's wrong there too, and flipping the light switch doesn't help as much as I expect. The face in the mirror is off—my own, almost, but there's something hollow about the eyes, and more gray in my hair than I remember.

For all the strangeness, routine is routine. I stop at each child's doorway. By the faint yellow-brown glow I see empty, carefully made beds in unnaturally tidy rooms.

I grab my lunch from the fridge, wondering if it will taste like smoke. The brown paper bag is unusually soft, and it doesn't crinkle like a paper bag should. At first its proportions seem too wide and too short, and its angles are odd, but I blink a couple of times and it looks normal.

It's time to leave.

Our home sits on the outskirts of town, near the base of a mountain and the edge of a forest. I have countless memories of watching the sun rise into a clear blue sky above evergreens and gray peaks, while ten thousand birds chirp and sing, and our whole world smells of pine, aspen, and scrub oak.

Now, in the smoky silence, those memories feel distant and unreal. The sounds of my truck's door closing and its engine starting are unnaturally loud.

My office is a Forest Service watchtower, thirteen miles in. The last ten miles are a primitive track that makes my four-wheel-drive Toyota a necessity, not a toy.

This morning, after the first mile, I see no other lights at all—not on the road or off, not on land or in the sky. The moon's gone, and I cannot see the countless stars. If I could, they'd be a lush blanket of lights such as no one ever sees in the city.

My burly Tundra is the only light source in this world. Its headlights make the surrounding darkness darker.

The forest should be full of wildlife, but after the second mile I see no animal, large or small. The reason's in my headlights, when they shine on what used to be aspens. Now they're naked trunks, forlorn shadows on the mountainsides, mostly black, with uncharred streaks of whitish bark.

The fire here was recent enough, but I never saw the flames, and I barely remember the smoke. The night shift watchman called it in. He saw the lightning bolt that started it, about the time I emerged from the mountains after my shift and noticed all the flashing lights on the freeway, a mile and a half away.

The storm brought mostly wind and lightning to the mountains, but there were sudden, heavy downpours in the valley. On the watery freeway five lives ended quickly in a multi-vehicle crash. Three of them were mine.

It wasn't Ann's fault, said the state troopers at the front door. She hadn't caused it. It was just bad luck. An accident. Nothing Anyone Could Do.

Everyone was so very, very sorry for my loss.

The fire in the forest was out by the time I returned to work, many days later.

Fog shrouds the road ahead, but when I reach it, it's dull and brownish, not reflective and white. I know it's smoke from 300 miles upwind, not from the forest I watch for fire, but my journey into smoky blackness is too familiar. I feel as if I should be accustomed to this nightmare, but I'm not.

How would one become accustomed to this?

I work alone, a 12-hour shift. Ty is nearly always there as I arrive, ending his own shift, but this morning there's just a note in his familiar scrawl. "Repeater down again. I'll reset it on the way home. Leaving early." The note itself is strange. I seem to remember him spelling *repeater* with all *e*'s and no *a*, and putting two *s*'s in *reset*. This morning, everything's right, and that's wrong.

Until he resets the repeater, I'm isolated. But it shouldn't be long. He lives on the other side of the mountains, a seventeen-mile drive from our post. The repeater sits just off the road and resets in two or three minutes.

In any case the rules are clear: even if communication fails, I stay at my post, except to report a fire.

When the sun climbs halfheartedly through the secondhand smoke, it's apparent that only the firebreak saved the watchtower itself when the forest burned. From the far edge of the cleared area to the jagged horizon, in every direction, I see a black, lifeless dreamscape, with practically nothing left to burn. Yet still we watch for fire.

This must be what hell is like. Alone, the smoke, the stench of charred forest, the meaningless drudgery, the silence.

I often stream music while I watch the horizon, but our internet connection depends on the same repeater. So I turn on the AM radio instead. Nothing happens, not even static. Fresh batteries don't help.

I could push back the silence by talking or singing, but I don't try. It would simply wait nearby for me to stop, and then it would return.

The repeater doesn't go back on line. No doubt, Ty will explain when he arrives for his shift, but that's hours away. In the meantime I doze. I dream of the same wasteland I see with waking eyes. It feels like a nightmare that has always been and will always be.

At noon I study my lunch bag. It's just a brown paper bag, used and reused until it's soft and verges on disintegration. I probably have new ones at home. Ann would know where.

Ty doesn't arrive for his 5:00 p.m. shift. It's been months since that happened. The rule says I'm to remain on station for an hour. Then, if he's still not here, I can leave and report.

I wait the extra hour, then two more. By then it's dark, and my drive home is through the same brown, black, smoky nightmare as my morning commute. The last two miles of forest are green and alive, but shrouded like the rest.

As I approach the valley, my phone finds a connection and vibrates with alerts. As soon as I'm home, I start with my voice mail. There are two messages from Ty. The repeater wouldn't reset, the power supply's fried, that was the spare, and a new one won't arrive until next week. Also his truck wouldn't start, so he'll be three or four hours late for his shift. But he'll be there. I text him, thanking him and wishing him luck.

Dinner is something from a can. Then I make tomorrow's lunch. I find more lunch bags in a cupboard, but they're worn soft too, so I use the one I used today. Showering washes the stench of burnt wood off me. Too bad I can't wash the air. Every light I see from my window is a dingy yellow.

At 8:30 p.m. I put on my pajamas and settle into bed. I used to pray at both ends of the day, but no more.

With the thoughtless efficiency of long habit, I tell Siri to set my phone alarm for 3:45 a.m. Then I give the last voice command of the night: "Play Ann Czerny."

Her words and voice are my refuge. Her accent is music.

"*The Tale of Peter Rabbit*, by Beatrix Potter. Read by Mum, for Jake and Amber."

She planned so carefully for her month-long trip home to Yorkshire, to help her father care for her mother after surgery. She wanted to take the children with her, but we couldn't make it work. So for the month before she left, to help them miss her a little less, she would record one story a day, every day they were in school. Twenty stories in all.

She recorded only one. Then the storm came, and she left for a different destination, and they went with her after all.

"Once upon a time, there were four little Rabbits, and their names were . . ."

If I'm lucky—I often am—I'll dream of her in bed beside me, with our children between us at first and then not. Of waking up early and giving her a hug and kiss, and standing in the children's doorways for a long moment, watching them sleep. Of going to work in a lush mountain forest that teems with life.

Falling Off My Shoes

WHEN MR. BINGHAM ASKED my history class, "Why did Nixon go to China?" I kept a straight face and raised my hand.

He nodded to me. "Ms. Morgenstern?"

"To make American Chinese food great again?"

Others laughed, but he didn't. "After class, please. Now, serious answer, anyone?"

I raised my hand. When no one else did, he nodded to me again.

"Why am I in trouble, but Mark isn't? His jokes haven't even been funny lately."

I knew the reason. Mark Williams was the teacher's pet.

Morons hooted behind me. Bingham pursed his lips. "Everyone, Monday will now feature a quiz. Fifty words on the significance of Nixon in China."

The class groaned. A nearby jock said, "Thanks a lot, S&M." That was their nasty nickname for me, Sandra Morgenstern—because, obviously, initials.

I went straight to Bingham's desk after the bell. I had a bus to catch. He put me off. "Three minutes. When things settle down."

I tried to appear calm as I waited. Inside I was fuming.

Bingham looked toward the door. "Mr. Williams, join us, please?"

For one shining moment I thought Mark was in trouble too. But when Bingham was finally ready, he said, "Ms. Morgenstern wonders why you don't get in trouble for joking around. Please tell her what I said the other day."

Tall-blond-and-dorky cleared his throat, shifted from one foot to the other, looked down at me, short-blonde-and-angry, and croaked a single word. "Timing."

"What's that supposed to mean?" Maybe my tone was too harsh. He was already embarrassed. This was junior high, and a boy was talking to a girl.

"I crack jokes when things are under control and going smoothly, not when it's rowdy or he's hurrying to beat the bell."

I glared at my captor. "Timing?"

Bingham shrugged. "Timing."

"Can I go?"

He nodded.

Tall-blond-and-dorky rushed to open the door for me, and I hurried toward my locker. It was at the opposite end of the building, and I was fighting the two-inch heels I'd worn for a church thing before school.

Ninth grade sucked. Heels sucked. Riding the bus sucked. Locker combinations sucked. Boys sucked—jocks, brains, teachers, all of them.

When I burst from the school, breathless, Bus Seven was roaring away.

"Crap!" I yelled after it. No one heard me. It was the last bus, and I had the loading area to myself. I took another step and fell off my shoes. I grabbed a railing, so I didn't fall hard on the sidewalk, but my open backpack spilled all over.

"Oh, crap," I whined.

I heard the school door open and close.

I knelt and started gathering my things. Someone handed me a book. I saw beat-up sneakers and jeans and looked up to say thanks.

"Oh, crap," I said instead, under my breath.

"You okay?" Mark Williams asked, blushing less than before.

"No! I just missed that bus."

"Yeah, me too."

"Seven?"

"Yeah."

"I've never seen you on it."

"Mom usually drives me," he said, "but her car's broken. Where do you live?"

"I'm not telling you that."

"Whatever."

I ignored his outstretched hand and picked myself up.

He was still there, so I asked him my question. "How do I get home now? It's too far to walk."

"Especially in those shoes."

"What's wrong with my shoes?"

"Nothing. They're nice. Just not for walking."

"My shoes are fine." I turned away and stumbled over them again. He grabbed my arm, steadying me, then quickly pulled his hand away.

Okay, he had a point about my shoes. And anyway, awkward!

"The activity bus leaves at 4:45," he said.

"Two hours? How do you know? Are you a jock?"

"Hardly. Sometimes I have a student council thing after school. Just a dumb committee. Appointed, not elected."

"Are you riding it?"

"Am now."

"It would take me home?"

"Where do you live?"

I looked up at him, then looked away. "Locust Lane, behind the high school."

"It stops at the high school."

"What are you doing until 4:45?" I asked.

"Catching up on history, I guess."

That was too much. "Seriously? Mr. Straight-A Teacher's Pet is behind in history?"

He hesitated. "Yeah. Got Ds on the last two chapter tests. Hadn't done the reading. Things got . . . complicated."

I fumed. Again. "Two Ds, and Bingham still lets you crack jokes? Unlike me, you may have noticed."

"I have timing," he said seriously. "You sure you're okay?"

My mood softened. "Yeah. Thanks for, um, rescuing me. I better text my mom now."

"Yeah, okay. See you on the bus."

When the bus came, he was first in line. Dorks did that to avoid asking someone if they could sit. My thing was being last in line, so I could spend the least possible time on the bus.

When I finally climbed the steps, seat after seat had a track star or two in it. I worked my way back to where Mark sat alone.

"Can I sit here?" I felt half-meek, half-sullen.

"Sure."

"Thanks." I left some space between us and looked straight ahead, as the bus pulled away.

"Why do they call you S&M?" he asked.

"Because they're jerks."

He looked puzzled.

"Sandra Morgenstern? S, M? My initials?"

"Oh, right. Those guys suck, Sandra."

"Thanks."

I looked straight ahead again, as the bus rattled through the streets.

At a stop, when things were quieter, he said, "Your Nixon joke was funny."

I glanced at him. "Thanks."

At the next stop, I looked again. He was watching me. He colored a little when I saw him, but he didn't look away.

I didn't like my heart beating faster, but it did. "Why are you staring?"

He blushed more and looked away. "Sorry."

"Seriously, why? Do I have a zit?"

He shook his head. "No, it's just, well, cute girls don't usually sit with me. Sorry for staring, Sandra."

When he finally looked again, I smiled very slightly.

"Mark?" My face felt warm.

"Yeah?"

"My friends call me Sandy."

If Only I

"**H**enry! Come up to dinner! Lights out on your way." Mom was always going on about the electric bill.

"Two minutes, Mom." I crossed out what I had just written and tried again.

> I watched you wipe a tear away
> And smile, when

"Wipe" was wrong. And "watched" and "when." I changed them all, then hurriedly scrawled the rest of the lines that had formed in my head on the school bus and during a snack break in the middle of my math homework. I didn't want to forget them.

> I saw you brush a tear away
> And smile, as notes began to fade.
> If ever there could come a day
> When I could be the one who made
> You smile, who dried your tears, I'd say
> God heard my heart, when silence prayed.

I sat back. It still wasn't quite right. "Notes" sounded wrong, but I didn't know very many music words.

"Henry, that's a long two minutes!"

"Sorry, Mom. Coming now." I locked my notebook in the drawer and took a moment to admire my desk. We'd seen it in a thrift store for $35, and I hadn't had to beg very much. Mom liked the real wood and the nice finish. Dad liked the small size, so it was easy for us to carry downstairs to my bedroom. I liked that it was mine, and one of the drawers had a lock—and the keys were taped inside.

Halfway up the stairs, I smelled Fried Chicken Friday. Once a month, Mom made her specialty, and Mike and I ate like we hadn't seen food since lunch.

"So Mom," Mike said with his mouth half-full, as he reached for more chicken, "our little Henry is finally growing up. He's using deodorant, and he showers every morning. He must like one of those little seventh-grade girls."

Mike was a jerk. He was only two and a half years older than me, but he acted like he was grown up already, not fifteen. It was worse when Dad was away on business, like he had to be the man of the house or something.

"Mike, don't embarrass him."

He snorted. "Too late for that, Mom."

He was right. I hated that I always blushed redder than Mike, and more often. I figured it was because my hair was blond like Dad's, and Mike's was brown like Mom's. Or because I had a soul.

Maybe the fried chicken would give him zits, just in time for his big Valentine's dance next Saturday. I could hope.

"So, bro, found any hair on—"

"Michael!"

He finished his question. "Your, um, chest yet?"

"Michael." This time it was more reproof than warning, which meant he was outnumbered for the moment. It was time to attack.

"It's okay, Mom," I said. "He picks on me to help him forget he's not a man yet, and actually not even enough of a boy to get a girlfriend."

"Shut up, loser!"

Yep, I'd found a sore spot. His latest crush had told him to take a hike at school on Monday. And Wednesday. And yesterday in a text.

I overheard things.

"Michael! Apologize to your brother. Henry, apologize to yours."

We looked at each other.

"I'm sorry you're such a loser," he said, with no trace of sarcasm.

"I'm sorry I'm so much like my brother," I said just as soberly.

"Michael! Henry! Last chance!" I knew without looking that her lips were pursed, her jaw was set, and her brown eyes were glaring at each of us in turn.

I looked him in the eye and shrugged. This time, sticking to my principles wasn't worth missing dessert. "Sorry."

"Sorry," he mumbled. Then his eyes glinted. "Who is she?"

"Who? The girl who doesn't like you? That's most of the girls on the planet. No, wait. I think it's *every* girl on the planet now. Except Mom."

I knew before Mom said it that I'd just lost dessert after all. It was worth it.

No way would I tell Mike that her first name was Rebecca—Becky—and her last name was Harmer, and her hair was the color of wheat that was ready to harvest, and her eyes were bluer than the sky on the brightest winter day, and just seeing her from two rows back in history class made me feel like I'd never felt before.

Not that she would ever know, or ever see what I wrote about her. And for her. And to her. Or ever care that I existed.

"Is your homework done, Henry?" Mom asked.

"All done."

"Good. Now you can enjoy the whole weekend. You know, Michael, there doesn't have to be a girl for a boy to want to present himself well."

"Maybe not, Mom. But there is. Look at his ears."

My ears were burning—as in hot.

"Of course he's embarrassed. That's what you wanted, isn't it? I wish you'd treat him better. He's your brother, and you were a lot like him, two or three years ago. Try being kind for a change."

I didn't want Mom defending me that much, but I was glad she was doing it. Which didn't make sense, but it was how I felt.

"So, Henry, was today that assembly at school?" she asked. "With the symphony?"

I swallowed before answering. "Yeah."

"How was it?"

"Good."

"What did they play?"

"*Star Wars*, *Pirates*, some other stuff."

Other stuff like the long song that made Becky cry, "Adagio for Violins" or something like that. I remembered the Italian word, but not what they said it meant. The song had no words, but somehow it said things in notes that I wanted my poems to say in words.

I'd sat so that Becky was a few rows ahead of me and a little toward the center, so I could watch her and still look toward the stage. For a while, as she watched and listened, she hardly moved a muscle. I could see her hair, but not her face.

The Adagio song started soft, slow, and gentle. It stayed slow but grew louder and louder. They'd told us another Italian word for that. Just when it was as loud and strong as it could get, I thought, it suddenly became soft again, but the melody didn't change.

Becky squared her shoulders and brushed her hair back, and I saw a little smile, but also the tracks of tears sparkling in the lights.

"What did you like best?" Mom asked.

Becky, I thought. "*Pirates*, maybe. The Adagio thing was good too."

"The what?"

"'Adagio for Violins,' I think."

"Probably 'Adagio for Strings,'" she said, "by Samuel Barber. It's famous. And very poignant. They used it at the end of a sad war movie once. Not sure which one."

Mike looked up from his fourth piece of chicken. "Our Henry is a lover, not a fighter, Mom."

"Good," she said. "The world needs more lovers. Fewer fighters too. Pass the potatoes, please." She turned to me. "We have it on CD. You should put it on after dinner."

Not where Mike might listen, I thought.

When the dinner dishes were done—my job was drying them—I retreated to my room and pulled out my notebook. Hours always passed like minutes, when I wrote and rewrote and rewrote.

> I wish that I were brave, that I
> Could say to you the words I know
> Will never reach your ears, your eyes,

Your heart—for if they did, I'd die.
Or would I live? Perhaps I'd fly
And feel and touch. If only I . . .

Before bed I found the CD, which was easy, because the whole album was called *Adagio for Strings*. I put that track on repeat in my room, set the sleep timer for an hour, and kept thinking about Becky.

She played flute in the school band. I knew from history class, because she usually had her flute with her in a small black case, and a cardboard folder of music with "Flute 1" written across the front in large, black letters. I wondered if there were any violins in our band.

· · · ● · ● · ● · · ·

A T SCHOOL ON MONDAY I saw a poster about a band concert on Wednesday at 6:00 p.m. It was free, and Mom said I could go. She offered to go with me, but I told her I just needed a ride. She said that was okay too.

I studied band instruments online, so I would know them when I got to the concert. They were confusing. Trombones and French horns were easy, but I wasn't sure I could tell a trumpet from a cornet, or a euphonium from a tuba, or an oboe from a clarinet. If they even had all those instruments. I read that a lot of bands didn't use them all. But the flute was the important one, and I was pretty sure I could tell it from a piccolo, if only because Becky would be playing it.

I sat four rows back in the auditorium. The band chairs on the stage were in half-circles, and Becky was at the end of the front row, so she was easy to see. She wore a black dress and low, black heels, and she'd done something nice with her hair. She looked grown up. And so pretty.

When the band teacher announced the first song, I thought its name sounded like some kind of pasta. I listened as carefully as I could to the flutes, and I tried really hard to like them, but I didn't. They were shrill, and a weird vibration made a lot of their notes sound bad. The louder they played, the worse it got. I hadn't heard that when the symphony came, and it wasn't the vibrato they had shown us. Maybe some of the flutes were broken, or they were playing the wrong notes.

When the teacher announced the second song, I only half-listened. It was something about a pasture in Ireland, I thought a minute later, when I tried to remember—after he said, "Our flute soloist is Becky Harmer."

It was a soft, haunting song, and Becky played the first thirty or forty notes by herself, before the rest of the band started playing. It was beautiful. She had a vibrato, just like the symphony players, with none of the nasty vibration. Maybe you had to have at least two flutes for that, because, when it happened, it sort of sounded like they were fighting.

At the end of the song the audience clapped, and the teacher had Becky stand up. She smiled shyly, blushed, and did a small, quick bow, and we clapped louder. Then she sat down.

I watched her for the rest of the concert and wished they'd let her play by herself again, but they didn't. I still didn't like the flutes, when they played together.

At the end I texted Mom to come get me and went out front to wait. I didn't see Becky anywhere. Maybe the band went out a different door. Or maybe they had to find out which flutes were broken.

In my head I tried to replay her solo that I liked, but I couldn't remember it clearly. I shook my head in frustration.

And froze.

She was standing a few feet away, like she was waiting for a ride too.

My ears went hot, and my mouth went dry. I had to talk to her.

"Hi," I croaked.

She looked at me without smiling. "Hi."

While I tried to think of something to say next, she looked away.

"Is it hard to be in the band?" I asked.

She turned back to me, and I felt warm all over. Not the way my ears felt warm.

"No. You just have to practice at home every night, and some of us take private lessons."

"I'd be too nervous to play in front of people."

Like I'm almost too nervous to talk, I thought. I should have a website for all the things I can't say out loud. I could call it Wish-I-Could-Tell-You-dot-com. I could make one about my brother at the same time and call it Mike-dot-loser.

"You get used to it," she said. "I've played since fourth grade, but I'm nervous sometimes, like tonight, when I had a solo. You could probably tell that from the first few notes."

"No, I couldn't. You were really good."

She smiled at me, and I knew that nothing so wonderful had ever happened to me before. "Thanks. Are you thinking of joining the band?"

"No, just curious."

"Okay. Do you have a brother or sister in the band?"

"No."

"You just came to the concert?"

"Yeah."

"Cool. I'm glad you liked it."

It was getting a little easier to talk. "I liked that band at the assembly too."

"What band at what assembly?"

It was a strange question. It was only a few days ago, and it made her cry. She couldn't have forgotten already.

"Last week? The symphony?"

She laughed, and I didn't know whether to be devastated that she was laughing at me or awestruck at the sound. It was like the brook that burbled through the park in my neighborhood, where I liked to write sometimes.

"That's not a band. It's an orchestra."

I felt stupid and small. I'd read about this, but I couldn't remember the details. "What's the difference?"

"Violins, mostly. And violas and cellos. Also string basses, but some bands have one of those." She waved energetically at an approaching car. "There's my dad."

"Didn't he go to the concert?"

"He did. But he didn't want me to have to walk all the way to the car in these heels. He's nice like that. So, uh, bye."

I was still trying to think of what to say next, when she turned back to me. "I don't know your name."

I don't either. No, wait. "Uh, Henry."

"I'm Becky. Bye, Henry."

"Bye."

I watched her get into the car, close her door, and ride away without looking back.

"Bye, Becky," I said under my breath, as their car turned a corner and zoomed away. "You're amazing."

Then it hit me.

Crap.

I should have opened the car door for her. Between that and my not being in the band or even knowing an orchestra wasn't a band, now she'd think I was a loser. Henry-dot-loser.

Mom came for me a few minutes later. I answered her questions about the concert without thinking very much. Then I retreated to my room, pulled out my notebook, and stared at it. All kinds of confusion swirled in my head. Finally it settled down, leaving only words, so I wrote them.

> To speak is torture, pain, a wall.
> My words, near-spoken, die unborn.
> I freely write as water falls,
> As wind blows through an open door.
> You'll never see these lines at all,
> Nor ever know that there was more.

· · · • · • · · ·

ON FRIDAY AFTERNOON, THE last hour of school was our Valentine's Dance in the gym. Becky spent most of it sitting on a chair, looking pretty in jeans and a colorful t-shirt that said "Seattle."

I was so nervous just looking at her that my legs felt shaky and my stomach hurt a lot, but I finally walked up to her and opened my mouth to ask her to dance.

What came out wasn't words. It was slimy, school lunch-flavored vomit, with cookie-colored chunks. I caught most of it with my hands, but when I looked down, I saw that some had escaped—and it wasn't on the floor. It was spattered on her shoes.

I tried to say "I'm sorry" with my eyes for about half a second, just before I ran for the big garbage can inside the nearest door. A minute later, I was in the restroom down the hall.

I cleaned my hands and face and tried not to think. I scrubbed a few spots on my shirt until they were just damp with water, not obviously smeared with vomit. By the time I was done, my stomach felt a lot better, but the rest of me wanted to die.

I'd barfed on Becky's shoes at the Valentine's dance.

The dance was almost over, and I didn't think I'd barf again, so I didn't go to the office and call Mom to pick me up. I just sat in a bathroom stall, waiting for the last bell to ring, so I could slip out and cower in the front seat of the bus, where no one would pay me any attention at all, I hoped.

I silently cursed whatever made me throw up. I cursed the Valentine's Dance. I cursed St. Valentine, whoever he was. I cursed the fifteen minutes they spent in all the seventh-grade homerooms, telling us how to act at our first dance—how to ask someone, how to accept when someone asks, why it's usually rude to say no, and how girl's choice works. I cursed the half-hour I spent at lunchtime, at a dance lesson they said we could go to if we wanted, because I'd learned just enough to think I could do it, even if it was scary. I cursed the school and the calendar. I cursed the whole universe, for having me in it.

Except Becky. I didn't curse Becky.

I was actually sick until at least the next Wednesday, and I managed to stretch that into a whole week out of school. I didn't think I could stretch it longer, and I was pretty sure Mom and Dad wouldn't agree to let me transfer to a new school, even if I was a laughingstock. Which they didn't know—but I could have told them I was the boy who barfed on a girl's shoes at the Valentine's Dance.

Back at school on Monday, I found out where her locker was and slipped a small envelope into it. The words hadn't come out very well on the card, though I'd worked on them all weekend. But I couldn't wait any longer.

Becky,

I'm sorry I barfed on your shoes instead of asking you to dance. I'm very, very sorry, and I'm very embarrassed. If your shoes are ruined, tell me how much I owe you, and I'll pay for new ones. I hope I didn't ruin Valentine's Day for you. Please accept my apology. I'll never embarrass you again.

Sincerely,

Henry P.

I expected kids to laugh at me a lot that day, but no one did. No one even mentioned it. Not a word for two days, not even at lunch, where there was always talk of barfing.

On Wednesday I sat in my usual corner for lunch and ate my sandwich. I tried to compose a few lines in my head, but I could only think about Becky, and I hadn't been able to write about her since the dance where I barfed on her shoes.

I didn't see a girl standing next to me until she spoke.

"You didn't ruin my shoes, Henry."

I turned to look, then realized who it was and avoided her eyes. "I didn't?"

"I just wiped them off."

"Oh. Uh, good, I guess. Definitely good."

"Thanks for the card."

I finally looked at her. "You're welcome. I'm very sorry."

"I know." I saw what I hoped was a little smile. "I never thought asking me to dance would make a boy throw up."

I hung my head and wanted to die. "It wasn't you. I was sick. I mean, I didn't know it until right then. I thought I was just nervous, but I was sick. I missed school for a whole week. Because I was sick."

I was a useless fool when I tried to talk.

"Are you better now?"

"Not sick. Still a laughingstock."

"Nobody's laughing. It was just me, remember? My friends were dancing. And I didn't tell anybody. Well, except my mom. You're not a laughingstock."

"I barfed on your shoes."

"My baby brother does that sometimes. It's not that big a deal."

Her baby brother? Kill me now.

"My cousin did it a lot worse once. That was gross. Hit my shoes, socks, jeans. He was drunk. And fifteen. My aunt and uncle grounded him for life, I think, mostly for trying to drive their car."

I just looked at her.

"I guess I understand," she said. "I'd be embarrassed too."

But you would never do that, I thought.

"I have band," she said, "but can I tell you something?"

"Okay."

She hesitated, and new color appeared in her cheeks. "Next time there's a dance, if you're not feeling sick, you could ask me again."

Not in a million years, I thought. I'm permanently and irrevocably mortified. And isn't it nice that I'm a poet, so I know lots of big words for that feeling?

She must have seen it in my face. Her shoulders slumped. "Not if you don't want to." She turned away.

"Okay, I will. I mean, I want to. I will."

She turned back, smiling slightly. "Okay. See you."

The warning bell rang, and I headed automatically for my next class. Mr. Robbins stopped me at the door.

"No food in the classroom," he said. "This you know."

I looked down and saw my half-eaten sandwich in my hand. I said I was sorry, and I stayed out in the hall until it was all in my mouth and I'd wiped my hand clean on my jeans.

· · · · ● · ● · · · ·

Bus 23 stopped at a corner near our house. Sometimes I took it to the library, and sometimes I just rode it. There were always things to see, and I got ideas for poems from the people, the shops, the houses, and the cars. And all the signs.

So I went for a ride the next Saturday, because I needed new ideas. I still couldn't write about anything else, and I couldn't write about her.

When the bus stopped in front of an especially boring gray building, I was watching a brown-skinned woman four seats in front of me, wondering if she was from India. I looked up, when the driver opened the door, and my eyes went wide.

Becky was showing the driver her bus pass. Then my heart fell. A boy I didn't know got on behind her. He was carrying her flute and her music folder.

I slouched, so she wouldn't see me if she looked toward the back.

The bus was full of old people, mostly, so Becky and the boy just stood in the aisle, near the front. They laughed and talked. She seemed relaxed and comfortable, and he seemed confident—in other words, nothing like me.

I missed my stop, because I didn't want to attract attention, and I wanted to see where they got off. That was a few blocks past my stop. I wrote the location on my hand: Porter Road at 23rd.

I rode to the end of the route and back, debating whether I should look out the window and try to see Becky. If she was outside, she might see me. Or she might be with that boy, and they might be holding hands or something. I decided not to look.

I looked anyway—and I saw her in the front yard of a house, carrying a big, black trash bag. The boy was there too, shoveling the walk.

I almost laughed aloud in my relief. He was probably her brother. No wonder they were so comfortable together. I wrote the house number on my hand. Not that knowing she lived at 2287 East Porter Road would ever do me any good.

At home I wrote her address in my notebook, then tried to start a poem. About anything.

Nothing happened.

I wanted her to talk and laugh and smile with me, like she did with him, and I wanted to write about it. Or anything at all. But still nothing.

In my nighttime prayer, besides the usual stuff, I asked God to help me write again. And I asked him to help me not be such a loser, so Becky would like me. I didn't know if God handled things like that, but I asked anyway.

· · · · ● · ● · · ·

A FEW DAYS LATER, I stayed behind after history class to make up the last short quiz I'd missed. On my way to the teacher's desk to hand it in, I saw a sheet of paper on the floor. We were supposed to pick up litter, and the teacher might have been watching, so I did.

It was a parental permission slip. Those were always going home for something—a field trip, an activity, some embarrassing subject they needed permission to talk about in class.

It was Becky's. She had filled in her name just below the warning in bold letters: "Must be signed and returned by March 7." It was for a band trip to an elementary school—and today was March 6.

"Thanks for letting me take the quiz, Mrs. Lowe," I said, all but running out of the room. Becky needed this paper today.

I didn't catch up to her, and I didn't see her near her locker or anywhere else, so I came up with another plan.

When I got home after school, no one was there. I left a note: "Going for a bus ride." Then I raced out the door to the bus stop.

Twenty minutes later, I walked up the sidewalk at 2287 East Porter Road and rang the bell. I told myself I was brave, standing there with weak knees and shaky hands. I was about to ring again, when the door scraped open.

"Yes?"

I had never seen so many wrinkles on one face, and the woman was shorter than me. Becky's great-grandmother, maybe?

"Is Becky home?"

"Who?" she asked too loudly.

I cringed and tried to talk louder. "Uh, Becky. I brought her something from school. I think she needs it tonight."

"There's no Becky here."

"Are you sure?"

"I've lived here forty-seven years, young man. I'd know if I had a Becky."

My heart sank.

"Do you, uh, know if anyone named Becky lives nearby?"

"Can't think of one. Good day, young man." She pushed the door closed.

I trudged halfway back to the street, then stopped and scanned the neighborhood. There were plenty of houses, even a few people outside, mostly children. But no Becky and no Becky's brother, if that's who he was. Had I written the address wrong? No, I recognized the rusty, miniature wheelbarrow in the flower bed.

The door opened behind me and I turned.

It was the old lady again. She spoke slowly but precisely. "Young man, you asked about a girl named Becky. Am I remembering correctly?"

"Yes, ma'am."

"The Harmers across the street have a girl about your age. Her name might be Rebecca, if I'm not confused. Could she be your Becky?"

My Becky. Something inside me came to life. "Across the street?"

"Not directly across. That white brick house belongs to the Smiths. The Harmers are in the stucco house next to them."

I pointed. "That one?"

"I can't see where you're pointing, when you're so far away, but from where we're standing, it's the house to the left of the white brick one."

"Thank you!"

Twenty seconds later, I couldn't remember looking both ways or crossing the street, but I was standing on Becky's front step, telling myself I was brave again, and ringing the bell. And the door was opening.

Becky was opening the door.

Her forehead wrinkled. "Henry? Hi."

"Hi."

When I didn't say anything else for half of forever, she asked, "What are you doing here?"

"I brought you this." I held out the paper, and she took it.

"My permission slip for band? How'd you get it?"

"On the floor in history, after everyone left. I guess you dropped it."

"Honey, who is it?" called a woman's voice.

She rolled her eyes. "Someone from school, Mom."

"Okay. Don't forget Madeline's cinnamon roll."

"In a minute, Mom."

She turned back to me. "Sorry. Parents. How did you know where I live?"

"I didn't."

She frowned a little. "You're here."

"Um, right. Um, one time on the bus, I saw you and a boy, maybe . . . maybe your brother, in front of that house." I pointed to 2287. "The old woman there said you might live here."

"That's Mrs. Kunz. I was helping Sean mow her lawn. He's her grandson. I'm supposed to take her a cinnamon roll right now, actually. Then I have to go shopping."

I was pretty sure she would only help a boy who wasn't her brother if she liked him. This was a disaster.

"I guess I don't know him," I said.

"He lives across town. He has piano lessons on Saturday at the same time I have flute lessons, and then he takes care of his grandma's yard, so I see him on the bus. I help him sometimes, when I need a service project for church."

"Seventh grader?" I blushed to suit the question I wanted to ask. Was he her boyfriend?

"Not sure. Eighth, maybe? Thanks for bringing this."

I shrugged. "It's for tomorrow. Looked important."

"It is, sort of. I'm glad you found it. Thanks, Henry." She was smiling now, and her eyes sparkled. She hadn't looked like that when she talked about Sean.

I didn't know what else to do, so I said, "Okay. You're welcome. Bye." I turned to go.

"Henry?"

I turned back. Her cheeks seemed redder.

"Do you like cinnamon rolls?"

"Um, yes."

"And you're not sick to your stomach or anything?"

My heart went cold, and my face went hot. But her smile was friendly, not mean.

"I feel okay."

"Want a huge cinnamon roll to take home? Mom just made some. We have plenty."

"Sure. Thanks."

"Wait here."

She disappeared into the house, then reappeared with a plate and a paper bag. "This one's for Mrs. Kunz." She held up the plate. The cinnamon roll was at least six inches across and maybe two-and-a-half inches tall. It was covered with plastic wrap.

She handed me the bag. "This one's yours. I wrapped it for you."

"Thanks."

"Want to help me deliver this one?"

"Okay."

"I have to hurry, so we can't stay, no matter how much she wants to talk."

I ended up hurrying too, because the bus turned a corner half a mile up the hill, just as Becky handed the plate to Mrs. Madeline Kunz.

All I could think about on the way home, once I convinced myself that I'd remembered to say goodbye to Becky and thank her again for the cinnamon roll, was what the old lady said when she saw us at her door.

"Oh, it's you. You found your Becky."

My Becky.

I thought about those two words during dinner, when they asked me about the cinnamon roll that was now on the kitchen counter.

I wasn't in trouble with Mom and Dad for going to her house, once I explained the important paper and reminded them that it really was almost entirely a bus ride.

Then there was Mike, who wasn't completely stupid. He knew right away that the girl in my story wasn't just any girl—which is why I said her name was Amanda. He said something I didn't understand, but I could tell he was teasing me about her, because Dad told him to watch his mouth, leave me alone, and eat.

Mom said I didn't have to share my cinnamon roll if I didn't want to. But it was huge, and I wanted to. She said that was very generous of me. I didn't tell her my big reason for sharing was so I could give Mike the smallest piece. He glared but didn't complain.

The cinnamon roll was fantastic.

Dad took Mike's place with the dishes and sent him to do homework. That usually meant Dad wanted to talk to me.

"You went right up to the edge of what we mean when we say it's okay for you to take bus rides alone," he said. "Assuming you're telling the truth."

"I lied about one thing."

"You lied to us?"

"Her name's not Amanda. It's Becky, but I don't want Mike to know."

Dad grinned. "From now on, Amanda will be her code name, if we need to mention her." He put down the scrubber. "Anything I can do to help?"

"Can you change Mike from a jerk into something better than a jerk?"

He chuckled. "Yes and no."

"What does that mean?"

"No, not in the way you're thinking. Yes, but it may take us a few more years. Until then, we have to try not to kill him."

On my way to the basement, Mom handed me a blank thank-you note and an envelope. "You know what to do," she said.

"What's this for?"

"A really big, homemade cinnamon roll."

"It was a thank-you cinnamon roll, for delivering her paper. Should I thank her for thanking me?"

"I guess you don't have to." She smiled. "But maybe you want to."

She had a point. I wrote out my message for the card in my notebook and worked on it until I liked it. That way, I wouldn't waste the card if I didn't like the first thing I wrote.

At the last minute I crossed out the part where I said I like to write poetry, so maybe I should have written it as a poem. If she knew I was a poet, she might want to see my latest poems—which would be disastrous, because they were all about her.

The last thing I had to decide was whether I could write the word *love* in the card at all, even if it described a cinnamon roll. I decided I could, and I felt brave again.

Dear Becky,

Thanks for the huge cinnamon roll. I shared it with
my family. We all loved it.

Sincerely,

Henry

I sealed the envelope, printed her name neatly on the front, and
turned back to my notebook. There I wrote what the old lady had
said, even though I could never forget it: "You found your Becky."
For a long time I read and reread the words, and replayed in my
mind the few minutes I'd spent with Becky, at and between front
doors.

For the first time in a long time, the words came. I leaned
forward and wrote.

> "My Becky"? Could it ever be
> That you would think or say of me
> That I am yours, and you are mine,
> And we are ours, till end of time?
>
> That's probably too much to get
> From just a cinnamon roll. And yet
> Your laugh, your smile, your azure eyes
> Are everything. If only I . . .

There Might Be Another Way

P IA HAD SLEPT AS late as she dared on a Sunday. She slipped into a pew halfway up the right side of the chapel just as the bishop stepped to the pulpit to begin the weekly sacrament meeting. She'd looked almost human in the mirror before leaving home, which was pretty good, considering.

She listened conscientiously to the announcements, which had little to do with her, then sang the opening hymn, "Jehovah, Lord of Heaven and Earth," with as much of her usual fervor as she could muster. Her focus drifted during the brief invocation by one of her neighbors. It drifted further during some quick items of congregation business. But she managed to keep trying, at least, to ponder the Savior and his sacrifice, as the deacons passed the Sacrament of the Lord's Supper to the congregation. Everyone at church called the bread and water simply "the sacrament," but in the privacy of her own thoughts she preferred the more solemn and evocative phrase.

The bishop announced the first speakers, a girl of about fourteen and an old man she'd seen on Sundays but didn't know, and she drifted away again. She flipped to the Notes app on her smart phone, where she'd composed a sort of letter in the wee, desperate hours—a letter full of things she could never say or send to Doug, her back fence neighbor.

She saw him in his usual place, across the chapel, sitting alone, one row further back, in a heather gray suit (her favorite) and a gorgeous green necktie. She tried to envision him sitting with a wife, when he had one, but she didn't know him then, and she'd never seen his ex.

She should have entered the chapel from the other side, even if it took half a minute longer to get to the other door. She could have asked to share his pew. He'd have agreed, of course, and she'd have been no more distracted than now. She should have left for church a minute earlier.

Doug's posture was attentive, but she recognized the expression of a man who was somewhere else. He often looked like that, though not when he was teaching the adult Sunday school class or chatting with her afterward, and usually not in their occasional conversations over their common fence.

What she'd written overnight, as if to him, was unthinkable, but she couldn't resist reading it again.

> Doug, I need to tell you something—not that I really can. But maybe if I write it just for myself, I can get some sleep. I need that too.
>
> I'm lonely. Not lonely for human company in general or for a man, and any decent man would do. I'm lonely for you.

Out of habit, her eyes checked in with the elderly speaker at the pulpit, but her thoughts didn't. What she wanted in the dark of night, she wanted by daylight too. She wanted it so badly that she was afraid to pray for it, afraid even to hope.

> I don't need you at this moment, if I'm to survive to the next moment. I'm not fourteen. (I'll turn 34 this year.) But I want you in my life. I want to be in your life. I want us to have a life together.

As if on cue, a familiar gurgling sound made her look up. Two rows to the front, a brown-haired baby girl rested her head on her mother's shoulder. Dark eyes watched Pia until their eyelids drooped and finally closed.

Pia returned to her reading. She knew what was next. So did the universe, apparently.

> You could help me make some new life. I didn't used to want that with anyone. I didn't think I deserved happiness. Plus I feared that any teenager of mine might be too much like its mother.

> I wish you were attracted to me. Maybe you would be, if I were the kind of woman you'd want to make long-term plans with.

Her year-and-a-half-old memory of their longest, most serious conversation filled her with a grateful warmth, as always.

> I don't regret telling you about my dark and sordid youth. I'm glad I knocked on your door that wintry afternoon, even more desperate than terrified, to

ask if you really believed what you said in Sunday school about God's love and mercy, if you really believed God's grace is sufficient for someone who did what I did, in the way and for the reasons that I did it. Thank you for helping to persuade me!

You said my heart is "long since changed," that I'm no longer the person who did those things. I'm really not, thank the Lord. But I was that person, and the effects persist.

Recently, not for the first time, even a rough outline of my past pushed away a good man I was dating, when we got serious enough that I needed to tell him. And that was just an outline, not the grisly details. Four people in the world, including you and me, know everything I told you that day.

You've done so much for me already. You don't have to want me as anything more than a neighbor and casual friend. If you don't want even that after this, I could move, or maybe the city would approve a taller fence.

That's why I'm awake when I should be asleep. I wish I could tell you.

Just to be safe, she deleted the note.

Seconds later, she shook her phone to activate the Undo function. Nothing happened. She tried two more times before remembering the Recently Deleted folder.

There it was. The screen said her outrageous note would stay there for thirty days before disappearing forever. She carefully moved it back to its proper folder. Otherwise, she might have to write it again next month.

She put her phone away and tried to pay attention to the meeting. The last speaker was Louisa, an articulate woman with a professional demeanor. She lived two blocks over, was only a few years older than Pia, and led the Young Women organization, which seemed appropriate, since she and Bryce had three teenage daughters. The whole family had shown up with a dozen other neighbors, two years ago, to help Pia move in. Louisa had smiled warmly and said, "My friends call me Lou."

Now Lou was describing her childhood. It was surprisingly grim. For her eighth birthday, her grandparents gave her an American Girls doll named Samantha, which immediately became her favorite thing in all the world. Two weeks later, her mom sold Samantha, along with Lou's favorite Disney videos, to buy heroin. Within a month, her mom was back in jail.

"I hated her then," said Lou, "besides loving her, of course. I prayed for her to get clean, to return each time she went away, to stay when she returned. I needed my mom, but God didn't seem interested in those prayers. I thought she probably deserved to have God ignore her, but I took his silent refusal to fix things for me as proof that I didn't interest Him either."

Pia brushed away a tear, then another. She had blamed God too. Her childhood was far better than Lou's—but she'd bet money that her teenage years were much worse.

Lou spoke with tranquil strength. "I learned too early, I guess, that life can be too difficult, in too many ways at once. But I also learned, so maybe it was worth it, that God's silence doesn't mean he's absent or disengaged. I learned that he makes us strong enough to do what we must do. I learned that he offers us some joy even as we struggle, and when we're finished here, he plans to make us glorious. I think he's made each of us a little bit glorious already, if only we had eyes to see."

Strength from God would be good, Pia thought, if she knew what to do with it. Some joy would be welcome too. She didn't feel even a little bit glorious.

In Sunday school she sat in the back, behind a tall woman and her taller husband, where Doug couldn't see her clearly as he taught the class. She was too tired to pay careful attention, let alone participate. When it ended, she escaped the building quickly.

For a few seconds the late-morning summer sun refreshed and restored her. Then it overwhelmed her, and she began to wilt, but the skyful of billowy clouds gave her an idea. She retreated to the shade of an old maple tree in the churchyard to wait for a cloud to cover the sun.

She stared at a page in her leather-bound scriptures, so she wouldn't appear to be waiting for Doug when he came this way. If he came this way. He usually did. A few others waved or called greetings as they left.

Five minutes passed, then ten. She considered the sky. A huge, slow-moving cloud might help in a few more minutes. She closed her thick book and pulled out her phone. Last night's note was still on the screen.

She jumped and all but screamed when Doug appeared, not three feet away. She hadn't heard the church doors open or close this time, let alone noticed his approach.

"Hi. Sorry I startled you. And interrupted your reading." He was always friendly; it meant nothing more.

"No worries," she said. She turned off her phone as casually as she could, wishing her hands didn't shake, and held it at her side.

"You were quiet in class today," he said. "You okay? You never sit on the back row."

He couldn't have read her screen, but what if some of it showed on her face? Something did; her face felt like the sun was on it, even in the shade.

"Just sleep-deprived," she said. A version of the truth was always best. "Short night."

What she saw in his face was familiar enough. His brown eyes always appeared slightly sunken, with little bags under them. Now they looked mildly concerned.

"And you showed up anyway," he said, loosening his necktie. "Good for you. Heading home?"

"I ordered shade for the walk." She indicated the cloud that was edging its way in front of the huge, round fire in the sky. "Looks like it's about to arrive."

"Would you mind some company?" he asked.

Her heart leapt. "Not at all."

"I'm not being chivalrous," he said as the sun disappeared. "I need to ask a favor."

Needing a favor from her was good. "What can I do for you?"

They moved toward the sidewalk.

"It's pretty big. I should buy you lunch if you agree. Or make you lunch or mow your lawn."

If he was giving her a choice, it was an easy one. "What favor is so big that you have to make me lunch?"

He hesitated. "It's kind of awkward. What if I tell you over lunch? You can still say no."

"It's a date," she said, blushing again. "So to speak. When were you thinking?"

"Soon. Could be today, if you don't have plans. I'm grilling salmon for myself, and there's plenty for two."

They agreed on lunch at his place in an hour. She spent half of the hour preparing one of her best salads and the other half deciding what to wear. After a light mist of her favorite tropical citrus body spray, she donned a black-and-white peasant blouse and white capris—attractive and even a bit flattering, but not aggressively so.

She spent the entire hour reviewing every twitch and syllable of their conversation, yearning for some hint that this could be more than a friend asking a favor. She found none. But at least she'd be with him for a while.

· · · ● · ● · ● · · ·

S HE WAS BARELY EXAGGERATING later, when she told him the salmon melted in her mouth. He praised her salad and took a large second helping.

Doug's home had a formal dining room furnished in dark oak, but he'd set their places at a smaller, round table by a window onto his back yard. Her home was in the background. Tall potted plants framed the view at either side. Three hanging plants across the top sent hopeful, white-blossomed tendrils halfway down to the table's edge.

"Lunch was amazing," she said, after he'd cleared their places and returned to the table. "Even the ambiance is charming. Thank you."

He smiled less than he might have. "Been practicing the salmon. Nice to have an audience." Then his smile disappeared altogether. "I was softening you up for what I'm about to ask."

Against her will, her voice trembled. "Mission accomplished. What is it?"

He just looked at her for a moment. Maybe it was the nerves in her voice.

"What do you know about online dating?" he asked. "I've heard you mention it a couple of times. I need to sign up, and I don't know what I'm doing."

Her heart fell, but she tried to hide it. "You've come to the right girl. I'm a veteran. Seasoned. Jaded."

He nodded grimly. "I think I've picked a reasonable platform for me, but I could use a second opinion. I drafted my profile, and someone at work took some photos, and I need another pair of eyes on all that too, before it goes live. Sympathetic, feminine eyes would be ideal."

Her sympathetic, feminine eyes wanted to weep. This favor wasn't just big. It was very nearly the last thing she'd have wanted to do for him. She'd do it anyway. And there would be little point in joining the same service. Even if the algorithm cooperated, he'd already met her.

"You decided you're ready to get back in the game," she said softly. "That was a huge step for me."

"I didn't decide anything, and I don't feel ready. I lost a bet with my sister."

"On what?"

"NBA finals."

"What did she put up?"

"Finally seeing a specialist about whatever's wrong with her foot. I didn't expect to lose." He blew out a breath. "I get to pick the platform, but I have to sign up, take my profile seriously, stay on it for sixty days, and at least look at anyone who responds. That might be all I do."

Or it might not. Pia didn't care about the NBA, and she'd never met his sister, but she'd managed to lose his bet too.

"Okay," she said. "Let's earn my lunch."

"I'm not ready for this," he said, opening his laptop on the table and turning it slightly toward her.

She scooted closer so she could see the screen, but not as close as she wanted.

His profile was positive but not overdone, and she praised it sincerely. He admitted spending a few hours studying best practices. She suggested some edits, which he made. Then she read it aloud one more time, mentally comparing it to the man she knew. It suggested his keen intelligence, but it could hardly convey his kindness and compassion. She didn't tell him that. It mentioned his faith and how important it was to him. But he would never believe, let alone boast to strangers, that people who knew him considered him an uncommonly Christian man. She didn't tell him that either.

She helped him choose the best photos. She tried to be conscientious, but she couldn't wait for this to end. Something wasn't sitting well in her gut, and it wasn't the salmon, the salad, or the sorbet he'd served for dessert.

It was clearly an excruciating half-hour for him too. She might have enjoyed his veiled suffering, since he was unwittingly causing hers, but she didn't.

He leaned back. "That's as good as it'll get and still be me. Thanks for helping."

"You're welcome."

He grimaced. "So this is how it's done in the 2020s, when you're in your late thirties."

"I'm in my mid-thirties," she said. "My early mid-thirties. But yeah."

"I was talking about myself," he said unnecessarily. "May I ask a personal question?"

"Sure."

"Do you feel like it's going to work for you?"

She hesitated. "No. I mean, I haven't given up. Not yet. I have doubts."

He nodded. "Then good luck to us both. Especially you. Thanks again."

"My pleasure," she lied, and her heart resumed breaking.

He poised a finger over the touchpad, then leaned back again and let his hand fall to his lap. "I'm a coward. I'm going to sit here and gather my courage. Then I'll click the fateful button." He stared at his hand, smiling faintly. "Say something encouraging, okay?"

"I remember the feeling," she said. "Maybe this will teach you not to bet on sports."

"This is how you help me be brave?" he asked too seriously.

"I'm no expert at that," she said.

But bravery was the issue, wasn't it? Could he hear her despair? What would she say, if she were brave? And why was she growing angry with him, and not with herself for her own cowardice?

The answer hit her and spilled out in the same moment. "What you lack is not courage."

Their eyes met, and she answered his unspoken question. "You're not taking this seriously enough. It's unfair and unkind. It's unlike you."

"What do you mean?"

"Women will see your profile and think you might be a really good guy, which you are. They'll feel a spark of hope in a part of their hearts that starves for hope, and they'll muster their own courage one more time and reach out and try to connect. But their hope will be wasted, and their courage too, because you're not there to connect with someone. You're just going through the motions, paying off a bet, and then you'll be gone, after barely being there in the first place."

His face went slack, and he averted his gaze—out the window in front of them, but it was a thousand-yard stare, aimed at nothing.

She covered her face with her hands. "I'm sorry. I shouldn't . . . It's none of . . . I'm sorry."

"No," he murmured after a moment. "You're right."

She lowered her hands enough to look at him. His face was still slack, but now his cheeks were slightly flushed, and his eyes were on hers. She attempted a wry smile. "Want your lunch back?"

"No. What should I do?" He sounded overwhelmed, not defensive.

"Why aren't you trying to connect with someone? Are you . . . attracted to women?"

Ohgodohgodohgod.

"Since I was twelve."

"Then why . . . Sorry, it's . . ."

"Pia?"

"Yes?" Would he invite her to leave now? She still hadn't said what she most wanted him to know. She'd used her bold moment to accuse him instead.

"It's not in my profile," he said, "but I'm pretty messed up. Have been for a while."

She hesitated. "Someone told me the divorce was devastating, but I don't know any details, and I'm just guessing it's that anyway."

"Six years, and I'm still part of the smoldering wreckage." He looked out the window again and said too evenly, "I failed at the most important thing I ever tried to do. And I didn't know I was failing until it was too late. I didn't know life with me was so miserable for her."

She yearned to take his hand. "I can only imagine how that hurts."

He nodded slowly.

"And you don't want to do that to yourself and someone you care about ever again."

"I really don't."

"What do you do when you feel something for a woman? Does that still happen?"

He spoke carefully. "I . . . resist it. Repress it, if that's the word. Fear it, obviously. I'm not dead, but feeling nothing is how I get through the nights. Some of the days too." He gestured toward his laptop. "What should I do?"

"I don't know," she said.

"I gave my sister my word. But if I'll be causing pain even to strangers . . . I don't want that."

She bowed her head and said nothing.

"I guess I could just click the submit button and take whatever happens next more seriously."

This was it: her best chance, maybe her last chance, to tell him what she couldn't tell him. She looked into his eyes and resisted the urge to bite her lower lip.

"What should I do?" he repeated.

Her internal organs quaked, but she spoke the words that came to her mind. "There might be another way." Her voice quaked too, and he looked concerned. "There is another way you could approach this."

"Better than advertising myself at Please-God-Help-Me-I-Am-So-Lonely-dot-com?"

She liked gallows humor, but she couldn't laugh. "I think it's better." She hesitated. "You may not agree."

"Tell me," he said. "Please."

She nodded slightly. "Since you said 'please' . . ." Her pulse pounded in her ears. She pushed the crucial words out quickly, before she could falter. "You could just forget all this online stuff and date me instead."

Her gaze clung to his, and she did, after all, bite her lower lip to stop it quivering. Her mind was beside itself. *OhGodohGodohGodohGod!*

He didn't visibly melt or reach for her hand or rush to embrace her. He froze. He didn't even smile. He stared, and she stared back.

His mouth barely moved. "I could . . . Is that an option?"

"Now you know," she said softly.

He nodded almost imperceptibly. "Is that what you want?"

Could he speak so evenly, so calmly at this moment, if he wanted it too?

"Yes," she declared, but her firmness didn't last. "I mean, if you . . ."

He stared a little longer before replying. "I'm nothing like the guys I've seen you date. You're young. Alive. You really want . . ."

Finally she saw a glint in his eyes. Was it interest? Hunger? Disdain? She was afraid to put a name on it, afraid to put the wrong name on it.

"I want two things." It was out there now, so she could talk about it—barely. "I want you to see me as more than your neighbor, if you possibly can. More than a friend you see at church. And I want you not to waste time worrying that I won't feel that way, because I already do."

OhGodohGodohGodohGod!

She saw his fear and responded to it. "And if that happens, I want us not to be afraid—of ourselves or each other. When one of us is afraid, which I guess makes four things, not two, I want us to face it together. Get through it together. That's what I want."

His voice was gentle. "How long?"

"How long have I wanted that?"

He nodded.

It was easier in someone else's words. "It has been coming on so gradually, that I hardly know when it began."

"Jane Austen?" His smile was faint, but she didn't imagine it, because then she saw it fade. "I have no Pemberley to offer you," he said. "I am in most ways Mr. Darcy's inferior. Up to and including the tall hat."

"I don't need Pemberley. And you're not inferior to him in any way I care about. Also, you're not fictional. Even your online dating profile is nonfiction."

"You really . . ."

"Yes," she said with untempered emotion.

"Wow," he said neutrally.

Her anxiety bubbled over. "I'm sorry, Doug. I don't know what that means. Is it wow, this neighbor woman is unimaginably brazen and repulsive? Wow, she's lost her mind? Wow, I'll never invite her to lunch again?"

She watched in vain for a response.

"Those options don't have to be mutually exclusive," she murmured, just to break the silence. Why was he silent?

When he spoke, he seemed dazed. "How about, wow, I . . ." He shrugged. "I don't know what. Not the bad things you listed. Maybe, wow, you're the bravest woman I know?"

It wasn't the answer she needed. Did he feel anything for her? Was he trying to dissuade her? Was her distant past getting in the way, even with him?"

"I'm pretty messed up too," she said. "As you know." She swallowed nervously. "Remember when we sat in your living room once, and you changed my life?"

He brightened. "You had already changed. You just needed to finish admitting it to yourself."

"In your Sunday school lesson that day, you said changed hearts are the greatest miracles you've ever seen."

"They are."

"And you saw that in me." Her chin trembled. "You know too much. How could you ever be seriously interested in me?"

There. She'd asked him directly. Maybe her whole future wouldn't turn on his answer, her mind advised, but the rest of her felt that it might.

"You're one of the best people I know," he said. "You're beautiful on the inside too. It's like Lou said today. You're a little bit glorious. More than a little bit."

"Thank you. I'm not sure that answers my question."

He said nothing.

"I'm sorry again," she said, "but I can't tell what you're feeling now, and I need to know. Even if you don't—can't—feel for me what I . . ." She stopped a sob half-formed. "Right now I can't see that you feel anything at all."

He frowned, and she feared his reply nearly as much as she needed it. After a long moment, he nodded solemnly and took a deep breath. "Pia, I'm sorry."

Her heart fell hard, and she looked away. She heard a quiet whimper and realized it was her own.

She had tried. It was a good try, better than she could have hoped for. Maybe now she could—

"When the emotions you could show are nearly always negative," he said slowly, "you learn not to show emotion, or it's hard for people to be around you. Hard to be around yourself. I will need to unlearn that." He took another deep breath. "I'm messed up, and it's already hurting you. I'm sorry." He hesitated. "I feel stunned," he said. "Elated. Terrified. Grateful."

She dared to meet his eyes again. "So many feelings at once," she mused, then smiled as best she could. "Who knew men were so complex emotionally?"

"I think I know what to do now. Thank you." He seemed to grow calm, and his voice turned decisive. "First step, as you said. Forget the online stuff." He shut his laptop with an exhilarating click. "It's forgotten."

Hope flared inside her, undaunted by the possibility that he was just giving up. "What about your bet?"

"If I get the next step right, it'll count."

Her eyes widened and her mouth fell open. *And date me instead.* That's what she'd said. That's what came next. And getting that right would mean . . .

He must have read it on her face. "Sounds like I have some catching up to do," he said. "Maybe less than you think."

"Are you serious? You're not just humoring me?"

A hint of a smile touched his eyes. "I have no pretension whatever," he said, "to that kind of elegance which consists in tormenting a respectable woman. I would rather be paid the compliment of being believed sincere."

His eyes repaid her smile with a full-blown twinkle.

"How do you know my favorite novel so well?" she asked. "You being a man and all."

"*Pride and Prejudice*? Good choice. My sister shamed me into reading it in high school, and I enjoyed it. This winter, when we couldn't get together for the holidays, she wanted us to reread it together, which we did. We discussed it over the phone almost every evening for two weeks. Even read some scenes aloud together."

"That's more fun than I had over the holidays," she said.

"I like it on its merits too. I finished the audio book again last week. I usually go with comfortable and familiar for my evening commute." He shook his head. "I'd be well schooled for new romance, if this were 200 years ago and one English-speaking empire to the east."

He still hadn't declared his feelings clearly, but she no longer feared to hope. "Did you ever think of me this way before?" she asked.

"I've liked you well enough since I met you."

"In a way that could turn into new romance?"

"Are you sure about me?" he asked with a pained expression. "I'm not . . . I'm a . . ."

"Everybody's messed up," she said. "You're a good man."

It took a moment, but he visibly relaxed. "Thanks for thinking my heart is . . . worth reviving."

She waited to see if there was more, perhaps something amazing like, "It's yours if you want it." Then she waited until she could speak. "Thank you for not abruptly showing me the door."

A gentle smile appeared. A fond smile. "I think you've made yourself . . . irrepressible."

She wanted to smile in response, but his smile passed too quickly, and he looked away. She saw despair, and it made her want to weep for him. "Doug, I need to tell you something, and it's not another ugly confession. There's something I can see, and it's real, and you need to see it too."

He met her eyes.

"I love that you see it in me," she said, and her voice began to tremble. "I need you to see it in yourself."

"See what?" His voice was soft and gruff.

"That Lou was right. You're already a little bit glorious." She managed a nervous smile. "If you ask me, and you should, it's more than a little. You're a good man with a good heart."

He didn't take his eyes off her. Something in his expression turned gradually from dark to light, and his wary diffidence fell away. Behind it came a warmth she could feel even before he spoke.

"So," he said. "Our first date. Tell me you're not busy after dinner tonight."

She beamed. "I am now. Hot, buttered popcorn, my sofa, and my choice of BBC video?"

"Perfect." He pushed his chair back, stood, and reached for her hand. "Come here, Pia. Please?"

She stood and turned toward him.

It wasn't a kiss. He pulled her to him, hesitantly at first, then firmly, and she held him so tightly her arms ached. She'd hugged him once before, briefly, in gratitude, after their long talk in his living room, but this was different. This felt like home, the sort of home you could spend a lifetime building, if you were lucky. The sort of home she'd never had, the sort of love . . .—but they could say that word when they were both ready.

In the safety of his arms, feeling overcame thought again, and she began to sob. They clung to each other as her sobs gained strength.

When his own breath became ragged and his chest began to shake, she felt it with her whole soul.

Nine Roses and Three

February 13

Dear Mary Beth,

I don't know whether they have the same holidays or even the same calendar where you are, or if time means anything there at all. I've heard that it doesn't. But it's Valentine's Day again here. Well, tomorrow is Valentine's Day.

I've been counting. Tomorrow will be the sixth Valentine's Day since you left. I still love you, and I still miss you every day and every night.

I spent today making preparations. You can imagine how that goes at my age. What I could have done in half an hour before, without a second thought, took the whole day. It was exhausting, and there were some frustrations. But it was a good day, because I was doing it for you.

They don't send out as many ads with the newspaper anymore, or in the mail either. I guess everything is on the Internet now. Every*one* is probably on the Internet too, except me. I'm too old to need an Internet. I'll be 87 in April, but you know that already. You'd have been a youthful 83 last month, but you know that too.

Without ads, it would take me a week to go to seven different stores, to pick up ads or check prices. I could do two in a day, but I'd need a full day of rest between such strenuous days.

I never wanted to grow old without you. I grew old with you for a while. That is, I grew old, and you grew more beautiful. Then you went away. I know it's not forever. You've just gone ahead. But I miss you. And most nights I go to sleep hoping to wake up where you are. Not that my life is bad. There are some joys. It's just that being here without you isn't one of them.

But I was telling you about my day. With no ads and no Internet, I spent the week collecting phone numbers for stores, which isn't as easy as it used to be. My phone book is older than some of the stores. I probably should have kept one of the new ones they've left on the porch in the past few years, instead of recycling those and sticking with the old one. Or maybe I shouldn't have lost the list of stores and phone numbers I made last year. As it was, I ended up calling Information. Don't worry, though. I know it costs money, so I don't do it often.

This morning, I called all seven stores. I asked if they were selling bouquets of a dozen red roses and, if so, for how much. They all were. I wrote down each price on my list of stores.

One of the grocery stores wanted $24.99. You're worth it, but I knew you'd disapprove if I went there, when Walmart was selling them for $15.99. That was the cheapest. So I went to Walmart.

I picked up a few other things, including a prescription, to save myself another exhausting trip. Then I spent a long time examining each bouquet of roses, to make sure I found the best, just like I did when I found you. They had 34 bouquets when I started choosing, but when I finished they were down to 29, including yours.

I won't say I was looking for flowers that were as beautiful as you, because they're just flowers. But I like them. I think you would like them. I hope they last at least a week. Do they ever let you come back for a few minutes and see things like that?

I made my purchases and was heading for the door, when my plastic shopping bag broke. It had everything in it but the flowers. One of the things which crashed to the floor was a jar of pickles. I know pickles have too much salt for me, but I like to have one sometimes, and the truth is, you're not around to tell me not to. I'd rather have you than occasional pickles, but I don't. I'm not blaming you.

I was certain someone was about to get on the intercom and call someone to come clean up the mess an old klutz made, when he dropped his jar of pickles. I know they wouldn't say it that way, but they'd be thinking that.

Here's a happy thing. The jar of pickles didn't break. I think I stared at it for at least twenty seconds, while it lay on the floor, just to be sure. Then, before I could start picking up my things, a young lady knelt down and began doing it for me. She was lovely, with brown hair like yours used to be. She must have been 25 or 30, not that I can tell such things. She had pretty eyes and a kind smile, but she looked tired. She was carrying a baby, and she also had an older girl, maybe four years old. I guess that explains looking tired.

When I saw them, I was glad the worst thing I said when the bag broke was "Fiddlesticks!" I'm sure they heard me.

The mother and the older girl picked up my things and put them in a new bag. I was embarrassed. They shouldn't have to clean up after an old, pathetic stranger, when he spills his groceries all over the floor.

I thanked them for their kindness. The mother started to hand me my bag, but I asked her to hold it for me for a moment. Then I pulled three roses out of the bouquet. I hope you don't mind. I was clumsy, and my hands don't work very well anymore, so it took a minute. Now that I think about it, I'm surprised I could do it without dropping the bouquet, but I managed.

I gave one rose to the older girl and told her it was for her, for helping me. Then I gave her another and told her it was for her baby sister. At least I hope the world hasn't changed so much that I can't assume a baby dressed in pink is a girl. Then I said to their mother, "I'm sure you have a charming husband to wish you happy Valentine's Day and buy you flowers, but please accept this rose from an old but grateful stranger."

I wish you could have seen her smile, when she thanked me.

Then her older daughter said, "She has my daddy. He's in the navy. He won't be home for a month."

I'm a silly old man. I wanted to thank them for their sacrifice and have them tell him thank you for his, but I was about to weep at the thought, and all I could do was nod and wish them good day. I turned away and shuffled a few steps toward the door. Then I turned around. The three young ladies were on their way to the side of the store where the groceries are, not watching me, but still carrying their roses. I watched them for a moment, but then I figured I'd better get moving before the new bag broke too.

On the way home I got honked at only twice for driving cautiously. I carried the flowers in, then rested, then carried the groceries in. Then I rested again. Then I put the groceries away.

I've put the roses in a vase on the dining room table, between my favorite pictures of you. There's the one I've always loved most from our wedding day, because your eyes and your smile . . . I don't know what to say about them. But you know the one. And there's the one from your last birthday, which you didn't like when I took it or when I framed it, because you said you looked so old. But you were still younger than me and a great deal prettier.

I'm sitting at the table as I write this. It's a few minutes to midnight now, because it takes me a long time to write anything. My hand shakes more than it used to, and I have to stop and think a lot and try to remember how I was going to end a sentence or why I started it in the first place. Don't worry about the hour, though. I usually can't fall asleep for another two hours anyway.

I remember you without stopping to look at the photos in front of me every few minutes, but I stop and look anyway. I have to rest my hand a lot, and besides that, I like to look at you. I always have, even when you thought I didn't.

I'll do as I always do, a little more slowly than last year, I suppose. I think I finished by 11:30 p.m. last year. When I'm done writing this letter, which I almost am, I'll put it in an envelope and write your name on it, and leave it by the flowers and the pictures. In a week or so, when the roses wilt, I'll throw them away. Then I'll put the letter in your top dresser drawer, with all the others, and I'll put your pictures back in their places in the living room until next time.

There's room in your top drawer for another five years of letters, at least. I hope it won't be that long.

Have a happy Valentine's Day. I hope to spend one with you soon. I don't suppose it will be tomorrow, but that would be nice.

I'm sorry your bouquet has only nine roses this year. I thought I should explain the reason, because, now that you know, I'm sure you don't mind.

Tonight, when I pray for other things, I believe I shall pray that three young ladies' valentine will come home safely and soon. I'm glad I could make them smile today. That's more good than I accomplish most days.

It's been a very good day for me. Thank you for that and many other things.

I wish you were here, or I were there.

All my love,

Henry

Beyond Ugly

A FTER 25 YEARS IT probably wasn't even the same door, but it could have been. It led to the same school, the same fetid swamp of teenage cruelty. My grasping the handle unleashed a fresh deluge of memories. My arm trembled, and my knees went weak.

Obviously, the decision I'd been defending was a mistake. But it was also too late. It was too late *not* to go to my 25th high school reunion, because I was here.

I'd arrived in Stirton an hour early, having somehow missed the promised freeway construction delays. I freshened up in the tolerably clean restroom of a convenience store, then made my way to the campus where I'd spent the worst dozen years of my education.

For the last half-hour of my drive, my older sister's voice in my hands-free car audio system had said pretty much what I'd told myself for weeks, even before I bought my reunion ticket online. Viv and I were both right: "Kat, this is a bad idea."

Stirton was a small town, where everyone knew everyone. Its only elementary school, only middle school, and only high school were right in a row, along one side of the state highway that doubled as Main Street. All three cinder block temples of learning had opened in the same decade, each just in time, give or take a year, for me to suffer in it.

I didn't pull the door open yet, but that was procrastination, not decision. I might open it later. For now, I walked around the outside of the school, starting with the library expansion that hadn't been here the last time I was. The outside wall was now labeled "Stirton Public Library." The dual use probably accounted for the extra landscaping, including a bronze statue of a child reading and several wrought iron benches under trees.

I'd told Viv I had things to prove: That I was past what my classmates did to me here from first grade through high school. That I had made a life for myself since then, no thanks to them, and now neither had nor needed any active, living connection with any of them. That I could attend my class reunion and feel like I was in a roomful of strangers, whose lives and cruel words no longer touched me in any meaningful way.

I hadn't seen my last therapist in five years, but I knew what she would say. Didn't my need to prove that I was past it constitute proof that I wasn't?

She may have been right. Maybe I could prove I was past it by *not* needing to prove it. Maybe it wasn't too late *not* to open the door.

I turned a corner and came face to face with a wall that hadn't been there before. There was probably a metaphor in that. I turned back and made my way to the furthest bench from the front doors of dear old Stirton High and sat in the welcoming shade of a locust tree.

A catering trailer and several cars, not just mine, were parked in front of the school, but I still hadn't seen any people. I tried to breathe slowly and deeply as I looked around. The trees were mature and beautiful. I remembered them as saplings that weren't good for much, but they had grown.

Stirton's only city park was across the street. A midblock crosswalk led from it directly to the schools. The lines on the asphalt looked freshly painted, just as I remembered from first grade, on the day when the crossing guard signaled a dozen of us to cross the street, and my classmate Tami Bates pushed me back onto the sidewalk and said, "You wait here. You're too ugly to cross with actual humans." She turned to her friends and said too loudly, "Ick! I touched it! What if it rubs off?" They all laughed and said more things to each other, which I knew I was meant to hear.

The leaves were turning then, so it was fall, so that would have been the beginning or nearly so. For the next twelve school years, ugly was my brand, and some kids acted like it was contagious. A few of them found it necessary to remind me almost daily—a little less often in high school—so maybe they thought I was stupid too. Or deaf.

"Why would you ever go back there?" Viv had demanded as I drove. "They treated you like a leper. Or one of those untouchables in old India."

She wasn't wrong.

Decades later, Tami's jabs were still the most memorable. Mrs. Martin's biology classroom, toward the rear of the building, behind the library, was the setting for a classic. "You're a failed human specimen," Tami said one day, when we were in the same small group for half an hour. "You should remove yourself from the gene pool. You know, in case some blind man, who can't smell either, by the way, loses his mind too and wants to reproduce with you."

I hadn't truly wallowed in school memories in ages. Now they made me queasy and revived my fantasy of finding a dark room somewhere and hiding in it forever. But there was really nothing to do but get up and walk toward the pain, as I had done here for twelve ugly years.

The next time I touched one of the door handles, I pulled the door open and walked in. It was still a bad idea, but I had paid for my ticket, and I had things to prove.

Full-color signs on easels directed me through the big common area inside the doors, then down a hall toward a cafeteria which also hadn't been there before. I still hadn't seen another living soul since I arrived. I paused to consider my reflection in the glass of an empty trophy case.

"You were on the plain side, like me," Viv had explained again, during our call. "But you weren't ugly. You weren't the worst-looking girl in your class, and they weren't ugly either. Nobody deserved any of that."

Ugly or not, when boys wanted to tease another boy, more cruelly than in fun, they teased him about having a crush on me, or me having a crush on him (which I sometimes did). Starting in about sixth grade, boys teased each other about having sex with me. It was the most disgusting thing they could imagine. By ninth grade, girls teased each other about that too.

They teased Donna a lot. She was my only true and constant friend through my school years, and she wouldn't be here tonight. We'd bought our tickets the same Sunday afternoon, while talking on the phone, but her first grandchild was in the NICU, having just arrived six weeks early, and her daughter was struggling too. She needed to be there, not here.

She'd have been the one obvious exception to my reunion full of classmates reborn as strangers. Other exceptions were possible, perhaps, a few kids who were never really my friends but didn't avoid me or torment me when they could.

I walked into the cafeteria and still saw almost no one, though I heard a muted clatter from the kitchen. By now I wasn't that early, but besides me it was just one guy with a receding hairline. No doubt I'd see more of those before the evening was over.

He sat at the nearest round table to the entry, the only one without place settings. He had a laptop, what might have been a tiny printer, and a sign that said, "Name tags here."

"Welcome," he said in the instant I recognized him as Nate McConnell. An unwelcome, inappropriate thrill raised the hairs on my neck.

"Are you the entire reunion committee?" I asked. He'd sent out all the e-mails. If it had been anyone else (besides Donna), I might not have opened them.

"The others are down the hall, setting up the self-guided tour. What's your name? Sorry I have to ask."

"Kat McCowan."

He looked puzzled, and I knew why, but I didn't help him.

"Are you class of '96?" he asked.

"Yes."

"Let me check my list, then I'll print you a name tag if I don't already have one for you. I'm sorry for not remembering you."

I summoned my courage. That felt thrilling too. "I remember you, Nate," I said. "For twelve years, plus kindergarten, you didn't treat me like something to scrape off the bottom of your shoes."

Recognition gradually informed his eyes. "Is McCowan your married name? I think I remember you as the girl with no vowels in her last name." He scanned the list. "Andrea Vrbs." He even said it right, after all these years: "VERB-us." He looked up. "You're Andi? Hello, former neighbor."

"Hi. I used my old name to buy my ticket, but I go by Kat now. From Kathryn, my middle name. And yes, McCowan is my married name, but the marriage is long gone."

"I'm sorry."

"Divorcing Mr. McCowan is one of the best things I've ever done. Looks like you've done better; I see a ring. Is your wife here?"

Sadness flashed across his face, then was gone. "She's ill. Can't travel."

"Sounds serious. Chronic?" I shouldn't have been so nosy, but I was.

"Lately, both. Her MS relapsed hard over the winter. She has MS. We keep hoping the next remission will start soon. Praying, really."

"Now I'm sorry," I said. "But here you are. Such worries at home, and you still crossed whole time zones for a reunion. Tennessee, right?"

"Yeah. She pretty much insisted. Said nobody's at death's door, which is true, and each day is pretty much like every other day. Her sister flew in to take care of her for the weekend."

"Must be good to get away," I said.

"This is the first time I've been more than fifty miles from home in months." He smiled faintly. "But I love being home."

"Not everyone could say that," I said too soberly. "Especially, you know."

He raised his eyebrows. "We have our joys. Our daily routine is unusual in some ways, but she'll be the first to tell you we have a good life."

I had to smile. "Will you be the second?"

"Absolutely."

My growing urge to confide in him was familiar from our school years. There were two differences now: I could actually do it, and he was confiding in me. "I almost didn't come tonight," I said with only minor difficulty.

He spoke cautiously. "Truth is, I was surprised to see you on the ticket list."

"I almost turned back at the front doors just now."

"I wouldn't have blamed you. Been thinking about you since I saw your name a few weeks ago. We were awful to you, all the way back to, what? Second grade?"

"I remember it as first grade."

"Forgive me, but I've been wondering. Why even come tonight? I mean, I'm glad you're here. But most of the memories must be unpleasant. Is this a profile in courage? Are you here to take your revenge somehow?"

I offered him a wan smile. "I think I'm here to prove that I got past all of that, and they didn't wreck my whole life."

He nodded thoughtfully. "To prove it or test it? Sorry. Not really my business."

I shrugged. "To test it? Yes. To prove it? I hope. I really hope."

"What would proof look like?"

"Maybe feeling no remaining connection to anyone, by the time I leave tonight, and snipping any last threads I may find."

"No one at all?"

Suddenly it felt like a sad thing, and I wavered. "At least not the ones who said cruel things, or the ones who laughed. Which was almost everyone. I remember you as one of the ones who didn't."

Instead of responding to that, he showed me the name tag he'd found in the box: Andrea Vrbs. Both me and no longer me. "Want me to reprint it as Kat McCowan? That's what I'm here for."

"Thank you, yes, please."

He turned his laptop so I could see the screen. "Check my spelling."

He'd guessed correctly about the *K*. "Perfect," I said with a nod. "Thank you."

"Will anyone here know you as Kat McCowan, besides me, now?"

"Donna would, if you remember her, but she's not coming. She bought a ticket, but there's a family situation. So nobody else, probably. Think anyone will recognize me?"

"I'll be surprised. You look . . . different. I see the resemblance, now that I know, but yeah, different. They'll just assume you're somebody's plus-one, probably, until you tell them otherwise."

I peeled the backing from my new name tag, attached it to my shirt, instantly felt more like my adult self and less like I was back in high school, and asked if I could keep him company. "For a while," I said. "If you don't mind." I was only a little bit afraid he might.

"Be my guest," he said. "I'll put you to work." He slid one of his two boxes of printed name tags to me. "You can have A through L, unless you prefer M through Z. It's by surname when we graduated, not married names."

"Works for me," I said, then hesitated. "If I'm here and they don't recognize me, they might think I'm your plus-one." It was a strange, awkward thing to say—but no guy in my class would have taken that risk when we were in high school.

He smiled faintly. "I'll live."

"Your wife won't mind? Is she the jealous type?" I was kidding, but I was also completely over the top. He gave me the puzzled look I deserved. "Sorry," I added meekly. "I don't know her name."

"Julia. We talked about you, when I saw you on the list. By your old name."

In high school world, people talking about me rarely turned out well, but an odd electricity raced through me. My voice was unsteady. "What did you say?"

He hesitated. "I don't—"

I interrupted him. "Tell me the truth. I can handle it." I hoped I could handle it.

I watched and waited for him to speak, but he didn't.

"Please," I said. "Please, Nate."

He nodded slowly. "The truth is, I'm ashamed of the truth. Some of it."

"Ashamed? You? On behalf of the whole class or something?"

"I told her we thought you were the dictionary definition of ugly, and I don't even know where that came from, back in first grade. We hardly knew what a dictionary was. I showed her my old class pictures and yearbooks. That's what I've been wondering about. Not the photos. Why did the ugly label stick back then, and for so long? Why did we ever see ugly in the first place? Why did we treat you the way we did?"

"I've wondered that ten thousand times," I said. "Not so much lately. Did you come up with anything?"

He didn't answer my question. "I'm sorry," he said. "Very sorry."

"Don't apologize for the others," I said. "That's on them."

"I'm apologizing for myself."

Forty-somethings began to appear at our table, and we were busy for the next twenty minutes. Several of them stopped to chat with Nate, like it was more of a reception line for him than a get-your-nametag line.

Some of our old classmates said hi to me and scrutinized my name tag, but no one seemed to recognize me. I recognized most of them, with the help of their names. The twinges of pain were fewer and less severe than I expected, so there was that.

I was relocating a misfiled name tag when I heard a familiar voice, and something froze inside me.

"Do you have one for Tami Bates Wilson?"

I looked up. I could see most of twenty-five additional years in her face and her figure, but she was still beautiful. And I still remembered the pain.

"There should be one for Tad Wilson too," she said. Tad hadn't been among the humane few either. Not even close. He'd also never been with Tami when we were in school, at least not that I recalled. That must have happened later.

I found her name tag. Nate found Tad's and handed it to me. Tad walked up beside Tami and put an arm around her waist. I held out their name tags, looked them in the eye, and said, "Welcome."

She smiled sweetly—I wanted it to be nasty, but it wasn't—and said, "Thank you."

"Thanks," echoed Tad, and they moved on.

I told my heart to stop pounding and my head to stop remembering, and congratulated myself on my exemplary adult behavior. Because I wanted to run, and I didn't. I wanted to shriek, and I didn't. I wanted to weep, and I didn't. I wanted to go vomit somewhere, and I didn't.

There was no one behind them. I took a deep breath and glanced at Nate. He was staring at me, looking concerned.

"How's your proof going?" he asked softly.

"Of complete disconnection?" I stalled for time, knowing it was pointless and wondering how vulnerable I could afford to be tonight.

"Yeah, that," he said.

"I think I was fooling myself."

"Yeah. Look, we spent 180 days a year for a dozen consecutive years with mostly the same people. Seems to me like cutting ourselves off from that completely would require cutting off big parts of ourselves. I don't mean to wax philosophical. But I've been thinking lately how many of these people affected my life, and how much, even though it was 25 years ago and I've hardly seen any of them since."

"You always were smart," I said.

"Takes smart to know smart. At least my high school memories are mostly happy ones. You're really brave to be here."

His phone vibrated. He glanced at it and smiled. "Sorry, I should take this." He tapped the screen. "Hi, Jules. Perfect timing. Having a lull at the name tag table. What's up?"

He sounded happy.

He listened for a moment, then said, "Bob Polzer's here; remember his toast at the groom's dinner?" He laughed softly. "I'll tell him. Wish you were here. Miss you."

I realized I was eavesdropping and tried to tune him out. Focusing on the remaining name tags helped. They were still in perfect alphabetical order, but checking them distracted me anyway—with unhappy memories.

"Sorry for the interruption, Kat," Nate said a minute later, after he put down his phone.

"No worries," I said. "How long have you been married?"

"Nineteen years last week."

"Happy anniversary. That's really great. Not the life you imagined, though. With her MS, I mean."

"Kind of has been, actually. She was diagnosed when we were dating. We knew it wouldn't be easy. I guess marriage never is, but in our case we knew a big reason up front."

"You must have loved her a lot."

"Still do," he said.

"I know. I heard it in your voice. I tried not to eavesdrop."

He just smiled. I could see his thoughts were still back at home.

"I only made it to six and a half years," I said, "and I'm not sure he ever loved me like that. You have kids?"

"Three," he said. "You?"

"Two. Do you like yours?"

He chuckled. "Yeah, most of the time."

"Me too. Forgive me for backtracking, but tell me why you said you were apologizing for yourself. Why would you need to?"

His smile disappeared. "Tell me why you think I wouldn't need to."

"That's easy," I said. "You never said an unkind word to me. You had more chances than most, living three doors down, and our parents being best friends and all. I never saw you laugh at me when someone else did. You never even refused to dance with me, when it was girl's choice. Why should you apologize?"

"I wanted to do those things," he said. "I'm glad I didn't. But I pretty much thought what they thought about you, even if I couldn't say it or act it out."

My surprise and dismay somehow caused a confession. "I had a crush on you for a while," I said.

"When I realized that," he said. "I tried to avoid you even more."

That brought a twinge of remembered pain. "I never saw you show any interest at all, and believe me, I was desperate to see some. Granted, you were usually interested in someone else. As I recall, it was always someone smart and pretty and kind. In fact, none of those girls ever mistreated me either."

"That wasn't one of my criteria," he said with a wry smile that didn't last. "Well, not directly. Unkind was a general turn-off."

"That narrowed the field for you quite severely," I noted with a clinical detachment I didn't feel.

"Yeah, but here's the thing. Even when I was between, well, interests," he said with obvious reluctance, "I wanted nothing to do with you. On the inside I was as bad as the others, and I'm sorry. So before you disconnect completely here tonight, please consider forgiving me."

His confession was worse than I expected, but there was a redemptive side to the memories too. Perhaps he'd forgotten. "I recall you defending me a couple of times," I said. "I heard of a few more times when I wasn't there to witness it. That's partly why I had a crush on you. You were my hero, even if you didn't want to be."

"I didn't want to be, and I wasn't heroic. I still thought what I thought." He shifted in his chair. "I mostly didn't want to be ashamed of myself when I saw your parents. I cared what they thought of me."

"How about now?" I asked.

"Your parents?"

"No. How about I forgive you now? And even if your thoughts were worse than I knew, thanks for telling me. And for not telling me back then."

More people came, and we were busy for a few minutes. Then we weren't.

He turned to me. "What if we had treated you better?"

"That would have been nice. What do you mean?"

"I guess, what if some of us had decided that you always being ostracized meant we should go out of our way to include you?

All the time and in the middle of things, not just on the fringes. Would you have welcomed that?"

"It's kind of a moot question."

"The thing is, Julia would have done that. She actually did."

"I'm sorry. She did what, exactly?"

"Her family moved a few times when she was a kid, and she says there was someone like that in her grade in every new school. Always a girl, someone all the kids thought was ugly and gross, with no real cause she could see. So she befriended them. I first heard about it from some of them at our wedding reception, so I asked her about it. She said it was easy to reach out to outsiders, because she was new, so she was an outsider too."

My stoicism was slipping away. I wanted to cry, and I was about to.

"We should have treated you better," he said. "We could have. We just didn't. I know hindsight doesn't help much, but as humans we kind of sucked. As Christians too, mostly."

Emotional detachment was my only hope of keeping it together. I thought of my last therapist—and the one before that, and the one before that. "I've been told it doesn't make sense to expect our younger selves to have already known what we learned in the process of becoming our older selves."

He looked like he was chewing on that. I was about to restate it more clearly, if I could, when he finally spoke.

"There's a lot of forgiveness in that, if you really believe it."

"My mind has believed it for a long time." I grimaced and looked around. "My heart wavers."

"Mine too. Mostly when I remember my own younger self. Seems easier with other people."

"I have to ask," I said. "Do you still remember me as being ugly then?"

He didn't hesitate. "No. I don't know what we were thinking."

I felt my cheeks flush. Before I could consider how he'd take it, I asked, "How about me now?"

His eyebrows arched. "You look good."

"You're not just saying that?"

"No."

"Why don't single men see me that way?" My eyes went wide. "Did I say that out loud?" Now I was really blushing. "I know I'm not a great beauty."

He smiled. "Here's some hard-won wisdom from the Gospel According to Nate. Some women are conventionally beautiful, superficially at least, in ways that are easy to see. Hard to miss, in some cases. Julia's like that for me, except her beauty is more than superficial. A lot of other women are like the Mona Lisa. If you look for a while, you learn to see the beauty other people miss. External beauty, I mean. If she's beautiful on the inside, and you get to see that too, it's that much better."

"So I have Mona Lisa beauty?" He must have heard my disbelief, with its undertone of wonder. We were talking about the most famous painting in the world.

"I'm going to say yes. But even at first glance, superficially, forty-three looks good on you."

I actually laughed. "Don't get ahead of yourself, cowboy. I'm forty-two for a few more weeks."

He smiled again. "My apologies. Forty-two looks good on you."

Another batch of classmates and their partners appeared. None of them recognized me, as far as I could tell. Then the formalities began, and dinner was announced.

"We tried to make this as different from our memories of school cafeteria food as we could," said our class president, Susan. She smiled at the ripple of laughter. "We hope you enjoy it."

Black-clad servers filed into the cafeteria, and before I knew it, one was at our table, smiling graciously. "Ma'am, sir, would you like us to serve you here, or did you want to move to one of the regular tables?"

"Here, if it's okay," Nate said.

"Works for me too," I said.

"Is anyone sitting there?" She indicated the third chair at our table.

"No," said Nate.

"I'll be back with two place settings and your salads."

He thanked her, and I turned to him. "So it's a working dinner for you."

"There may be stragglers. But any dinner I don't have to make is not a working dinner. I shouldn't say that. My kids are pretty good in the kitchen."

"Mine are dedicated consumers but poor producers," I said. I summoned my courage again, which seemed to involve alerting every last nerve. "Back to that other topic. Short version of a longer story: My freshman year of college, my roommates gradually did a makeover on me—looks and clothes first, but socially too. First they sat me down and told me they could see I was prettier than I looked, and we needed to fix that.

"It's the nicest thing anyone ever did for me. They changed my life. They taught me how to look different. Still myself, but better. The dark side is, as grateful as I am to them, I retroactively hated everyone who didn't do that for me sooner. My mom, my older sister, girls at church who didn't shun me. Church youth leaders, even my female schoolteachers. Any of them could have seen what my roommates saw. They could have done the same thing for me years earlier, but no one tried."

"Do you still hate them?" he asked.

"No. I gradually realized some of them did try, in their own ways, but I resisted. So it was partly my fault that I didn't get rescued from myself until college."

"Did you hate yourself for that, just to be consistent?" I couldn't tell whether his tone was gently ironic or just gentle.

"Not just to be consistent," I said.

He winced. "Do you still? Is that too personal?"

"I seem to have grown out of it about halfway through law school."

"Good," he said.

As the serving began, so did the introductions. They passed a microphone from table to table, so everyone could take half a minute to reintroduce themselves and introduce a partner, if they brought one. Our table was last—so I had time to escape, and I wanted to, but I didn't.

I tried to sound casual and confident. I'd worked on what to say, when I was driving and not on the phone. "I'm Kat McCowan. You don't recognize my name, because Kat is from my middle name, and McCowan is from my ex-husband. You knew me as Andi Vrbs, the girl with no vowels in her last name."

I heard a gasp from the nearest table. Tami was there with her husband and some old friends, staring at me, looking stunned and distressed. Others had milder responses. I instinctively believed the scattered whispers were mean.

"I have two boys and two cats," I continued, "and approximately two-thirds of a grandchild. I went back to school part-time when the younger boy hit middle school, got my law degree at Denver."

This time the murmurs sounded appreciative.

"Now I work as a civilian attorney attached to the Air Force Judge Advocate General Corps, assigned to Peterson Air Force Base at Colorado Springs. I guess that's about it."

I wasn't tempted to say it was good to see all of them. But I had survived the introductions, even mine.

For a lightning bolt from a clear blue sky, what happened next came quietly. I was finishing my very respectable chicken scampi when a soft voice asked from beside me, "Andi, sorry, Kat, could I talk to you for a minute?"

It was Tami, but in a meek, earnest version I'd never met. My heart was all confused, and my head with it. I nodded automatically. "You mean here?"

"Sure," she said.

"Kat, should I excuse myself for a few minutes?" Nate asked.

I glanced at him and back at Tami, who had never needed privacy to talk to me before. "No need." To Tami I said, "Have a seat. Talk."

"Thanks." She sat, and I told my heart to stop pounding. I wasn't alone in the Alaskan wilderness, face to face with an angry grizzly bear, like my ex-husband in his most tiresome old story.

"We were just talking about you," she said. "I didn't recognize you before. You look really great."

"I get it," I said. "I think I'm actually flattered that you didn't recognize me." I could see in her eyes that my words hurt her. Or maybe it was my tone.

"Kat, we were awful to you, and I was the worst. I'm so sorry."

"Lots of kids were awful," I said.

"He wasn't." She pointed at Nate.

"He was no knight in shining armor either," he said.

She put her hand on mine, and I was too shocked to pull away. "I was married to a man for a while who told me I was ugly almost daily for more than a year," she said. "That's what it took for me to learn what I did to you."

It was her tears that made me say it. Her tears and the way she just let them roll down her cheeks, instead of wiping them away. "He was lying," I said. "Or blind."

She nodded slowly. "So was I."

I saw the notecards in her hand just as our class president spoke again. "Tami Bates Wilson, a member of our reunion committee, will speak to us for a few minutes and introduce what comes next."

There was applause, but Tami didn't move. She just stared at me. "I'm sorry. Excuse me. I have to go do my thing." She hesitated. "I've been working on this little speech for a month, and it's still not ready."

Eyes still wet, she stepped to the mic and looked down at her cards. Then she looked toward me, and I broke into a cold sweat.

She held up her cards with a sheepish smile. "Hi, everybody. I can barely see my notes. It's so good to see all of you twenty-five years later, to see the people you've become and hear about the things you've done and the things you've endured. You're amazing, all of you.

"We weren't always kind to each other in school." Her voice had a higher pitch now. "For example, I was incredibly stuck up and frequently cruel. I thought most of you were losers. I don't think that anymore—about any of you. So please forgive me for that, if you would."

We could have heard a cloth napkin drop.

"I think I needed time and some big struggles of my own. I didn't mention before that I flunked out of college the first time. My first husband was a huge mistake. And I started drinking on the way home from work, until I scared myself by almost hitting my little boys in the driveway once."

I heard gasps. Her voice was steadier when she continued. "I got my 15-year chip last month."

She smiled at the applause. "Thank you. I'm pretty proud of that. My depression and anxiety got a lot better too, when I stopped self-medicating. And even if it took me too many years to grow up, I'm so happy to have finally learned to look for the good in people, the beauty. I love seeing it in you. It's easy to see, and there's a lot of it. I wish I'd seen it sooner.

"I want to tell you how wonderful you are, in case no one has told you that lately, and because I'm sure I never did. Thank you for being forgiving enough to share a happy reunion with me."

She sniffed and swiped at her eyes.

"This video we're about to see is a montage of photos and videos sent in by a lot of you, plus some things the yearbook still has on file, plus a tribute to five of us who have passed away, one as recently as last month, as you know. It's about ten minutes long, and I don't know about you, but I'm going to cry even more when I watch it. So at least I got to give my little speech before the video.

"I have these two quotes I want to read, and then I'm done. If I can read them." She wiped her eyes again.

"The great writer Kurt Vonnegut said, 'True terror is to wake up one morning and realize that your high school class is running the country.'"

There was a burst of laughter and applause. Her smile seemed shy at first but rapidly grew almost to the megawattage I remembered. Strangely, I remembered it without pain.

"Nelson Mandela said, 'There is nothing like returning to a place that remains unchanged to find the ways in which you yourself have altered.'"

No one laughed at that. I saw some nods.

"Thank you," she said. "For listening to me and for being part of my life, then and now. Thank you."

She returned to her table. I found myself applauding with the rest.

They had technical difficulties with the video. Some lights went back up, and Tami reappeared at our table while they worked on it.

"Hi," she said meekly. "Me again." She looked at Nate. "I'm sorry your wife couldn't come tonight."

"She missed a fine speech," he said.

I thought Tami should appreciate something about Nate. "His Julia is home with MS," I said. "She's had it a long time."

Tami looked at Nate with concern. "All those meetings, and you never told us. That must be so difficult."

"I try not to compare people's struggles," he said.

She just looked at him for a moment, then nodded slowly.

"Besides," he added, "I have a perfect excuse to spend lots of extra time at home with an amazing woman."

He was a freaking saint, I thought but didn't say. He wouldn't like it. Or believe it.

Someone announced that the video was about to start "for real, this time," and the lights were about to go down. Tami looked at Nate, then me. "Thanks for coming. Both of you. And helping with the name tags. And Nate, everything else you did. Excuse me." She returned to her table.

I wasn't in the video, which was fortunate. I felt enough like an outsider that I could watch without crying. I really needed not to cry.

Nate smiled through the whole thing, until the tributes to deceased classmates. The pictures reminded me that one of them had been his closest friend. When the lights went back up, I pretended not to notice his tears, until he could dry them.

"Are you staying for any of the dancing and mingling?" I asked, as the buzz of conversation rose above the many sniffles around us.

"I have an early flight," he said. "I met everybody on their way in. Talked to a lot of them when we were planning this too."

"Back to Julia."

"And three teenagers," he said.

"As difficult as it is, you really do miss her tonight, don't you?"

He didn't get all the way to a smile. "Is that pathetic? I'm only away for one night."

"I think it's sweet."

Now he smiled a little, and I waxed bold. "Before you go, could I talk you into a dance or two, when the music starts?"

He hesitated, then nodded. "Yeah, I think you could."

They served dessert, and Nate excused himself to chat with some old friends at other tables. The music had barely started when he returned.

"Now?" he asked.

"No, but soon. I'll let you know."

"Okay." He took his seat.

"I'm not stalling," I explained. "I'm waiting for a slow dance. Not to be romantic. I just look stupid trying to fast-dance. I'll keep my distance, I promise."

They played a slow song next. He leapt to his feet, held out his hand, and said, "Andi, Kat, may I have this dance?"

I wondered if he realized my smile was thanking him for asking me, as I always hoped he'd do when we were in school.

We danced in silence, until I couldn't bear it.

"I don't have a crush on you anymore," I said.

"That's probably for the best," he said.

"But I think you're a very good man. I'm glad we could get reacquainted."

He smiled the same little smile as before. "Thank you. So am I. Good to catch up."

"I saw the Mona Lisa once," I said. "I think I need to see her again. For longer this time."

The song was ending. "One more for the road?" he asked. "If it's slow?"

"Sure," I said. "Thank you."

It was slow, but the first few measures turned something inside me dark and cold. "No, actually. No. I can't. Thank you, though." I started back toward our table, and he followed.

"Are you okay?" he asked, as he pulled out my chair for me.

"They should put trigger warnings on these old songs," I said, dismayed at my voice for trembling again.

I sat, and so did he. "Is this Celine Dion?" he asked.

"Yes. 'To Love You More.'"

"A penny for your thoughts," he said. "A quarter, since they seem painful. And for inflation."

I stared at him with what I imagined were hooded eyes. I couldn't and shouldn't be too specific.

"You don't have to tell me," he said. "I don't think I have a quarter anyway."

We listened to the song for a while. Or he looked like he was listening. I was Andi again, and I shriveled inside.

I finally spoke. "For a while this song was kind of the dark anthem of my life."

"Uh-oh," he said. "Bad memories?"

"There was this guy once, and this was our song. My song, actually. I was waiting for him, so I thought. To notice me that way. I wanted to be the one to love him. I knew I could do it better than the girl he was with."

"Yeah," he said. "That would hurt."

"I don't know why it was so intense at the time, but I was in agony for, well, it seemed like a long time. I guess everything's exaggerated when we're teenagers."

Oops. Too specific as to time.

"Yeah, you're right," he said.

He didn't appear to suspect he was the guy. I didn't remind him that "To Love You More" had been the theme of one of our school dances. He'd asked a girl I didn't know he liked, a pretty athlete from the girls' basketball team. A different guy asked me a week in advance, then told me it was a joke at the last minute, when he was due to pick me up for dinner. He said I was an idiot to believe anyone would ever want to go out with me.

In lieu of dinner I cried for a couple of hours, sitting in my best dress, then went to the dance alone just to spite him. Or to spite myself. I wasn't sure. I spent at least half an hour there, sitting in my dark corner, stealthily weeping, watching Nate and his date. They danced to my song like it was their song. They were in their own little world, a happy, beautiful place, a paradise clearly visible from my corner of hell. I went home without even sampling the refreshments.

Nate snapped me back to the present. "Why does getting past everything have to mean disconnecting?" he asked. "Is it just too painful otherwise?"

"Funny thing," I said. "The pain tonight is less than I remember."

"I just watched you during that song," he said. "I'm not sure I believe you."

If he only knew.

"It's not all gone," I admitted. "Maybe it never will be. Maybe that's okay." I attempted a smile.

"So what's the status of your proof now?" he asked. "If you don't mind my asking again."

"You may be onto something," I said. "I'm starting to think there's a necessary step after severing all the bad connections. I'm kind of making this up as I go along."

I didn't continue right away, and he didn't jump in to ask.

"I think the next step"—I hesitated, checking to see if I really did think it, and I did—"might be to replace the old, bad connections with new, good connections. With some of the same people, if possible, bizarre as that feels."

This time, it was a big smile. "Sounds like you're glad you came," he said.

"I kind of am. Thanks for letting me hang out. It helped."

"I enjoyed it. Thanks for forgiving me. And the rest of us. Not kidding." He stood. "I should go."

I stood too. "You sound tired," I said. "But I'm glad you got to come. Have a safe flight home tomorrow."

"Thanks. You driving home tonight?"

"It's only an hour," I said. "Ish."

"Be safe." He took my hand and squeezed it, and for an instant I was Andi—but the Andi I'd wanted to be, not the Andi I was.

I knew he didn't mean anything romantic. I was Kat now, a realist who specifically didn't marinate anymore in old, impossible, long-expired hopes.

"When you see the Mona Lisa," he said, "tell her I said hi. It's been a while, and it's probably going to be a while."

We hugged awkwardly and said goodbye. I stayed a little longer and actually talked with a few old classmates near the refreshment table. No one else offered any apologies, but they were friendly, which felt somewhat apologetic to me. Two of them asked if I knew where Donna was and how she was doing, so I caught them up.

I walked out to my car, sat behind the wheel, inserted the key in the ignition . . . but didn't turn it. Not yet. I needed to cry my eyes out, for completely contradictory reasons. The old pain. The new, different feelings. Nate caring for his ailing wife and loving her so much all these years. Tami, of all people, apologizing to me. Tami conquering her own demons. Classmates remembering Donna and caring enough about her to ask. Five classmates who were no longer alive.

I waited for the tears to start, but they didn't. Dark memories lurked nearby but out of reach, and happy thoughts hovered just beyond my grasp. I sat and wondered what it all meant.

I smiled faintly in the darkness.

"See you at our thirtieth?" Nate had asked. "You better come."

"I will," I'd promised with a restrained but honest smile. "You better bring Julia. I hope she can. I'll pray for her, if that's okay."

He said it was, thanks.

I started my car and headed home.

Rhonda VII

WHAT I WANTED TO say was, "I'm a football player, not a popsicle." What I said was, "This is what you want us to wear to the Homecoming dance?"

School had been out for half an hour, when Haylee pulled me into a short, dead-end hallway to talk about formal wear. I stared at her phone in my hand. The disaster she was planning filled the screen.

"This is what I'm wearing," she said, "and because you're my boyfriend and we're probably going to be Homecoming King and Queen, we should coordinate."

The models on the website had coordinated. His tux was as pink as her dress.

"It's not just the color," Haylee explained. "It's the style and the fabrics too. My gown and your tux were made to go together. Wait till you see everything in person."

I returned her phone, shaking my head.

"Is there a problem, Ty?" she asked semi-sweetly. The color rising in her cheeks contrasted starkly with her blonde, very very blonde hair.

"Yeah, there's a problem. I'm not wearing a pink tux. Especially not for $228."

Her big, sad, brown eyes didn't affect me like they usually did. I may have been in shock from all the pink. Besides, lately Haylee was just too . . . Haylee. Maybe that was the real problem.

Her lower lip quivered, and that didn't work on me either. "If it's about the money, I'll help. I know you don't have a lot."

"Seriously? I wouldn't wear that if they paid me."

"You rent the whole ensemble for that price, including shoes."

I hadn't noticed those. I reached for her phone again.

They were pink too.

"No, thanks," I said, and gave her phone back.

"You're not being very nice to me right now," she complained.

"I'm . . . You're . . . What?" I sputtered. "You showed me that picture. Was that nice? How do I get all that pink out of my head? I have a game tonight."

I was overdoing it. I'd be fine, assuming I never wore that tux. Or those shoes.

Sometimes calmness moved over her face like a wave, when she decided to compose herself.

She put away her phone, slipped an arm around my waist, and leaned into me, which also didn't distract me as much as usual. Her voice was gentle and sincere. "Ever since I was a little girl, I've dreamed of being Homecoming Queen and wearing an amazing pink gown, and being escorted by a handsome Homecoming King in a matching pink tuxedo. I started planning for it before I even got my—"

"Sorry to interrupt, but this is your crazy pink fantasy, not mine."

I gently freed myself from her grip and turned to face her, keeping some air between us. She reached up to put her arms around my neck, but I covered her hands with mine and held them a few inches away.

After a moment, she seemed to understand. She pulled her hands away, I let go, and she folded her arms across her chest.

Her eyes were hard. "Why are you so mean to me?" There were still a few kids in the halls, or she might have yelled.

I answered calmly. "It's not mean, just because you don't get your way."

"I thought you wanted to take me to Homecoming." Now she just sounded hurt. She could go through more emotions more quickly than anyone I knew.

The truth was, I'd been looking forward to it. We'd been an item since May, and this would be our first big dance together. Homecoming in the fall was almost as big as Prom in the spring. So I could make one more serious try.

"Don't other colors go with pink?" I asked. "Maybe black?"

"No black."

I waited, but she didn't explain.

"Maybe white or baby blue," I said, "with a pink vest or cummerbund. And a pink bow tie." I could see it in my head. It wasn't me, but I might have done it.

"Not in the evening," she said. "Plus you'd stand out more than me."

"Yeah. Can't have that."

"The idea is to stand out as a couple."

"What about that dark red color? Like your last prom dress?" We weren't together then, but I had noticed.

"Ma–roon?" She said it slowly, like I was stupid.

"Yeah. I could do maroon. For you. Maybe with a pink shirt. Maroon goes with pink, right?"

"Yes," she said quietly. "It just doesn't go with me to Homecoming."

"So I wear pink or nothing?" I blushed at that accidental image, which was also too pink. "I mean, pink, or we don't go to Homecoming together?"

"Your choice."

I looked at her and tried to imagine her in a pink homecoming gown, all gorgeous and sparkling, with me by her side and just as pink. All I could see was the girl standing in front of me, in jeans and a pinkish-orangish top. (She'd said the color was salmon.) She looked great, as usual, except for the scowl.

That's when I realized it. I just didn't care anymore. So it didn't feel like this might be an ending. It felt like we'd already ended.

"Fine," I said. "Let's not go to Homecoming together. Let's not go anywhere together at all. Starting now."

Her cheeks flushed, and her tone could have drawn blood. "You're breaking up with me?" I'd seen her this ticked off with other people plenty of times, but never with me.

"You know what? Yeah. I just did."

"Seriously, Ty? Social suicide over a tuxedo? How dumb is that? We've been together for what, five months now?"

"It's not just a tux." I didn't want to yell at her, but I couldn't help raising my voice a little. "I'm tired of being an accessory in your—what do you call it?—your ensemble. I'm tired of you reminding me how my family has less money than yours. Everybody's family has less money than yours! I'm tired of trying to care what everybody thinks about your shoes or your hair or your flawless paint job or your intergalactically awesome curves. Five months is plenty."

"Paint job" was a cheap shot. She was an artist with makeup.

She put on a pout I'd never seen. It might have been sincere.

"Who is she?" Her voice shook.

"Who is who?"

"The other girl. How long have you been cheating on me?"

"There's no other girl. I wouldn't do that. But if there was, you know who she'd be?"

"A tr–amp?" She said that slowly too.

"No. She'd be someone who . . . She'd care about me as a person, not just an accessory. And I wouldn't have to keep reminding myself there's a decent girl under there somewhere."

"I care about you. And I'm not a bad person!"

"Mostly, Haylee, you care about yourself. Maybe I'm no better, but . . . whatever."

When the weather changed again, her new mood wasn't exactly resignation. It was more of a strategic retreat, like the Russians in 1812. We were studying that in history. They couldn't beat Napoleon's army in a fair fight, so they destroyed everything in its path and beat it later. Starving, half-frozen invaders were easier to defeat.

"You'll still have to escort me for the ceremony, if we win. We'll have to dance once as King and Queen, with everybody watching."

I'd faced max blitz packages on fourth-and-long with the clock winding down and the game on the line. I could dance with her one more time with everybody watching. "Okay, but I won't be in a pink tux."

"Why do you suddenly hate me? Did something happen at practice today? Is Coach benching you? Is it because of your grades?"

Thanks for assuming it's my problem, I thought.

"I don't hate you, Haylee. I just don't want to date you anymore. In any color. And we don't have practice on game day. If we did, I'd be there now."

Her face, which I had studied so devotedly for months, went through a few more emotions. One of them looked like rage. She settled on pretending not to care.

"Good luck finding that other girl, or even a date for Homecoming, after the whole school hears how you treated me. You better be there for the ceremony anyway, even if you have to go alone. And you better dress up."

She whirled away. I watched her stalk to the main hallway and around the corner. Then I just stood there, arms at my sides, trying to think of ways I could have handled it better. I really was tired of those things, and I didn't want to wear a pink tux. I hadn't planned to break up with her, but the strange thing was, I felt pretty good about the result.

"I'll go to the dance with you," said a girl's voice.

I looked up, saw no one, and decided I'd imagined it.

The next time was louder. "I'll go to the dance with you, if you want. If you don't mind the rumors that I'm a lesbian."

This time, I could tell the voice came from behind me. I turned and saw a girl, I thought, but her black hair was cut short like a boy's. She wore black jeans and a faded black Pittsburgh Steelers shirt.

"What? Who are you?" I'd thought Haylee and I were alone.

"I said, I'll go to—"

"I heard that part. How long were you standing there? Who are you?"

"Since before you and the princess arrived. My locker's here." She hefted a black backpack. "I wouldn't have eavesdropped, but I couldn't help it. I couldn't get away without interrupting you." She jerked her thumb at the doors behind her, at the end of the short hall. "Those doors are for emergencies, which this wasn't quite."

"I didn't see you before."

"I'm mostly invisible to star athletes and future Homecoming royalty."

"You're not invisible. Who are you?"

I could have sworn she said her name was Rhonda VII, complete with Roman numerals, like they use with the Super Bowl.

"Rhonda VII?"

"Yes."

I snorted. "What went wrong with Rhondas I through VI?" I instantly regretted my tone.

"Yeah, haven't heard that one before," she said dryly.

"Sorry. Seven's your last name?"

"S–e–v–u–n."

"Okay. You want to go to the dance?"

She didn't seem smitten with me. She seemed businesslike, and she hadn't smiled at all. "I'll go with you if you want."

"I don't even know you."

"You can get to know me."

"You don't know me," I said.

"Everybody knows you," she said. "You're the big macho quarterbacker guy."

Apparently, wearing a football team's shirt didn't mean she knew football. It was faded enough to be secondhand anyway.

"Quarterback," I said.

"Oh. Quarterback."

My head felt weird. Maybe breaking up with my girlfriend was sinking in.

"Look, it's a good idea," I said. "Nice of you to offer. Can I think about it? I just . . ."

Her mouth twitched, like she was trying not to frown, and the look in her eyes grew distant.

"Sure. I get it," she said. "I'm not . . . It's not fair to catch you on the rebound like that."

She hefted her backpack and started to walk around me, toward the main hall. "See you around, maybe."

"Wait a second, okay?"

She stopped and half-turned.

"Can I walk you to your car or the bus or whatever?"

She looked at me for a heartbeat or two. "Sure, if you want to."

"Can I carry your backpack?"

She shook her head. "I can carry it."

"Didn't say you couldn't." I reached out anyway, and she handed it to me. It weighed a ton.

"What's in here?"

"Physics, chemistry, English. No math today. Some books for a report." She smiled a little. "Too heavy for you?"

I swung it onto my shoulder. "No, but I have wide receivers who weigh less than this."

"Are those football players?"

"Yeah. Mostly little guys, plus a tall, skinny one. They run around, and I throw them the ball. Then the other team tries to break them in half."

"Eww."

"I try to throw to them when that won't happen. Parking lot or bus stop? I could give you a ride home."

"Parking lot, please. I have my car."

We didn't say much as we walked, but I thought as fast as I could. I wanted to go to Homecoming. I should, in case I won the royalty vote. Most of the girls I knew had dates already. If Haylee got to the others first, and she would, the rest of them might say no.

This girl wasn't even in Haylee's universe. Plus she'd actually volunteered, and she was decent-looking. Kind of nerdy, but she seemed interesting so far. Also, she didn't hate me, at least not yet.

She stopped next to a black compact that was losing the paint on its roof and hood.

"This is my car," she said. "Thanks for carrying that."

I slid her backpack off my shoulder but didn't give it to her yet. She reached for it and caught hold of one strap.

"I thought about the dance already," I said. "I suddenly need a date, so I guess, if you want . . ."

She raised her eyebrows and still didn't smile. It wasn't my best guy moment.

"You sure can sweep a girl off her feet." There was a catch in her voice. "You don't have to take me to Homecoming if you don't want to. You're on the rebound. It's not fair to you."

"Rebound or not, I still need a date."

"You should ask someone you already know. And like." Her blush was as cute as Haylee's, even if her face was thinner.

"I'll know you by the time dinner's over," I said. "And I like you so far. Are you afraid I'm trying to make the princess jealous?"

"No. A little. Are you? May I have my backpack now, please?"

I surrendered it. "I don't care what she thinks anymore. I should go to the dance, and going with you will be fun."

"You don't know that."

"You think it won't?" I asked.

She shrugged. "I'm more afraid you're asking because I didn't give you much of a choice, and you don't really want to, but you also don't want to be mean or hurt my feelings or whatever."

"At least that makes me a decent guy. So will you go with me or not?" I was starting to care about her answer.

"I don't know. Maybe."

"How can I persuade you?"

She looked away. "This is Friday. Give yourself two days. If you haven't asked someone else by Sunday afternoon, and you still want to, text me, and I'll probably say yes. If you change your mind, don't text me."

Her eyes met mine. "I suppose you'll want my phone number, just in case." There was a little tremor in her voice.

I smiled, and she smiled back, sort of. We typed our names and numbers into each other's phone, then said an awkward goodbye.

I stood in the parking lot and watched her drive away. It was strange to feel so off balance with her, but so calm about suddenly breaking up with Haylee.

She wasn't out of sight when I set an alarm for 3 p.m. Sunday. I already knew what I'd text her: "After school, near your locker?"

I didn't know exactly which locker was hers, but I knew which little hall it was in. And I wanted to ask her properly.

· · · ● · ● · ● · · ·

O N SUNDAY AFTERNOON HER whole reply to my text message was "OK." I didn't know what to think. I decided just to be glad she agreed.

She smiled when she saw me Monday afternoon, and she might have blushed a little. The first thing she said was, "Hi, Tyler. There's a problem. You know, if you're asking me again."

Her eyes didn't look like there was a problem, and I wasn't worried. "You're a lesbian?"

"That's just a rumor. The problem is, I only have one nice dress."

"So?"

"It's pink."

I laughed. "If I don't have to wear it, I don't see the problem."

I saw a hint of a smile. "Wouldn't fit you. I like your navy pinstripe, but wear what you want."

"Okay, Rhonda VII stalker-girl, I'm here to do this right. Would you please go to Homecoming with me?"

"Yes." She sounded serious, but her eyes sparkled. "Thanks for asking again. I haven't stalked you. You guys wear suits to school for away games, and girls notice."

"Thanks for not trying to make me wear a pink one."

"Quarterbackers shouldn't wear that much pink. Even I know that. I shouldn't either, but at least I'm a girl."

I took a few seconds and just looked at her. She was in black jeans and a black t-shirt again, but this shirt wasn't faded.

Her short hair was neat and stylish. She had a few freckles under each eye. Princess Haylee would have covered them with makeup, so they wouldn't ruin her perfect complexion, but they were cute.

She used some pretty dark eye shadow, but it worked. Her lips were somewhere between gray and black, like before. Haylee might not have done that even on Halloween.

Her look was a lot of black, but I didn't see any extra piercings, and she wasn't wearing any clunky jewelry I could see. She didn't look Goth.

She watched me and looked calm, even if she probably wasn't.

"I like your shirt," I said, and read it aloud. "'Underestimate me. That'll be fun.'"

"Thanks," she said. "I got it for my dad to give me for my birthday."

"I'll bet you look really nice in pink," I said.

Her cheeks turned pink, and her eyes looked away.

"Are there details we should work out?" she asked. "I've never had a date for a dance before."

"A few. Is dinner okay before the dance? You pick the place."

"I'd like that. But anywhere's fine. You should pick. Doesn't have to be expensive."

"Okay. What's your favorite color?"

"Why?"

"Corsage."

Her eyes lit up again. Hadn't anyone ever given this girl flowers either?

"Black. But I wouldn't want black flowers. Can you even get those?"

"I'll take care of it. Send me a photo of your dress, at least the color, and I'll see what the florist can do. Pink and white flowers with a black ribbon, maybe."

"Thank you. That sounds beautiful. Should I get you one of those flowers for your lapel?"

"A boutonniere? If you want."

"Something that matches?"

"Usually, yeah." My question came from nowhere. "Why are you going with me?"

"You asked. After I asked you, sort of. But you asked."

"If I'd asked you last week, before that scene with Haylee, would you have said yes?"

"Last week you were just some revolting, testosterone-poisoned football star."

"I'm still a football star. Not sure about that other thing."

She laughed. It was soft, deep, and musical, and it lasted only a second or two. I wanted to hear it again.

"I liked how you stood up to the princess," she said. "Nobody does that. You seem like a decent guy. And some of what you said was pretty cool. Besides, I should go to one dance while I'm in high school."

"You really should. Is it okay if we go alone? I had a group, but it was hers. I think I'm on my own now."

"That's fine. I have three good friends, but so far none of them are going."

"Only three?"

"Three's a lot of friends," she said. "Not a lot, maybe, but three more than some kids have."

"Guess you're right. Thanks for saying yes."

Her cheeks dimpled, and her gray-black lips parted to reveal almost perfect teeth. But it was her light green eyes that pulled me in. I couldn't remember seeing eyes like hers before.

"Thanks for asking again," she said.

"Can I tell you something, Rhonda VII?"

"I'll look okay in pink?"

"No. Yes. Better than okay. But you're pretty cute in black too." I gestured toward her outfit.

"Thank you." She smiled again. A guy could get used to that.

· · · · **·** · **·** · · ·

O N TUESDAY A GIRL named Bea, one of Haylee's friends, told me I could ask her to Homecoming if I wanted. I was pretty sure she already had a date, which meant she was testing me for Haylee. I should have done it, to see what she'd say, but I didn't think of it soon enough. I just said, "Sorry, I have a date."

She didn't seem to mind.

On Wednesday a girl named Alli did the same thing. She was only on the fringes of the popular crowd, but I figured Haylee sent her too. She was a better actress. She managed to act disappointed.

· · · · **·** · **·** · · ·

T HE HOMECOMING GAME WAS Friday night. The other team wasn't good, so we were supposed to win big, and we did. I threw three touchdown passes in the first half and one just after halftime, before Coach pulled me.

From the sideline I mostly paid attention to the game like we were supposed to, but when I could, I checked the crowd for Rhonda VII. I didn't see her. I could have missed her, but she probably wasn't there.

My backup, Chandler Lynch, threw for a touchdown and ran for one. I'd beaten him for the starting job by working harder at practice, knowing the offense better, and spending more time studying film, but I could never beat his looks. I was handsome because I was the starting quarterback. He was just handsome. Maybe even hot.

After the game I saw him with the princess. They looked good together, which was probably why she moved on to him within hours of our breakup. I did him the favor of asking some of the guys to vote for him for Homecoming King, if they planned to vote for me.

I won anyway. So did Haylee.

· · · ● · ● · · ·

W HEN I ARRIVED TO pick up Rhonda VII on Saturday night, a man opened the door in a police uniform. A silver pin above one pocket said, "Sevun."

She hadn't mentioned her dad was a cop.

"I'm, uh, Tyler." I stammered. "Pleased to meet you, Officer Sevun."

"It's Lieutenant. Come in."

Before I could apologize for getting his rank wrong, he said, "I told my daughter, if she didn't get at least one date on her own each semester this year, I'd arrange some for her. So she goes out and brings home the star quarterback, who's also the Homecoming King. Can you explain this? All she would tell me is, you asked."

While I tried to think of something to say, he continued.

"Seems like I saw you with a pretty blonde in tow, last time I worked security for one of your games."

I knew where to start now. "Rhonda's pretty."

He raised his eyebrows. "I think so. And?"

"I broke up with that girl."

"And?"

"Rhonda kind of saw us break up. Then she said she'd go with me, if I wanted."

He chuckled and shook his head. "Sometimes I think that girl's timid and shy, and then . . . Anyway, she says you're a good guy. So do the other people I asked this week. Make sure she's right."

"Thank you, sir. I will."

"If you'll drive safely and have her home by midnight, I'll try not to find something to arrest you for."

"Thank you, sir."

I heard a door open somewhere, and Rhonda VII appeared. She looked worried or maybe queasy, but when she saw me smiling, she smiled too. She smiled more when she saw her wrist corsage. It had pink and white flowers, with a baby red rose accent and a wide, black ribbon. I'd never seen Haylee so happy over flowers.

I put it on her arm. She lifted it to her nose and closed her eyes.

"They smell so pretty. Thank you. Here, smell them." She held them up to me.

They smelled like flowers.

Her hands shook as she pinned my boutonniere to my lapel, but I didn't say anything.

Her biggest smile was for her dad. They didn't actually say goodbye. She beamed at him, and he smiled faintly and nodded. Then she said quietly, "Let's go."

"You didn't tell me your dad's a cop," I said as we drove away.

"You didn't ask. Were you shocked?" She sounded amused.

"Yeah."

"Is it important?"

"No. I never even had a traffic ticket. Some parking tickets, which I paid, but that's different."

We ate at a busy Mexican place, where the service was slow and I was glad. Talking with Rhonda VII was more fun than talking with the princess lately, or maybe ever. Looking at her was good too. Her light pink dress was simple but nice. She looked like a pretty girl, not a princess. She couldn't do much with her hair, as short as it was—she said that's why she kept it that way, when long hair was the fashion—but she didn't need to do anything. She was cute.

Her lips weren't gray or black like before. They were deep red, and I was distracted for a while, admiring them. I didn't know what to call the color. It was nothing like the princess's glossy pink. It was like the baby red rose in her corsage—and I was afraid of what she'd think if I asked.

Her lips were red and velvety and comfortable and—

She looked up, and I looked down at my plate.

· · · · ● · ● · · · ·

THE NEXT THING I knew, we were in the school gym, at the dance. We'd already danced a little and talked some more, and I was telling her I was sorry, but I had to go do the royalty thing.

Soon I was waiting to step onto the little stage, with the princess on my arm. She could be cold up close but smile sweetly for the crowd. I tried to ignore the chill and be a gentleman.

"Who's your little pink date?" she asked with acid in her tone. I'd heard worse.

"Her name's Rhonda."

"Where'd you find her? She looks like a lesbian. Or a boy. Are you gay?"

I smiled and shook my head. "You didn't see her?"

"See her where?"

"When we ducked into that little hallway last week to talk about pink tuxes, she was like ten feet away, at her locker. She heard every word. We blocked her escape."

"There was nobody else there."

"I only saw her after you left. We started talking, and she's pretty cool."

"How nice for you. Not much to look at, though. Part of the world really is flat. Who knew?"

"I think she's cute."

"Yeah, whatever."

"You know what I really like?" I asked. "Thanks for helping me see this. I like that she's not trying to impress everybody, and she doesn't need everyone to admire her." I almost said it was refreshing.

"You're trying to insult me."

"I'm trying to tell you what I think."

"It's insulting."

"Sorry. Did you send Bea to ask me to Homecoming as a test? And Alli?"

She pursed her lips. "I sent Bea. Alli did it on her own. She'll regret it."

I forced myself to speak calmly. "If you do anything to Alli—or Rhonda—because of me, I'll make sure you get worse. We dated for five months. I won't even have to make anything up."

Not even that disturbed her poise. She looked and sounded like we were talking about yesterday's lunch or something. "Are you threatening me? That's not like you."

"Only if you attack someone else because of me."

"We'll see."

I was relieved. That usually meant she was dropping the subject.

"Is she your girlfriend now?" she asked after a moment.

"Rhonda? Just my date. Is Lynch your boyfriend now?"

"Chandler and I have already kissed. He's very affectionate. More than you ever were."

I stopped myself from saying, "So I've heard."

"I'm glad you're happy, Haylee. Is he wearing pink tonight? I forgot to notice."

"He's wearing a gorgeous, light gray tux, but his vest and bow tie match my dress."

I could have worn light gray, but I kept that thought to myself. Things had worked out fine anyway.

"It's our turn," she said. "Stand up straight and take short steps, so I can keep up."

I managed a smile. "Of course, Your Majesty. Congratulations."

She was radiant as they crowned her with a tiara, and more radiant when they finished. I was glad they didn't have a crown for me.

The King-and-Queen dance started with just us. Then they added the attendants. By the time they invited everyone to the floor, she was dancing way too close. That was fun when we were dating, but now I didn't want to be seen that way with her—by anyone, but especially Rhonda VII.

"I miss you," said the princess, as I gently tried to put a few millimeters between us. "You're handsome, even in this navy pin-stripe. The pink tie's nice too. I might take you back, if you apologize for how you treated me."

"No, thank you," I said, and tried for a few more millimeters. Finally, as gently as I could, I moved her arms from around my neck, until we were in a ballroom dancing position I'd learned once. Some other couples were already dancing like that.

She compressed her lips, and her cheeks colored, but she kept her head up and kept dancing, all poised and regal.

I thought she was reluctant to let go of me at the end. Maybe I imagined it. Then she just looked at me.

"Thanks for the dance," I said. "Congrats again. Nice win."

She didn't thank or congratulate me. "Ty, look at me."

I looked her in the eye. Where some girls had freckles, she had glitter tonight.

"Not just my eyes. All of me." She pointed her hands at herself, sweeping them downward from her shoulders and past her hips, like a salesperson in a showroom.

I stayed focused on her eyes.

She shrugged. "Have it your way. But this is really your last chance. I'm Homecoming Queen. And I've got curves your little Rhonda never dreamed of."

She was right about having them. She was wrong to think I still cared. "They really are quite lovely," I said. "I know your backup quarterback likes them. You should go back to him, and I'll go back to my date."

"Yeah," she said, and her nose twitched. "Do that. Be a loser. Go back to your loser date."

I found Rhonda VII where I'd left her, on a chair at the edge of the floor. She gave me a little smile. I needed air, so I asked her to come outside with me, and she did.

We sat on a bench under a street lamp which blotted out the stars. It was warm for October, so I thought she wouldn't be cold.

"Sorry, but I had to get out of there for a minute," I said, staring out across the parking lot. "Sorry you had to watch that."

"I didn't necessarily have to watch." I couldn't read her tone yet. I worried that she was angry or frustrated with me. "But since I did, what are you sorry about, exactly?"

"Lots of things."

"Like what?"

I couldn't read her expression either. She might have been a little sad, or just serious.

"I'm your date," I said, "but when everybody was watching, I danced with her."

I faced straight ahead again.

"You had to. It's ceremonial or whatever. It didn't bother me."

"Even when she practically molested me for a minute?"

"I noticed you stopped her without making a scene. You were a gentleman."

Too many thoughts spun in my head for any one of them to make sense, if I let it out. Homecoming, Haylee, football, dancing, gentleman, Rhonda VII. Mostly Rhonda VII.

"What are you thinking?" she asked.

"I guess I'm . . . One thing is, I . . . I sort of wish it bothered you. Some of it. A little bit."

Which was true, but it hadn't sunk in until I heard myself say it.

"I don't understand. You wanted that to bother me?"

"No. I mean . . . I don't know how to say it."

She waited and watched. She didn't seem sad or happy, just interested.

I couldn't look her in the eye and say it, so I stared at her corsage.

"Ten days ago, I didn't know you existed. Wouldn't have cared. Now we're at Homecoming together, and it's fun. I guess I was hoping you liked me enough that seeing me with the princess would bother you a little. I didn't do it to make you jealous. I did it because I had to, like you said. I wished it was you the whole time. You're a lot nicer. But you probably would have hated it. I just thought . . . I don't know. I'm not saying this very well."

"You're saying it fine," she murmured. "Are you more comfortable talking to girls because you have more practice than other boys, or is that just the way you are?"

It was a loaded question, but I didn't think she meant it that way. Even if she did, the truth was the truth. "Lots of practice, I guess. Wouldn't say I'm all that comfortable."

"Well, you're good at it. And it did bother me a little, when she danced so close. Not too much, I guess, because you didn't seem to like it."

I brightened instantly. "Sounds like you like me."

I looked up and saw a gentle smile. "Maybe a little," she said.

"I'm not just the next worst thing to your dad picking your dates?"

She winced. "He told you about that?"

"Yeah. Said he might look for reasons to arrest me too."

"I'm sorry," she said. "He wouldn't really do that. I don't think he would. He just worries about me."

"Can I tell you something else, since you maybe like me a little?"
She smiled. "Sure."

I stared into the night. "Haylee already got pretty frisky with Lynch. He's the backup quarterback. Stuff I never did with her."

Rhonda VII didn't answer for a few seconds, which gave me time to realize how different what I said was from what I meant to say.

She spoke softly. "I don't think I needed to know that."

"Sorry. What I meant is, she has a new boyfriend. But she told me she might dump him if I apologize and come back to her. I said no, thanks."

"What did she say to that?"

I turned to face her. "It was my last chance, and I should re-member she's Homecoming Queen, and she has curves . . . other girls . . . never dreamed of."

Rhonda VII just looked at me seriously, so I continued.

"I said her curves are quite lovely—I got 'quite lovely' from a movie—and I was going back to my date. She called us losers. She gets mean when she's angry."

Rhonda VII nodded and started to say something, then stopped and looked down. I began to worry. I wasn't sure about what. Maybe I shouldn't have said the part about us being losers.

She looked at her hands. "Was it really curves I never dreamed of?"

"Yeah. She called you my 'little pink date.'"

"Your little pink loser date. What else did she say?"

"Nothing true. And we're not losers. And it's kind of dumb for her to call you little, when you're taller."

Seconds passed.

"Tyler, I won't say I never dreamed of looking like her, but I don't have anything close to those curves you like. Obviously."

"I don't care," I said firmly.

More seconds passed.

"I don't believe you," she whispered.

"You don't believe me?"

"I don't believe you."

"It's the truth."

She looked up. "I believe you think it's the truth. But tell me this. When you stared at me at dinner, were you comparing me to the princess?"

She'd caught me after all.

"I was. Yes. Sorry."

She looked down again, frowning deeply. "I thought so." Some sort of light was gone from her face, and I wanted nothing more than to get it back.

"You did better than you think," I said.

Her voice shook. "You don't know what I think."

"I do this time, poker face. But you don't know what I was thinking." The emotion in my own voice surprised me.

"I know she's gorgeous, and I'm not. I know she's like an hourglass, and I'm more like a surfboard or a light pole."

"I should tell you what I thought. Because it wasn't that."

"No need." She turned away, which hurt me somewhere deep inside. Would she ask me to take her home now? Maybe call her dad for a ride? That would hurt too.

"Please? I want to tell you," I said. "I'll tell you the truth. It won't be bad, I promise. Please?"

After what seemed like forever, she turned back toward me, without looking up. She still frowned and said nothing.

I had to get this right. Because, apparently, I wasn't the only one who'd thought of us lasting longer than tonight. Any other time, I might have teased her about that, but not now.

I had to get this right.

"Her hair's long and blonde," I said, "and pretty. She works really hard on it. But your black hair's pretty too. I like the short cut, whatever it's called. It's cute."

"Pixie," she said softly. "My real color's sort of medium brown, but I like black."

"Black looks good on you. So do real eyebrows. And you have freckles, where she puts glitter."

"I don't do glitter."

"I like that too. You're about five-seven, right?"

"In flats. Probably five-eight tonight."

"She's five-seven in five-inch heels, which she wears even though they make her feet hurt, and her back too, and she tells you all about her suffering. You win that one for about three reasons."

"Her face belongs on a fashion magazine," she said.

I blushed, but I had to say this. "Your face is pretty. I like your eyes a lot." I took a deep breath. "What I looked at most at dinner was your . . . your lips. Hers are, uh, glossy and pink. Usually sticky. Sorry, too much information. Yours are . . . I don't know how to say this either . . . They're like dark red velvet tonight. They're really pretty. Distractingly pretty."

I wanted to kiss her on those lips. I wanted her to want me to kiss her.

"There's glossy lipstick, but the sticky part's lip gloss," she said. Her voice had more life in it, and there was color in her cheeks. "You probably know that. My lipstick's a matte. That's why it's not shiny. I don't wear lip gloss." She glanced up at me. "I'm glad you like it."

"I like it a lot. What's the color called?"

She blushed instantly.

"My Red Velvet ran out, even though I don't use it very often. This is the closest thing from Mom's collection."

"What is it?"

"I'll tell you, but don't draw any conclusions."

"Okay."

"It's called 'Naughty.'"

I didn't laugh, but she could see me trying not to. "I see what you mean," I said. "I was thinking soft, comfortable, luxurious."

Inviting, I added in my head and blushed again.

She was smiling. Not exactly beaming; it was milder than that. It was sweet. It sort of melted me.

"Rhonda VII?"

"Yeah?"

"Does it bug you when I call you that?"

"It's my name."

"Yeah, but when I say it, I'm still thinking Roman numerals, not S–e–v–u–n."

"Like I'm a spacecraft?"

"Or a Super Bowl."

"I like spacecraft, and you must like Super Bowls. So unless you're thinking of me as your seventh conquest or something, I think it's cute."

For some reason I remembered hefting her backpack, and everything she said was in it.

She interrupted my thoughts. "Did you have more to say about the princess? Or should we call her the Queen now?"

"Yeah, and I'm the King. Don't remind me." I could do this, I thought. "She asked if you're my new girlfriend. I said you're my date."

"That's true."

It took all my courage to turn and look at her while I said the rest.

"I was thinking, it doesn't have to be true forever. We could spend more time together. If you want. Have you thought about that too?"

She hesitated, then nodded without looking up. "I kept telling myself you couldn't possibly be as nice as you seemed, and I can't possibly measure up to what you expect in a girl."

A knot tightened in my gut. "What I expect?"

She finally looked at me. "How many girlfriends have you had, just in high school?"

"Three. Four, if you count one that started in junior high. One of them twice."

"How many were gorgeous?"

"Three. Four, if you count . . . Four."

"See my point?"

The knot got tighter and somehow bigger at the same time. I hung my head, which I never did. I had thought we were getting somewhere good together, but now we were pushing ourselves further apart.

She wasn't finished. "How many of them were popular before they were your girlfriends?"

"Four."

"I'm not popular. I don't want to be. I probably never could be anyway."

"I'm okay with that."

"I don't see how you could stay okay with that. You're the star quarterbacker. You're automatically popular. It's like a law of nature."

"I don't love it like people think I do."

"People like me?"

"You tell me." I looked up long enough to say, "None of them were conquests."

Neither of us spoke for a while. I didn't know what else to say. The knot inside was more of a lead weight now, and I thought I knew why. Something in me yearned to get close to Rhonda

VII and stay there. It wasn't just physical. It wasn't even mostly physical. The lead weight was there to tell me not to get my hopes up.

I looked out over the parking lot, which reminded me of her car, which reminded me of her backpack again. What was in it was pretty good evidence, once I thought about it, that she was a lot smarter than me. Which was already obvious anyway.

She thought she wasn't pretty enough for me, but she was. And I didn't care if she wasn't popular. But what if I wasn't smart enough for her? She had to see that, with all the stupid, awkward things that kept spilling out of my mouth. Even if she was too nice to say it.

When she finally broke the silence, her voice shook again. "I'm so stupid," she said. "I convinced you, didn't I?"

"I don't understand."

"Of all the idiotic things for a girl like me to do on her first date with a nice guy." She sighed. "My first date ever. I told you that, right?"

"Rhonda VII, what are you talking about?"

"I made a pretty convincing case," she said. "You're sitting there thinking I'm right, aren't you? That I'm not pretty enough or popular enough? Please be honest. I'd rather hear the truth."

That was so different from what I was thinking that at first I couldn't even think of the wrong thing to say.

"Please, Tyler? Just tell me. I know who I am. I'll be okay."

The look in her eyes broke my heart and sort of made it come alive at the same time.

"You're wrong," I said. "I wasn't thinking any of that."

She just looked at me.

"My backpack is never that heavy," I said. "Not even close."

"Your backpack? What?"

"I'm not smart like you," I said. "I don't take physics or chemistry or any of that hard stuff. Mostly I'm just a dumb football player. That's what I was thinking."

"Wait. You think you're not smart enough for me? Are you serious?"

I frowned and nodded.

"Shouldn't I get to decide that for myself?" she asked.

"I don't know. Maybe."

"Dad says you have to be smart to be a good quarterbacker."

"It's quarterback."

"Right. Sorry. Anyway, he says you're a really good . . . quarterback. He says you have to study a lot to be that good, even in the summer."

"Just offenses and defenses, not chemistry or physics."

"You're smarter than me about flowers too," she said.

We fell silent again. I didn't feel any better, maybe, but I didn't feel any worse.

"You're not very much like the football player reputation," she finally said.

"I just love playing football, and I'm good at it. I don't love being Homecoming King or alpha male or whatever."

"You do make a handsome Homecoming King."

"Thanks," I said, and felt a glimmer of hope, like when it's third-and-25 or worse, but you have a long pass play called that sometimes works.

It didn't last.

"You stayed with her for five months. She must not be all bad."

Just that quickly, the pocket collapsed, leaving me scrambling and about to be sacked. I wanted to talk about Rhonda and me, but we kept getting stuck on Haylee and me. Which was probably my fault, but still.

"She's not all bad." I leaned forward and buried my face in my hands. "I wish I knew how to do this, Rhonda VII, but I don't."

"Do what?"

Two deep breaths didn't help me.

"There's this girl I just met. She sort of asked me out. I like talking with her and looking at her. But I keep saying dumb things, and I don't know how to convince her that I like who she is, and I don't care who she's not."

No girl had ever reduced me to this—and it was only our first date. Probably our last date too. I was sandwiched between two big linemen, about to hit the turf.

"Tyler, I'm not sure it's possible for you to convince me of that. Not completely."

I hung my head even lower.

"Not tonight," she said. I heard the nerves in her voice. "Not completely."

It took me a few seconds to realize she'd just given me hope. Throw up a prayer and your guy actually catches it hope.

"Not tonight?" I asked without looking up.

"Yeah."

I sat up and looked at her. I couldn't get the words out quickly enough. "Could we go out again?"

Her sad smile was adorable, but it didn't have to mean anything good.

"I don't know. Do I really make you feel like you're not smart enough? I hate that. I know I take hard classes and get good grades, but I don't want you to feel that way." She hesitated. "Do you have to feel that way? Could you maybe not?"

"How does that work, exactly?" I sounded pretty skeptical.

She blushed, and I wasn't sure why. "I guess I have one idea," she said.

"I'm glad one of us does."

She stared at me with big green eyes and pressed her red velvet lips together. "If I say I'm not pretty enough or popular enough for you, which I did, what's your response?"

"My response is, that's crap." I smiled faintly. "And shouldn't I get to decide that for myself?"

"Good," she said. "So when you say you're not smart enough for me, I get to say that's crap too. It's only fair. Tyler, that's crap."

I wanted to believe her, just like I wanted her to believe me. "Your idea is to say we're both full of crap?"

She met my eyes. "Not full, exactly. I was going to say it this way. Maybe we could trust each other. I could trust that you think I'm pretty, and you could trust that you're smart enough, because you are."

"I like that," I said. I blew out a breath and a thought struck me. "I like that you can be really smart and not think I'm stupid. That way I can be happy you're so smart, and maybe not feel . . . what's the word?"

"Threatened?"

"Yeah, that. And you should believe you're pretty, because you are, and not feel threatened because other girls are pretty too."

She looked at me for a moment. Then she started to smile. "You know what? Those are really smart thoughts."

"Thanks. Can we go out again?"

Her smile got even sweeter. "I'll agree up front to two more dates, if you want," she said, "in case the next one flops for some reason beyond your control. That's from a movie too. But there's one condition."

"I won't wear a pink tux, even for you."

She giggled. "What I mean is, football players don't have a great reputation with girls. Star football players have a terrible reputation."

"I'm not like that. You can ask the princess."

"I believe you. We're trusting each other, remember? But I'm telling you anyway. I'm happy to be your date. And your friend, if you want. I really am. I will not be your private recreation area. And there better not be any locker room talk about me that's not true. You guys have no idea how much that stuff hurts girls, even the girls who don't get talked about. Maybe that's two conditions."

"Okay."

"It's not because I'm a lesbian. I'm totally not. It's just dumb. My mom's gone, and Dad has a dangerous job, and I may have to take care of myself sooner rather than later. I don't want to take stupid risks and mess that up. I have to do well enough in high school to pay for college, and I have to go to a good college and graduate. There's no room for big mistakes with boys. Not even kind, handsome quarterbackers. Sorry, quarterbacks."

"I'm okay with that." I swallowed nervously. "If a guy likes you, is letting him hold your hand one of the things you won't do?"

"No. You could do it sometime, if you want."

"How about now? I really want to."

She looked up soberly and nodded. "Now would be very nice." She moved her hand closer to me, resting it on her knee.

I couldn't remember the last time I was nervous reaching for a girl's hand, but I was. Even with permission.

We sat quietly, looking out over the parking lot and into the night. I didn't think about anything. I just enjoyed her hand in mine. It started out timid and nervous, like mine, but then it felt calm and strong. Like mine, only smaller.

I turned toward her and just looked. She faced straight ahead. She didn't smile or frown. She seemed to be thinking. I already knew she puckered her lips a bit when she was lost in thought. I couldn't take my eyes off them.

Her mom's lipstick. Well, hers now. Her mom was gone, she'd said.

She closed her eyes and blushed just enough that I could see it by the street lamp.

"You're looking at me again?" she asked, not moving at all.

"Yeah."

"Are you comparing me to someone?"

"I think I'm done with that," I said.

She nodded once. "This is fun for you?"

"Yeah."

She took a deep breath. "Will you tell me what you're thinking?"

"Are you sure?"

She turned to face me. "No. Tell me anyway." Her voice was husky and low. It made me want to tell her every happy thought I could possibly think about her.

"Two things, I guess. The first one is, I'm learning to see your beauty. I feel pretty happy about that. Lucky too."

She made a little sound, almost a whimper. Her green eyes got really big, and her cheeks turned red. "Thank you," she almost whispered. "What's the second thing?"

I said it as gently as I could. "When you said your mom's gone, did you mean she . . . passed away?"

Her eyes filled with pain, and most of the color left her cheeks. She looked down, and I thought her chin quivered.

I wanted to kick myself. Or punch myself in the nose. She couldn't have expected me to be thinking about her mom, especially after what I'd just said. I was a moron.

"Cancer," she said without looking up. "I was twelve."

I squeezed her hand. "I'm so sorry. I can't even imagine."

"I miss her every day," she said quietly. "So does Dad. I miss him too, in a way. I think she took part of him with her. I missed her a lot today."

"I'm sorry."

"Thanks, but you already said that."

"What was she like?"

Her eyes met mine. "I don't know. She was . . . She was Mom."

She looked stricken and sad, but I saw no tears. Maybe you eventually run out of tears for some things.

"I'm really sorry for asking about her. I wasn't smart enough not to ask, and I hurt you. I don't want to hurt you ever."

She squeezed my hand for a long time. "I asked you what you were thinking, and you told me. It's okay. It's something you should know about me."

"Are you sure?"

"I think about her all the time, but I hardly ever talk about her anymore." She turned to me. "I think trusting you is working."

She looked away again and asked, "What about your parents?"

"They're divorced," I said.

"That must suck," she said.

"It did for a while. But they both remarried, and they're happier now, and the stepmom and stepdad are pretty cool. The best part is, Mom and Dad both try to spoil me a little."

We sat in silence after that. I tried to think of a way to rescue our Homecoming date from all the dumb things I shouldn't have said. I was about to say I was sorry for saying and doing so many things I had to say I was sorry for, but she spoke first.

What she said was, "Mom would like you."

What I heard was that all that stuff was behind us, including the dumb things I said, and how I made her sad.

Hope and relief made my heart beat faster. "You really think so?"

"She'd also like that I put her favorite lipstick to good use. Her black hair was real, by the way."

"Would she like that you used her lipstick for a date with a football player? Your dad didn't seem thrilled."

"She'd care that you're a good guy. That's what Dad cares about too. He'll figure it out. He played football too, by the way."

"Thanks for thinking I'm a good guy," I said.

"You are a good guy," she said. Then she grinned. "Who knew?"

I had never wanted to kiss a girl as much as I wanted to kiss her right then.

"Rhonda VII?" My throat was tight, and I sounded nervous.

"Yeah?"

I took a deep breath and tried to be smart for once.

"I don't mean right now, but what would you and your mom think if, sometime in the future, not tonight . . . if I tried to steal a kiss? Would that be a big problem?"

She giggled again, and I saw mischief in her eyes. "Just to be clear, since we're sort of pretending she's still around, you'd be kissing me, not Mom?"

I gave her the look you give a girl you want to kiss, when she jokes about you kissing her mom.

"Would she have to see it?" She sounded happy. Maybe even playful.

The lead weight in my gut finally disappeared, and I broke into a grin of my own.

"No. Just you and me."

Her smile was a gentle, red velvet curve. "Then sometime in the future, if you still like me, she . . . and I . . . might think that would be appropriate. But you're right. Not tonight. And Dad may have his own opinion, so don't ask him. He carries a gun, among other things."

"I'm not asking for tonight. I just wanted to know if I could hope for sometime in the future."

"I've never kissed a boy. Have you kissed lots of girls?"

That might have been another tricky question, but somehow kissing was easier to talk about, once we knew it wouldn't be tonight.

"A few, including the princess. Not as much as you think. Or as many."

"You don't know what I think." This time, when she said it, she wasn't defensive or upset. Her smile warmed me like a blanket.

"You said we have a reputation."

"You said you're not like that, and I believe you."

"I'm not."

A cool breeze began to blow, and she shivered.

"You're cold," I said. "Let's go back in."

"You know what?" she asked, as we headed for the doors, hand in hand.

"What?"

"Let's dance some more. Could we dance the slow ones like you and the princess did at the end? It looks classy and decent and non-bad-reputation-quarterbacky."

For the last half-hour we danced to every song and talked when the music wasn't too loud. I wasn't much of a dancer, and she wasn't either, but that was okay. The longer we danced, the more distant the difficult parts of our outdoor conversation felt.

"I almost wish this wasn't the last dance," I said when it was. "This was really fun." Then I wished I hadn't said "almost," because it sounded bad and it wasn't true. But it didn't seem to bother her.

"Of course it was fun," she murmured. "It's Homecoming, and you're the King."

"That wasn't the best part of tonight, Rhonda VII. Not even close."

I saw and felt her breathe deeply.

"I know," she said softly. Then she came closer, and instead of looking at me with her green eyes and her velvety, dark red smile while we danced, she rested her head on my shoulder, and I wished the song would never end.

After I took her home, said good night to her and her dad, drove back to my place, and checked in with my parents, my phone vibrated with a message.

> Tyler, thanks again for tonight. It was a really good first date and first dance for me. I like talking with you. I hope I see you soon. You know where my locker is, more or less. And don't worry. I checked, and my personal police lieutenant has never actually shot anybody, even when he wanted to. Good night! Rhonda VII

Marie

I MET MARIE IN the hallway after school. "The race is tomorrow," I said. "We should sign up."

"The three-legged race?"

"Yeah."

Running the three-legged race together was what seventh-grade couples did on the next-to-last day of school, at the Outdoor Games.

For two months Marie and I had sat together at lunch, in assemblies, and on field trips. Being a couple was way better than her poking me in the back with her pencil in Algebra. I'd never been so happy. I had already prepared something to write in her yearbook on the last day of school—right after the morning movie, where I hoped to hold her hand for the first time.

"I'm sorry, Kenny." Her big, brown eyes matched her words.

"You don't want to race?"

"No, I do."

"I don't understand."

I thought I saw her chin quiver, and she looked down. "I already signed up."

"Oh, good. I didn't know. Think we'll win?"

I liked her blond curls, her sprinkling of freckles, and her smile, but she wasn't smiling now.

"Not with you. With Bobby."

Maybe my heart didn't stop, but it started to hurt—for two reasons. The second one was, Bobby was my best friend.

"With . . . with Bobby?"

She seemed relieved. "I'm sorry. I didn't know how to tell you."

Later I was glad that what I said next wasn't angry or mean.

"Well, you told me." I started to turn away, then turned back. "Um, good luck. You know. In the race. With, um, you know."

Then I did turn away. She said she was sorry again. I nodded without looking back.

I walked home in a daze, told Mom I was sick and wouldn't want dinner, collapsed on my bed, tried not to cry, and thought about how much it hurt.

I must have fallen asleep eventually, and Mom or Dad must have pulled a thin blanket over me. It was dark when I awoke, and the house was quiet. I couldn't get back to sleep.

Instead, I had daydreams. I figured they were still daydreams, even at night, because I was awake.

In my first daydream I cheered for Bobby and Marie, and they won. After they untied their legs, Marie ran to hug me, not Bobby, and we walked away, holding hands.

In my second daydream Bobby hugged April, the girl he had liked before. Marie kissed my cheek in front of everybody.

In my third daydream she hugged me, then pulled me away, and we went and sat under a tree. She apologized (tearfully) and said Bobby was nice (which I knew), but I was the boy she really liked. Then she kissed me on both cheeks. I dried her tears with the clean handkerchief Mom made me keep in my pocket, which I hadn't pulled out at school since kindergarten, because it was embarrassing, except when I used it to dry a girl's tears.

What actually happened was, in the morning I told Mom I was still sick. I didn't want to eat, so she believed me. I watched World War II documentaries on the History Channel all day.

On the last half-day of school, I sat at the front of the cafeteria for the movie, *Camelot*, so I couldn't see Marie sitting with Bobby.

Afterward, I picked up my yearbook, flipped through it, and decided not to stay for the signing. On my way to the front doors I ran into Marie. She was alone. Her eyes were big, and her voice was soft.

"Hi, Kenny."

"Hi."

"Did you like the movie?"

I shrugged. "The first part was fun."

"The last part was too sad," she said.

"Did you win the race?" I asked.

"No, but it was fun. Are you okay? They said you were sick."

"A little better today."

"That's good."

We both saw Bobby approaching. "So, uh, see you later," she said. "Have a nice summer."

"You too."

As soon as I was outside, I broke into a run.

At home I dropped my yearbook on the kitchen table—I wanted to throw it at the wall—and sat on my bed, updating my daydreams so Marie visited me at home, since school was out for the summer.

I must have fallen asleep again. I awoke when Mom knocked and opened my door.

"Still sick, honey?"

"Yeah."

"I'm sorry. You came home before anyone signed your year-book?"

"Yeah."

"A girl came by while you were asleep. Mary? Marie? She wanted to sign it, and she seemed nice, so I let her. She left hers for you to sign. She'll pick it up later."

"She signed my yearbook?"

"Yes. Shall I get it?"

"Yeah. Thanks."

She brought both yearbooks and a pen, then stood in the doorway, watching me.

"Thanks, Mom. I'll sign it later."

"Okay."

"Did you read what she wrote?" I asked.

"Not without permission. It's not my yearbook."

"Okay."

She finally left.

I sat up and tried to invent a daydream about Marie being my eighth-grade girlfriend. I couldn't make it work. Finally I reached for my yearbook and opened the front cover.

There it was.

Kenny,

You're a good guy, and we had a fun year. Have a great summer!

Your friend, Marie

A week earlier, she would have dotted the *i*'s in "friend" and "Marie" with little hearts. Now they were just dots.

I thought I should at least look at my picture, so I turned to the seventh grade section. When I found the page with me on it, there was a note tucked between the pages. I recognized Marie's handwriting and her favorite stationery.

Dear Kenny,

I didn't want to write this in your yearbook for other people to see.

I'm sorry I made you sad. Please don't hate Bobby. Sometimes things just happen.

I need to thank you for something. When you saw me today, you didn't pretend I wasn't there, and you weren't angry or mean. You talked to me, and when I said have a nice summer, you said, you too.

You really are a good guy.

Your friend, Marie

I closed my yearbook with her note still in it, opened her yearbook, didn't look for what Bobby had written, found my picture, and wrote in the margin next to it.

Marie, it was a fun year. Have a happy summer.
Kenny

I looked at the words for a long time. Then I closed the book. It was over. My daydreams were stupid. And it hurt.

I Am Chuck Steak

"**I**T'S A MEAT MARKET, Amber."

My roommate's face in the mirror looks a little hurt, because I'm complaining about church.

I'm in her room, tying one of my gym shoes, while she adds a little more curl to her long hair. I have a lunch date with a treadmill. She has an actual date.

"The whole YSA ward thing's a meat market, or just the pool party?" she asks calmly, not interrupting her work.

"The whole thing. The pool party itself is like the meat market's huge Labor Day sidewalk sale."

"Having a separate congregation for young single adults isn't just about marrying us off," she says, parroting the official line. It's familiar, but I listen anyway. She always listens to me. "We get more opportunities for leadership and service, and the activities and programs can focus on our needs and interests."

I cinch up the other shoe. "Plus we don't have to go to church with all those women who have husbands and babies already, and be reminded that we don't," I add helpfully. Sort of helpfully.

"We don't *yet*." Amber's an optimist.

"Right. Sorry. I shouldn't complain. Again."

She glances at me, smiling faintly, and turns back to the mirror. "It's okay. I know you like it less than I do. But you're still giving it a chance for a while, right?"

"Yeah." For her sake I wish I could remove the cynicism from my tone, but it doesn't work that way. "Let's review. The first Sunday we went to church here, two guys asked you out. Last Sunday, two more. Plus they've already put you to work in the ward. I'm happy for you. I really am. Meanwhile, nobody even noticed I was there. Tomorrow will be our third Sunday, with more of the same. In the grand meat market scheme of things, you're prime steak, and I'm day-old, marked-down stew meat."

She stops working and stares at my reflection. Her eyebrows are knit, and the little smile is gone. I'm criticizing her friend—me. She takes that personally.

I join her at the mirror. "I don't resent you for it. You're beautiful and sweet. I'm cranky and cynical. And my butt's too big."

"Shel—ly." She draws out my name. "You're not always cranky. And even if you were stew meat, which you're not, people like stews. Including, you know, guys. But you're not stew meat. I should know, right?"

I have to smile. She's my best friend, even after two years of rooming together. We're on our third apartment. And her family raises beef. "Then I'm a rump roast."

"Rump's a good roast," she says. "But we're talking about steak. There's lots of different kinds, including some with better flavor than the cuts everyone knows."

I'm feeling conciliatory. "What's a cut that's kind of tough but tastes good?"

"There's round steak. You have to cook it just right and slice it thin and at an angle, or it's tough."

"Do we ever have that?"

"No, Dad brings us the fancier cuts. I could ask for some. I love London broil."

"Okay, so round steak could be me on good days. Tough, and be sure to slice me thin. And I have to be at the right angle. Other days, I'm rump roast, for the obvious matching pair of reasons."

She turns to face me. "If it's bad for them to treat us like cuts of meat, how is it okay for you? And stop saying your butt's too big."

She doesn't say it's not, just that I should stop saying it is. She's not blind.

I shrug. "Maybe it's not okay."

"It's not. Remember that at the pool party next Saturday."

"Oh, yippee," I say dryly.

"It'll be fun."

If I wasn't whining already, I am now. "I get that a lot of us are new, and they want us to get acquainted, but this is a church thing. Does it really have to start with how we look in swimwear?"

She unplugs her curling iron and sets it down. "I think we wanted an activity people would come to."

"All you need for that is food and publicity. But the activities committee, quite naturally, is filled with people who look good in swimsuits, including you. People who think pool parties are great fun. What about the rest of us?"

"Good question," she says softly. "You could wear something else and not swim."

"That could happen. I still don't have a suit."

"Let's go shopping again," she says with more enthusiasm than I ever feel for clothes shopping.

"We tried that. Eighteen stores, was it?"

"It was seven. Some of the suits you tried were pretty nice."

"I need the one I wore freshman year for water aerobics."

"Where is it?" she asks. "Does it still fit?"

"It should, but it's in Nebraska. Let's go there instead of the party."

"Let's call your Mom and have her send it, so you can wear it to the party."

Her brown, puppy dog eyes win the day. I nod. "I'll call after the gym."

"How about now, before the gym?" No pushover, my friend Amber. She gets her way gently, but she gets her way. I call, and Mom promises to send it today.

Amber's delighted. "So you're coming?"

Deep breath.

"If it gets here in time and still fits, and if I still like me in it—at all—I might come."

She gives me a squeeze. "That's good enough for now."

She may be right about it being good enough. My old emerald green one-piece flatters my chest without making my butt look any bigger than necessary. I'm not sure the color matters, but we didn't find a suit of any color in our shopping that flattered me that way. I know it's not entirely the suits' fault.

I'm eager to change the subject. "Who's today's date?"

"Brian, but he introduced himself as Adam. It was cute. I mean, I guess it was a pickup line, but I liked it. He said, 'Hi, I'm Adam. I saw you and thought you might be Eve.'"

I facepalm. "Oh, Amber!"

She looks hurt. I'm not watching her, but I hear it in her voice. "Are you thinking I'm dumb now too?"

I've never thought that about her, but it's been a sore point since her high school reunion last month. A former classmate who just started some third-tier law school had to say, "Elementary Ed? Really? We always thought you were smarter than that."

Amber's barely twenty-three. She graduated high school early and raced through her teaching degree, with an eighteen-month break for a church mission. Now she's living her dream. She just started her second year teaching first-graders.

I un-facepalm. "You're not dumb. Not even close. I'm thinking you're way too smart to fall for a line like that."

"I didn't fall for it. I don't care that much about his pickup line. He seems nice."

This time I give her a squeeze. "I don't know what you get out of our friendship, but you're really good for me."

Her smile is back, radiant and sweet. "Aww. What do you mean?"

"You're like sunshine to my dark clouds."

"You're not all dark clouds."

"Also, you're a teacher. You work for the angels. I serve the devil."

She chuckles. "Marketing's not serving the devil. Go to the gym already. Exercise cheers you up. I'd go with you, but...you know."

I let go. "On my way. Have a nice lunch."

Not for the first time, as I walk out the door, I think there's a really lucky roomful of first graders at her school.

• • • • • • • • • • •

I'M AT THE GYM—SPEAKING of meat markets—on one of 56 identical treadmills with "Life Fitness" scrawled in a pseudo-handwritten font across their control panels. It's my usual routine: stretch, warm up, 30 minutes at 10 degrees elevation and 3.5 miles per hour, then warm down and stretch again.

I've forgotten my over-the-ear headphones, and my phone battery's down to six percent. I can't even read an e-book on it for the next half hour. And there's nothing on the TVs worth watching without audio. That leaves watching the people in front of me—and that includes watching their butts.

I'm in the second row of treadmills. In the first row, in front of me, are a woman, a girl, and a man. In front of them, elevated on four stair-steppers for optimal visibility, are three women and a man.

We won't think about the people behind me. I should stick to the last row of treadmills as a public service.

I'm not totally obsessed with butts, but I used to be, starting when I was thirteen and began noticeably putting the "max" in gluteus maximus. Now I'm only occasionally obsessed. Like before pool parties I can't avoid.

I have the butt and hips of a generously curvy woman at least six feet tall. On a bad day I think it might be 6'8". The problem is, I'm two inches shorter than Amber, and she's only 5'4".

As every civilized gym-goer knows, "eyes in front" is the unspoken rule. So I watch Stairstepper Three, a gorgeous twenty-something with pretty brown hair falling straight to her shoulder blades. She's in a navy-blue long-sleeve t-shirt with the sleeves rolled up a little. It's not tight anywhere, and it's loose enough around her waist that it bunches at her hips with casual perfection.

She must be nearly six feet tall, but the curvy six-footer I would be, if my height even tried to fit my width, is the opposite of her. She's trim, with just enough hip and butt to look completely fantastic. My supermax rear would be a crime of nature on her, compelling proof that there is no God, or that he/she/it is outright malicious.

But clearly there is a God. He's a gifted sculptor who totally rocks as a minimalist.

I watch her move. Her leggings are as tight as her shirt is loose. They'd show every line and jiggle, if there were any. Teenage me would have died of jealousy already, even before I could hate her properly. I hated a lot back then. At least I'm over that.

She hitches up her shirt and puts her hands on her hips. It's almost breathtaking—and I'm straight, so this is aesthetic, not sexual. That's why I watch her instead of Stairstepper Four. His loose gray shirt and black shorts don't need to be tight to show off a nice physique. If I watched his butt for more than, say, ten seconds, I might have inappropriate thoughts.

Stairstepper Two, to the left of Perfect Three, is in tight gray shorts and black leggings. Her pink halter top doesn't seem daring but shows off some nice shoulders. She's curvier than Three, but her hips are still much smaller than mine, and she's probably 5'8". Her butt doesn't approach the utter perfection to her right, but it's respectable.

To her left, Stairstepper One is about 5'6" and looks fit. Her ample curves are still noticeably less ample than mine. She's pretty enough, but she won't get a second glance from guys, when she's next to Two or anywhere in the same ZIP code as Three.

I'm still not watching Stairstepper Four. Nice haircut, not long. Excellent biceps. No visible tattoos. Good chin. I wouldn't mind seeing his eyes, but I'm behind him. And my ten seconds are up.

I keep returning to Three. Eyes in front.

Between the stairstepper row and me, I make Treadmill One as mid-thirties or older, and Treadmill Two is clearly her teenage daughter. They have the same face and the same blond hair with dark roots, even the same ponytail. The mom's in a modest, medium blue sleeveless shirt, but I can tell she has a generous chest, almost my size, and she's a few inches taller than me.

Her ankle-length sweats aren't skin-tight, but they're revealing enough. When she pauses her treadmill and bends over to adjust her shoe, I have to conclude she has a good butt. It's almost my size and about right for the rest of her curves. There's some extra weight around her waist, but not much. If I look that good at her age, after at least one pregnancy, I'll be awfully lucky.

I don't watch Treadmill Three at all. By the time I get to him, I've realized Treadmill One and Two are his wife and daughter. He's in great shape, but I won't knowingly drill my gaze into the butt cheeks of another woman's husband. Besides, he looks like he's pushing fifty.

Of the seven people in front of me, Stairstepper Three—Perfect Three—is the last to leave, after almost half an hour.

I finish too. On my way out, at the other end of the treadmill section, I see some competition for Perfect Three. I designate her Treadmill Four. She has a pretty green shirt, black leggings, and long, black, amazing hair with shampoo-commercial shine, cascading down past her waist. She looks a lot like Three, but she's shorter and a little curvier.

Near the front desk, still on my way out, I see the same girl, almost, but blonde and in stylish purple and silver spandex, with a buff trophy guy at her side.

Then there's me, in the mirrors near the front doors. I don't compare well to the perfection I've just witnessed, but I keep fit, and I have a waist. My black shirt, shorts, and leggings don't betray me too badly. And I regularly thank whatever gods there be, or maybe it's genetics, for endowing me with an excellent chest. Anything smaller, paired with my expansive rear, and I'd look like a total freak.

Amber's right. I'm not all dark clouds. I almost smile. Difficult as it is to accept, the truth here is inoffensive enough. I'm not freakishly beautiful, but I'm not a complete aberration in the other direction. I look pretty good, even on a typical Saturday at the gym. Even without my magic green swimsuit.

Another basic truth is, I need a guy. Please, God? I'm already twenty-five.

I half-snort, half-giggle. You'd think my butt's gravity alone would attract—

I imagine another hurt look from Amber and try again.

I need a good guy who thinks my curves are beautiful and sexy. And, of course, loves me for my sharp mind, delightful wit, and intermittently pleasing personality.

I watch myself produce a wry smile. Would I tell him before, during, or after the honeymoon about spending my afternoon watching women's butts at the gym? How does a girl start that conversation? "Honey, we're both eager for you to have your way with me, but before this goes any further, you need to know the history of my butt."

Someone's coming, so I move on. In the parking lot I relax for a minute in my Hyundai. Then my phone rings. It's down to two percent.

"Hi, Mom."

"Hi, honey. Having a good afternoon?"

"Just finished at the gym."

I know what she'd say if I told her I'd been studying butts. Obsessing on my butt, and therefore other women's butts, like I did as a teenager, is not healthy. She'd ask how she could help. Another therapist, maybe?

Because that worked so well before. Because my big butt is all in my head.

I shift in my seat.

Not. Anyway, she's already helping.

"Only have a minute, but I found your swimsuit. Sent it Priority, so probably by Thursday. I'd forgotten how pretty it is. Quite modest for a swimsuit. Wait, doorbell. Hang on."

In fact, my suit is about as modest a one-piece as a girl would want to wear after, say, 1960 or so. The thing is, it flatters me like nothing else I've ever worn. I should wear it at my hypothetical future wedding.

It will still fit next week. Odds are I won't have enough of an excuse to skip the pool party. And maybe that's okay.

At church they said there are about 120 girls and 100 guys in my YSA ward. We're all out of high school, and none of us is over thirty. I don't know most of them, because Amber and I just moved from the next town over, and most of the younger ones just arrived for the new school year anyway.

It's true that encouraging marriage isn't the only reason my church makes special congregations for young singles. It's harder that way for us to slip through the cracks and drift away, which people my age pretty much do in droves anyway. But marrying us off is the most celebrated goal.

Despite my complaints, getting acquainted with guys isn't a bad idea. I want to marry eventually, so I need to be around single guys and practice not repelling them. And since the surest route to a guy's heart and brain—except food, perhaps—begins with his eyeballs, my green swimsuit may help.

What I did buy, when Amber and I went shopping, was a nice off-white, sheerish wrap to wear over a suit when I'm not swimming. It has the desired effect without interfering too much with certain other desired effects.

"I'm back," Mom says. "I sent it to your office. Less likely to get stolen that way. It probably still fits, right?"

"Yup. You're totally the best Mom I ever had."

"You know it. And you're welcome. Send me a picture."

"I probably won't."

"Whatever. Gotta run."

"Thanks, Mom."

• • • ● • ● • ● • •

For a few days I'm too busy with work, mostly, to think much about swimsuits and large body parts, even when I'm at the gym first thing in the mornings. Thursday morning's a little different; the thought that my green swimsuit will arrive today cheers me all the way to the treadmill. The mood lingers as I start my workout, dial up my daily podcast of industry news, and lock into work world.

By the time Amber's home from parent-teacher conferences that evening, I've nibbled a light dinner, because I'm fooling myself that a regular dinner would show when I model my swimsuit for her. The still-unopened box from Mom is on our kitchen table, and I've retreated to my room with something I didn't even imagine when I left for work this morning. I hear the front door open and wonder how long I have just to admire myself in the mirror.

It's a few minutes before she calls, "Knock, knock. I'm opening your door."

Hinges squeak, and I turn toward her. She's holding my green swimsuit and looking at it, not me, as she enters.

"I had to open your box, which I think is a federal crime. I love this!" She double-takes. "Holy crap, Shelly! That's gorgeous! You look amazing! New dress, or did your mom send it too?"

"I went shopping at lunch. I was celebrating." To myself I sound almost dazed. I'm not used to looking this good. Or shopping for clothes, when I can avoid it.

"What are we celebrating?"

While I tell her about the big, old client I didn't know needed saving, but I saved them anyway, and my raise and bonus and promotion, she turns me this way and that, commenting as much to herself as to me. "Surplice neckline. I don't have the chest for this, but you sure do. Tea length, rosette. Half-sleeves. The navy's just right. The waist is perfect for your shape, since you're so in shape."

Her tone changes. Now she's talking to me. "Honey, how did this happen?"

"Their CMO told our VP that I communicate, I don't blow smoke up their skirts when I don't know something, I spell the company name correctly every time—believe it or not, that was an issue before—I see the whole picture, and I know what I'm doing. Oh, and they like my sense of humor. They were shopping for another agency, but they're not anymore. It's a big save. So I am now Digital Marketing Supervisor, which might be a little grander than it sounds."

"Sounds great to me. Congratulations! But I meant, how did this dress happen? And really, it's not just the dress. You're beautiful. Are these the tags?"

She picks them up from my dresser. "Okay, Dillard's. Two hundred fifteen dollars? Good thing you got a bonus. You actually went shopping?"

"I found the right section at Dillard's, told the lady I wanted to look fantastic in a work-safe sort of way, and asked if she had anything that might achieve that. She looked at me from ten different angles and said, and I quote, 'I have something we should try. You might just pull it off.' Long story short, she may have a customer for life."

Amber has a conspiratorial smile. "How big's the raise? And the bonus?"

"Ten thousand and two thousand, respectively. I should pay two-thirds of our rent after this, if not seventy percent," I say. We're at 60-40 now, because our incomes are so different. "I want to. Please?"

"That's not why I asked, but thank you. I was wondering how much you can shop on your own before your head explodes."

"Maybe a little more now," I say. "Is this modest enough for church?"

She turns me to face her and pokes out her lips while she considers my question.

"Yes," she says.

"Do I get more than one word?"

"It doesn't show any cleavage, though it's pretty obvious that it's hiding some, which is part of why it works so well. It's long enough. It has a back. So yes, it's fine for church. And before you ask me if it makes your butt look big, because you always do, it's perfect in that department. I'm a little jealous. No way could I look this good in this dress. I don't have the curves."

"You're jealous of me? Are we laying it on a little thick?" I ask, but I'm grinning.

"Don't pretend you don't believe me, for once. You're radiant. It's not just the dress."

I nod. "Unbelievable as it sounds, yeah. I believe you. This time."

She hugs me, then practically dances toward the door. "Put on the swimsuit while I make myself a little salad. Wait. Were you done telling me about your amazing workday?"

"Their CMO told his team, 'In Shelly we trust.' Ann the VP said she might put that on a plaque or something."

"Know what? My salad can wait." She hands me the old green swimsuit. "Tell me more."

Three minutes later I'm turning this way and that, again, but I'm a little more self-conscious. When she pronounces judgment, I believe her. Again.

"Honey, at least half the straight guys at the party will think you're sexy. The ones with taste. It still won't be just the suit, but it doesn't hurt."

All the straight guys will think she's sexy, but I'm okay with that. I don't need them all. I don't even want them all.

I change into sweats and a t-shirt and look at the other things Mom sent—junk mail, chocolate, girly soaps—while Amber nibbles absently at her salad. I've watched her for maybe half a minute when she stops and looks up at me. Her smile is strained.

"Are you okay?" I ask.

"Do I seem sad?" She's genuinely curious. "I was trying not to. It's such a happy day."

"You do, a little. What's wrong?"

"You won't be angry and call me spoiled?"

"Have I ever been angry and called you spoiled?"

"No." She takes a deep breath. "I am sad. About something else. I'm really happy for you tonight."

"So why are you sad, and how can I help?"

"Okay. So. Three Sundays at church. Four dates, four different guys. Another tomorrow night. All of them kind of eye candy, you know? But there's not much going on in their heads, and I have doubts about their hearts too. Like whether they have hearts."

She's rarely so negative about people. This is serious.

"They only care how I look," she says. "Not who I am inside."

"Did one of them hurt you? I'll kill him. Was it Adam?"

"No. What hurts is there's nothing there. I attract emptiness. I know I sound ungrateful. You haven't had a date here yet, which is another reason to think these guys may not have souls. And I'm starting to agree about the meat market. All they want is a decent steak. What if they're scaring away the better guys? Or I am somehow? If there are any better guys."

"Amber, you're the best cut of steak, whatever that is. USDA Prime."

She looks hurt. "It's all just meat."

"Let me finish. If they can't see you're amazing on the inside too, and they don't love that even more, they're shallow. Overgrown children. Losers."

"I could be all kinds of amazing inside, and they'll never see it."

"You are all kinds of amazing inside. Sooner or later we'll discover some real men, and they'll find you irresistible for all the right reasons, and you'll forget about the pretty boys you've been dating."

A faint smile flickers and dies. "Maybe. Where do you suppose we'll find these real men?"

· · · · ● · ● · · · ·

ON SATURDAY WE ARRIVE at the party early, because Amber's on the activities committee. I offer to help, but they're already overstaffed. So I stake my claim to a deck chair and head for the pool, before it gets crowded. I'm in my green swimsuit, looking good. I'm a successful marketing professional, sought after by people who love my work and my sense of humor and don't care at all about the size of my butt.

Guys begin to gather around Amber. That's normal. I'm a tiny bit jealous but mostly worried. She's been kind of sad since Thursday night, and her date last night didn't help—and none of these guys looks like a philosopher.

We're at somebody's parents' place in the foothills, and it's spectacular. Behind their mansion is their own little box canyon, where steep sandstone walls shade an Olympic-size pool with a wide patio around it, and beautiful landscaping around that. The built-in grill is nearly as big as our kitchen. Matching deck chairs line three sides of the pool, but they're not just deck chairs. They're chaise lounges, all adjustable and with pillows for your head. I can't imagine having this much money.

The canyon walls might lean slightly inward—I'm not sure—but I'm not claustrophobic. The acoustics are incredibly live, almost like an indoor pool. Amber says they have music recitals here.

The acoustics are squirrelly too. I soon discover a certain corner of the pool where I can hear people talking clearly in some of the seats across the pool. For a while I look for another spot, where I can eavesdrop on Amber and her gaggle. I want to hear how they treat her. But no such luck.

I tread water in the magic corner for a minute and listen to four guys. They're looking my way, more or less, so I can't stare long enough to see who's saying what.

"Target-rich environment," one says. "See anything you like?"

"You mean anyone? Don't be a jerk," says another.

"He can't help it," says a third.

"Anyone, if that makes you happy," says the jerk.

"Too many blondes here," says a fourth voice. "Wonder how many are real."

"I'm not picky about hair color," says the jerk. "I need curves. Serious curves. Curves that need to be posted, or they'll wreck you."

"Do all the curves have to be real?" one of them asks.

I'm all for guys liking curves, especially real ones, but I can only listen to meat market shoppers for so long before my mind wanders. Then again, it doesn't wander very far.

What if I'd caught a few guys' attention before I got into the pool, and they preferred dark hair and major curves, and they were watching me and hoping I'd get out soon? Not that it would ever happen, but what if it did?

Something in my head would say I should be offended. They'd be interested in my body, not my delightful personality, my blossoming career, etc. But what if I ignored that voice and obeyed the one that whispered to wait ten seconds, then give them a show? Ten-Mississippi, nine-Mississippi, eight-Mississippi . . .

One-Mississippi. It's time to get out anyway.

I reach the side of the pool, put my hands on the edge, lift myself up, and hold that position with my arms extended for a few seconds. Then I raise my left leg, put my foot up on the edge, and casually climb out of the pool. I change my mind, turn around, and sit at the edge, dangling my feet in the water.

I'm at the fringe of the acoustic sweet spot. The four guys' voices are muffled but still audible.

"Over there," one says. "Near the corner, just got out of the pool. Green suit."

"I know. I'm watching," says the jerk. "And yearning."

Holy crap.

I don't stop to think. I lean back, arms extended behind me, with my palms flat on the concrete.

"Dangerous enough for you?" asks the first guy.

"Holy tabernacles, Batman! I could totally marry that for time and all eternity."

"Yeah, you're a pig. She's a she, not a that. A daughter of God."

"Too chunky for me," one says. "Some of those curves should be continued on the next daughter of God."

I can't say I haven't thought that about myself.

"You're a pig too," says my defender. Without being too obvious, I try to see which one he is, but I can't tell.

"The God who made that must really love his sons," says the jerk. "Think I'll go say hi. Maybe I should call the temple and schedule a wedding first."

"A pig like you? They probably won't let you near the temple."

I want to hear more, but I probably can't act natural if I stay, so I stand up and walk away. I feel their eyes on me—some admiring, some not. By the time I've reached donned my wrap, stretched out on my chaise lounge, spread my towel over my legs to dry, and put on my sunglasses so I can study the guys across the pool, I might be blushing all the way to my toes.

They look young and preppy, and none of them is on his way to meet me yet. Probably not my type anyway. Probably twenty and just off their two-year missions, with some serious growing up to do in the real world.

But I will have to thank Mom again for sending my suit.

When their heads turn in unison to follow a pretty redhead, I twist myself to the left in my chair, so I can adjust my suit a bit at the rear. I love the feel of the fabric, and I pause for a few seconds with my hand on my butt.

Yes, there's plenty of me there. But the whole package looks okay today.

That—of course—is when I hear a guy's voice from my right, sort of behind my behind, under the circumstances. "Pardon me. Is this seat taken?"

I blush at the double entendre—it has to be accidental—but mostly because my hand is where it is, as he can plainly see. I remove it, straighten out, and look up at him. Maybe he'll think my face is sunburned.

He smiles, which is nice, and I recognize him. He spoke in church last Sunday, and he was very good. Which means half the girls in the ward now have a crush on him. A totally pure, doctrinally sound, very spiritual crush, of course.

I'm suddenly aware that there are plenty of empty seats and lots of pretty girls around, but he wants to sit next to me. I smile at him. "Be my guest."

He's dark-haired, shorter than average height, which I like, and stocky but not chubby. He resembles the sweet Italian boyfriend-turned-husband in my favorite movie, *Brooklyn*. The one who loves the baseball team and the sweet, clever Irish girl.

I watch him sit. It's not like he's wearing a speedo at a church thing. In fact, he's in khaki knee-length shorts and a polo shirt. But definitely callipygian. If he has a brain and a heart too, like he seemed to on Sunday . . .

"I'm Adam," he says, and my heart crashes to the concrete.

"And you saw me and thought I might be Eve? You guys need better pickup lines."

"No," he says patiently. "My name's really Adam."

"That's not what the sacrament meeting program said. That was you, right?"

"They used my first name, Philip. I go by my middle name. And did you hear me use a pickup line?"

He has a point. "So you didn't go out with Amber Nilsson this week?"

"I don't know anyone named Amber," he says. "Why?"

"Some guy used the Adam and Eve line on her. She's my roommate. But his real name was Brad or Brian or something. Seriously, couldn't he look at least a little further into the Old Testament for his material?"

"Like Isaac and Rebekah?"

I pick a name at random, which is a mistake. "Or Solomon."

He gives me a mischievous little smile. "That could be fun. 'Hi, I'm Solomon. May I sing about you? Do you want to see my really big, uh, temple?'"

My unladylike snort makes him grin.

"You're the one who made that comment in Sunday school, right?" he asks. "The one where you disagreed with the teacher, among others?"

I know the one he means. "About how it doesn't make sense to think however we're born is perfect, because God doesn't make our bodies, our parents' genes do?"

"Yeah. I thought it was smart—and brave. Anyway, I'm Adam. You're probably not Eve. If you are, that's okay. What's your name?"

"Nice to meet you, Adam. Most people call me Shelly. Short for Rachel. Well, not short, exactly."

He chuckles. "Rachel? You're kidding."

"What's so funny?"

"As in Jacob and Rachel? Speaking of the Old Testament."

"So?"

"My last name's Isaacson. They got that right in the program. *Isaac*son, and my mom's Rebecca. Think about it."

He's reaching a little, but Jacob, the son of Isaac and Rebekah, married Rachel. I don't know whether to laugh or wince. I force a smile.

"Then it's fate," I proclaim. "I'm to marry your brother Jacob. Will I have to bear all twelve sons myself, do you think, or will he have other wives to help me, like the original Jacob did? I'd prefer to be the first, but I suppose we could negotiate. Shouldn't your name be Esau?"

He laughs heartily, and sincerely, I think. "My only brother, Jim, has one wife and one little daughter," he finally says. "I'll introduce you if you want, but don't get your hopes up. Besides, Holly might kill you. And him. And me."

"Well, if he has the wrong name . . ." I concede. "Why aren't you dressed for a pool party?" I kind of want to see him in swim trunks, preferably without a shirt.

"Cut my leg the other day, working on my sister's car. Seventeen stitches' worth of stupidity. Can't swim for about a month."

"Youch. I'm sorry. But hey, you had a perfect excuse, and you're here anyway."

"It's a ward activity. The whole thing has a meat market vibe, maybe, but the food looks good." He grimaces. "Sorry. The actual food."

"Thought I might look into that, when I'm done swimming." I check the pool. It's way too crowded now. "Which I probably am."

"Can I bring you something?" he asks.

"You can come with me."

"Best offer I've had all day," he says.

"How many offers have you had today? I'll save our seats with my towel."

I stand up and spread my towel across both chairs, nudging them closer in the process.

I consider taking off my wrap. As in, holy crap, I'm trying to be meat.

"Good idea," he says. It takes me a second to realize he means the towel, not my unspoken thoughts about the wrap. It stays on, and we head for the food.

"Sorry about the meat market crack," he says. "Hope I didn't offend you."

"You kidding? I had the whole meat market discussion with Amber this week, not for the first time. She's prime steak, by the way. At least a ribeye."

"If she's a ribeye, what kind of steak are you?"

I'm still not used to thinking I look good. I answer out of habit. "Compared to her, I'm hamburger."

We're at the food table, and I'm reaching for the buns—no, the hamburger buns, I tell myself—when he holds up a charbroiled patty with the tongs. He looks back and forth between it and me, kind of checking me out in the process. "Nope. Not hamburger."

"What, then?" I almost suggest rump roast.

"Have to think about that. Lots of different kinds of steak. All good, if you cook them right."

"Speaking from experience?"

"First thing I did in my new apartment was get a good grill and a heavy cast iron skillet. Before furniture, even. I'm getting pretty good." He grinned. "I practice a lot. And I share, so my roommates like it."

"This isn't just a really awful metaphor, is it?"

"It's an actual grill. I mean, half the time I just make burgers or hot dogs, and I'm not crazy about brats, but in between it's steak, fish, chicken. Or a good pork chop."

"Doesn't sound like a student budget."

"It's not. Been there, done that. Now I work for a living. Worked then too, but you know."

Twenty minutes later, back at our chairs, I spear the last chunk of cantaloupe on my plate. I'm actively trying not to look at him for a whole minute. I've been looking a lot, as we chat, and I think my eyes are starting to betray me. They feel eager. Radiant. Friendly. Interested.

"So Rachel, Shelly, want to do lunch next Saturday?"

"Sure, I guess." I'm more enthusiastic than I show. "When and where?" Maybe it's someplace I can wear my new dress.

"Let's grill something at my place. Bring a salad, if you want, or we can just make one. We can double with your roommate, so it won't just be us, in case my roommates are out. Or somebody else."

I'm strangely nervous. I scramble for a neutral question.

"What will you grill for us?"

"I do a lot of chuck steak, so maybe that."

I've never seen any of that in our freezer. "You're the expert."

"It's not fancy, but the flavor's great, and it looks fine. A lot of it's really tender, and the rest isn't bad. Just need teeth."

I resist the temptation to think he's talking about me, whether he knows it or not.

"Will these do?" I'm not faking my big, toothy smile.

He smiles too. "Yeah."

"Then I'm in. Thanks!"

My next temptation is to think he might be a better match for Amber, because beef.

"Pleasure's mine," he says.

"What shall I wear? Will there be swimming? Oh, wait. Not with your leg."

"You could swim if you want. There's a pool in the courtyard."

"I don't need to swim. It's not my best look anyway."

I try not to look shocked that I would say that—or that I actually kind of think that, since Thursday.

He raises his eyebrows and looks like he wants to say something, but he doesn't.

"What?"

I get a tiny shrug but no words.

"Just say it."

He hesitates. "Okay. That's . . . hard to imagine."

"What's . . . wait. You mean . . ." My cheeks warm.

I'm not fishing for a compliment. I'm really not. And I'm totally going shopping again this week. Same place, same Marta the wizard lady. Same price range, if necessary. Something more casual than my amazing new dress.

"Sorry," he says. "I try not to be a meat market guy."

I'm not sorry. And I have an idea. "I'll test you right now, just to be sure. You seem to like how I look. Is that true?"

"Yeah."

My smile's involuntary, but I'm okay with it. "Is that why you wanted to sit by me? And ask me out?"

"No. Doesn't hurt. But you seem smart, like I said. And you're fun to talk to."

"Okay, the results are in. We can both relax. You're not a meat market guy. Now tell me more about me being smart and fun. Start with smart."

"In Sunday school I was trying to think how to say what you said, but you got there first. My cousin would have hugged you, if she'd been there to hear it."

"Your cousin?"

"She's blind. Born that way. My aunt got the measles at the wrong time. Guess sometimes the vaccines don't work. She says she fully intends to have perfect eyesight in the resurrection, so obviously she was born flawed, and it's condescending and stupid to pretend it's perfect that her eyes don't work.

"One time, somebody heard her say that and thought she didn't believe in God, which she totally does. Anyway, you were more diplomatic about it than she usually is."

"I felt a little harsh," I confess.

"For applying rational thought to their fluffy little doctrinal fantasy? I couldn't believe the teacher." He mimics her low, soothing voice, and it isn't flattering. "'Don't you think that's unkind?' You just said—I don't remember exactly. But you sounded calm, not hurt, and not confrontational at all."

"I think I said, 'It's not kind or unkind. It's the truth.'"

"Sounds right. Then you sat quietly and didn't look ruffled when they went back to the same silliness you'd just called out for them. I was one row behind you and about four seats over. I waited for somebody else to take your side, but nobody did. I should have. Guess I'm less courageous than you."

"Probably wouldn't have made a difference," I say. "They weren't exactly open to new thoughts. Or, you know, thoughts. It wasn't the point of the lesson anyway."

"See, you are kind," he says.

"Sometimes I try. Wait. That was kind?"

"To me. Maybe not to them."

"Yeah. So why do you think I'm funny?" I ask. "Or fun. Whatever you said."

"You liked my Solomon joke."

"It was good. Bit edgy for a church activity."

"You liked that too."

I nod. "I really did."

"Plus we're at a pool party, and I'm in shorts and you're in a swimsuit, and we got through all that meat market talk okay. I think that shows we both don't take ourselves too seriously."

I feel my eyes twinkling. "Are you saying our bodies are imperfect?"

His eyes widen. "No. Yes. Mine is."

"And mine?"

His mouth opens, but no words come out. Finally he says, "I assume there must be something. Pollen allergy, crooked molar, hangnail. A genetic tendency toward male pattern baldness, which won't affect you, but your sons will be billiard balls."

I giggle, which I haven't done with a guy in quite a while. "You want the whole list?"

"I don't want any of the list. Can I get you some dessert?"

"Do I look like a girl who eats dessert?"

That flusters him again. "I—you—you look great. I didn't mean . . ." On the plus side, he recovers quickly. "Do you want dessert or not?"

Now it's a laugh, not a giggle, and my smile is a few levels above please-bring-my-dessert-already. He visibly relaxes, and I answer like I have manners after all. "Yes, please. Whatever has the most chocolate? But no coconut. It's not an allergy, just an attitude."

His smile is crooked, and his eyes sparkle. "Be right back." He stands, but before he walks away, he turns to me. "Thanks for saying yes to lunch."

"It's the least Rachel could do for the son of Isaac."

"Wouldn't that be fetching me a drink of water from the well?"

He does know his Genesis. "Go away," I say.

Hurry back, I think.

While he's gone, one of the guys I overheard from across the pool catches my eye. He's on my side of the pool now, a few yards away and possibly coming to see me. I wonder if he's the jerk, my defender, the continued-on-the-next-girl critic, or the other one. Probably not the critic.

I take a moment to appreciate the view. He's tall and tanned, lanky and dirty blond. His bright, beautiful green eyes match my swimsuit. He may not have an actual six-pack, but there's a pack there. His suit's almost knee-length, with a mesmerizing pattern of dark and medium blues. The same pattern in greens would be even better on him, because green eyes.

If Adam is cute and verging on handsome, this guy's objectively hot, gods forgive me.

"Hi, I'm, uh, Jake."

Okay, that makes it easier.

"Of course you are," I say. "Is that your real name?"

He's taken aback. "Yeah. Well, Jacob."

"Do you know my name?"

He recovers quickly too. "I . . . hope to know it soon?"

"I'm Rachel. Don't let that give you any ideas."

"What do you mean?"

"Genesis? Jacob and Rachel? Never mind. How old are you?"

"Almost 21."

"Just off your mission to . . ."

"Ecuador. Would you like to go out sometime?"

I've heard enough to be sure. He's the good guy, the one who insisted I was a "she," not a "that." He called those other guys pigs for me.

"Good for you, Jake! Look, you seem like a nice guy, even if your Old Testament needs some work. No stupid pickup lines, and you get straight to the point. But I'm almost 26, and I'm sorry, but almost 21 is too young for me even to try being interested anymore."

His shoulders sag a little, and I feel harsh again. He nods slowly. "Okay. That's fair."

"You in school?" I ask, almost as an apology. Also, now I'm on a mission.

"Mechanical engineering," he says.

I've known some engineering students. "Do you love it or hate it so far?"

"After one week I think I'm the only first-year who even likes it so far."

"Lot of math, right?"

"I can handle the math."

"I believe you. Tell you what, Jake. See the pretty blonde over there?" I look in Amber's general direction.

"Seriously? Which one?"

"No kidding. At the drink table. Blue swimsuit, nice figure, great legs, curls, sunglasses. Baseball cap." Amber's the only girl wearing a cap, but it totally works for her. I could have saved my breath and mentioned it first, but I'm advertising now.

"What about her?" he asks.

"She's my roommate, Amber. Closer to your age, and she's sweet. Smart too. And like I said, you seem like a nice guy. Just ignore those guys around her, because she's not attached to any of them, and go say hi."

I think I see a flicker of hope in his eyes. "Okay, I will. Thanks. Nice to meet you, Rachel."

I enjoy watching him go. He's plenty callipygian too. But mostly I'm pleased with myself for finding a potentially good guy for Amber to meet.

Adam returns with a big, chocolate-frosted brownie and a chocolate chunk cookie which might be more chocolate than cookie—and he gives me the choice. I waffle, but he won't tell me which he prefers. "This is about you, not me," he says. "I'm happy either way."

We split both, and our half-brownies disappear first. I'm about to demolish the last bite of my half-cookie, when I notice he's not eating his half. He's just talking some and watching me.

The sun seems warmer on my face. Except we're in the shade. "So . . . chuck steak," I say.

"If that's okay."

"Sounds great. We are what we eat. Or vice versa."

Again: holy crap. Did I just say that? And what does it mean?

He hesitates. "My turn to ask. Are we in the middle of a really bad metaphor?"

I totally blush. "It might not be so bad. But not speaking metaphorically at all, you should finish your dessert, so I feel better about inhaling mine. It's going straight to my hips, in case you want to think twice about asking me out."

His eyes follow my hand to my hip. Which wasn't my plan, but okay.

I sort of expect a witty reply, or a charming, well-mannered one, or both. Instead, he blushes and gets all shy. I'm so hooked.

"Look, I'm sorry for the meat market thing," he says with his eyes on mine again. "Like I said, I asked you out because you're smart and fun, not just—"

He's bright red now, and his isn't sunburn either.

I'm not helpful. "Not just . . ."

"Not just nice to look at."

I haven't put the towel back over my legs. Now I wriggle out of my wrap, fold it loosely, and set it aside. "It's getting warm out here," I explain.

I'm slightly breathless.

I'm also lying like a rug. The canyon's cool enough.

He smiles, and it's different. I hope it's about me, but I'm tempted to turn around, in case some other, prettier girl is walking up behind me.

"May I take your plate, etc.?" he asks after a moment.

"Sure. Thanks. May I save your seat, etc.?"

He smiles again. "Please. Be right back."

I admire him shamelessly as he walks away, until an Amber-size thump jars my chair and I find her sitting at my knees.

"Hi!" I say with uncharacteristic cheer.

"Hi yourself." She has a knowing smile. "How's it going?"

"I am chuck steak."

Her smiled fades. "You're better than that."

"No, it's just right. Adam—real Adam, my Adam"—I thrill at the possessive—"he'll be back in a minute—he explained it to me. Often overlooked, but great flavor. Some parts might be a little tough, but some of it's really tender. I am chuck steak."

"Okay. Did he really say all that about you?"

"He was talking about actual beef. We talked about the meat market though. He started it. I said you're a prime ribeye or better, so he asked me what I am. Turns out he grills a lot. Speaking of which, you're invited to lunch with me at his place next Saturday. Bring a date. We're having actual steak from his grill."

"Fun! Thanks! I will. You didn't tell him you're a rump roast, I hope."

"I started with hamburger, so he put me next to a hamburger patty. Couldn't see the resemblance."

She giggles. "This is pretty weird, Shelly. But he sounds fun. Anyway, I came to thank you for sending Jake. He's cute, and he's a gentleman. I think he might be smart. Can I bring him on Saturday?"

"Of course."

"I only ask"—her eyes sparkle—"because he says you rejected him, which makes him your leftovers."

"I liked him too."

"Good. Thanks for the referral! Oh, your guy's coming back. A real Adam, huh? I'm outa here."

I pretend not to notice his approach. I lean back, half-close my eyes, stretch a little, and clasp my hands behind my head for full frontal effect.

At this moment I don't know whether I've joined the meat market or transcended it. I catch him admiring me, before he sits back down, but he's not leering. Is that why this feels like it's about more than meat?

Anyway, God bless my green swimsuit and the underpaid Developing World piece workers who probably made it. I hope they're not slaves or political prisoners. God save them if they are. God bless all the women with smaller butts, or any size butts, who didn't buy it, so I could find it on the clearance rack at my favorite mall in Omaha.

And while I'm at it, God bless Marta at Dillard's, for being a genius at her job. And Amber, my smart knockout of a roommate. She's said more good things about me in two years than I've said bad things about myself, and she never lets the obvious fact that she's freaking gorgeous go to her head.

I look cautiously in Adam's direction. He's reclined his chair to match mine, and his eyes are closed. I like his relaxed little smile.

I start plotting how to get him to sit by me at church tomorrow. I'll definitely wear my new dress.

Maybe I could just ask.

I've already seen him in a white shirt and tie, with long pants, so I don't have to imagine what he'll look like, but it's too bad so much good stuff will be obscured. He's in construction management, but he looks like he does plenty of the actual constructing.

A different question comes out. "So tell me," I say. "Who exactly is Adam Isaacson, besides a guy who sheds his own blood to help his sister, gives a good talk in church, and likes to grill things?"

He says something about himself, and I should listen more carefully, but I'm admiring his upper arms again. And his lower legs. And thinking, if it's really thought, What kind of steak are you?

Yeah, I'm probably going to hell.

Unmanned

"LOOK, A SQUIRREL!"

Luke, my ten-year-old, pointed to the trunk of a tall pine tree at the edge of our campsite.

"I think it's a flying squirrel," said Ryan, his best friend. Ryan's father, Joe, was my best friend, and we were neighbors.

"Now how can you tell that?" I asked, more skeptically than I meant to. Neither boy answered.

We followed the squirrel with our flashlights as it climbed up into a tree-shaped space that seemed darker than the sky.

Joe and I weren't the camping type, but our ten-year-old sons had begged and pleaded and even done extra chores, so we had to take them.

They'd mocked our suggestion that we get a bucket of fried chicken or some pizzas on our way to the canyon. So we ate unevenly cooked tin foil meals, then s'mores. Then we did our best to clean up, locking our garbage and leftovers in Joe's SUV. We didn't want to attract the bears which, according to three signs in our campsite alone, had not been seen in the area but could be attracted by food.

Joe's walnuts were the only edible thing left in camp. They came from a tree in his yard, and he'd brought a small bag of them. He cracked one after another with his trademark brass nutcracker.

He offered me some, as he always did when we sat in his back yard, but walnuts weren't my thing. We didn't worry about them being the bears' thing either.

Our flashlights caught the squirrel spreading its wings—flaps, whatever—and leaping into the air. It flew through the darkness, eerily illumined, like a spotlit B-17 over Germany, until it landed in the next tree.

"It's flying! It's flying! Awesome!" sang the boy choir.

"That's pretty cool," said Joe. "But you know it wasn't flying, right? It was just—"

"*Toy Story*, Dad? Really?" asked Ryan. Even by the flickering firelight, I could see the boys roll their eyes in unison.

Joe shrugged and went back to his nuts.

I'd heard that fire repelled animals—bears, coyotes, bobcats, and mountain lions. But eventually we'd have to extinguish it, and I knew that humans were the least adapted to darkness of all the forest's predators.

When the boys stopped trying to scare each other with grisly stories and announced that they were ready for bed, I made them help me police the campsite one more time by flashlight, looking for anything that might attract bears. Joe kept cracking his nuts.

They assured us they didn't need any help with their tent and sleeping bags, so we stayed at the fire and listened to them. Their chatter and laughter took a full half hour to die down.

Every few minutes, Joe cracked another nut. I stared into the fire, wondering what there was about it that supposedly scared wild animals. Why would a bear be intimidated by a campfire? A forest fire, probably, but a campfire? That hadn't even scared the squirrel.

At 1:00 a.m. we reluctantly doused the fire and headed to our individual tents. I lay awake for a long time after that.

Joe was already snoring—would that attract large mammals or repel them?—but in between his seismic scrapings, every distant animal noise or nearby rustling of trees or brush riveted my attention. I listened for a pattern that would suggest something approaching our defenseless campsite. At times I thought I heard a large animal walking around, but the sound never seemed to get closer.

The screams awakened me.

The boys were screaming, but something in my panicked brain said they were screaming because Joe was screaming.

Joe was definitely screaming, and something was thrashing around out there. My mind flashed back to a news story years ago about a bear attacking someone through the wall of a tent and dragging him away and killing him—in this very canyon. For the first time in my life, I understood why people owned guns, and I no longer understood why I didn't.

Some of Joe's screams were intelligible. "My nuts!" he shrieked. "He's got my nuts! Aaaaah! He's got my nuts!"

Instinctively I grabbed my oversized flashlight, unzipped my tent, and rushed to rescue Joe. I passed the boys' intact tent on the way. It was still zipped.

As I approached Joe's tent, my brain advised me that I had no weapon, just a lightweight, plastic flashlight. It might have been useful for aiming a weapon, if I'd had one, but it would be of no use by itself against large, attacking mammals.

Joe's tent was partly unzipped. The upper half of his body protruded from the opening.

I screamed. Then I screamed again. As I turned to find a good place to vomit, I realized that I had seen no blood, no severed limbs, and no fierce animal. There was just Joe, not the least bit disemboweled, prone and pounding on the dirt with his fist.

"What's going on?" I asked, panting.

"Stupid raccoon. Unzipped my tent, grabbed my nuts, hissed at me, and ran off with the whole bag. Camping sucks! He got my nuts!"

"Your nuts?"

"My walnuts."

By now the boys were standing beside me, looking down at the spectacle.

"Wow, Dad," said Ryan sarcastically. "Nice one."

"What's that supposed to mean?" Joe asked heatedly. "One of you want to help me?"

"Just wow, Dad." He turned to Luke. "Let's go back to bed. Sorry my dad is such a freaking coward."

"It's not like mine is much better," Luke said, as if I weren't standing right there. "Must suck to go camping and come home without your nuts." They howled with laughter.

I opened my mouth to object to their disrespect, but Ryan spoke first.

"Next time we go camping, let's bring our moms instead."

"Deal," said my own traitorous offspring.

I closed my mouth, helped Joe up, and went to revive the fire, so I could sit by it until morning.

Not That Jason

MY BROTHER PUT HIS hand on my shoulder. "Sarah, almost there. Wake up."

"Not asleep," I groaned. "Leave me alone, Jason."

"Sorry, thought you were. Since the airport, actually."

"No." The pain struck again as I spoke. It was familiar, but that didn't make it less severe.

It had begun as we walked to baggage claim. Then it got worse. The ride to our hotel was excruciating. "Wide awake the whole time," I said.

The better to appreciate my impending death, I thought.

"You don't sound too good."

Master of the obvious, my brother. But not of the language. "*Well*. I don't sound too *well*."

"That too. Can I help? What's wrong?"

My little brother wasn't smaller than me, but he was younger by two years. That made him eighteen. I'd called him a loser at least a thousand times in the last several years, and I meant it. He was immature and annoying, not someone I enjoyed spending time with.

I knew the magic word to shut down the conversation. It had the added virtue of being true.

"Cramps," I said.

"Cramps?" he asked, with more compassion than revulsion. That meant he didn't get it. This was the boy who was still grossed out by packs of feminine hygiene products in the grocery cart.

Plan B was too much information. Way too much.

"Cramps. The monthly kind. Bad ones. Beyond the power of Midol." Cramps all the way to my knees, I didn't say. "Pain like endometriosis or maybe fibroids, if you ever heard of those. But my gynecologist says it's just bad monthly cramps."

I opened my eyes to check. His ears were the reddest part.

"Sorry," he said, but kept talking anyway. He was trying to be nice. "What I can do?"

"I have one idea. I hear they go away during pregnancy, and supposedly they're not so bad after it. Want to help me find a sperm donor?"

"Yeah, gross. Is this you telling me there's nothing I can do?"

"Up to you. Won't help for today, but if you find me someone in the next couple of weeks, when I ovulate again, we might prevent the next time."

By now he was less a deer in the headlights than a hapless boy caught in the unearthly beam of a descending UFO with an all–female crew.

I felt a tiny pang of guilt. He was kind, for once, and I was torturing him as I always had. But guilt was unbecoming an older sister, and it only lasted until the next wave of pain anyway. "He doesn't have to be rich or terribly handsome," I groaned, "as long as he's not sterile or impotent, and he doesn't poison the gene pool too badly."

Disgust had replaced horror on his face. "You know what, Sarah? I'm glad you're home from school for a couple of weeks. But right now, not so much. Some people can just be sick. You have to be gross. As if sisters weren't gross enough already."

"Who's being gross?" I gasped. "It's just plumbing." I closed my eyes. I'd seen enough of his glares when I lived at home. The older he got, the more he hated how easily I could push his buttons.

For a minute neither of us spoke. I concentrated on surviving the next several seconds, then the next, then the next.

"Isn't morning sickness worse?" he asked. He didn't sound angry after all. His voice seemed gentle.

"It lasts longer. And the way Mom did it, which means I probably will too, it's bad. But the second trimester will be great. No morning sickness by then, and no cramps. And after the baby's born, supposedly things might go better with the plumbing."

"Yeah, it'll be great," he scoffed. "Just another human growing inside you, and then labor. Then diapers and tantrums and barfing and parent-teacher conferences and daring acts of teenage rebellion."

"You left out colic and teething. The donor can have full custody, if he wants."

"I'll mention that in my tweets. Is a trimester three months?"

"One-third of forty weeks would be thirteen weeks, two days, and eight hours."

"Show-off." In the past he'd have elbowed me or punched my arm or something. I was glad he didn't.

The limo turned into what was probably a driveway, and I opened my eyes again. Sure enough, we were at a hotel. The words were in large, polished gold script: "Continental Grand."

The pain hit again, and I resisted the urge to writhe. "I guess we're here," I said. "Now I need to concentrate on getting out and walking into the hotel."

I didn't want to get out of the car, for the obvious reason that I was in pain. Also, it was a real limo. We'd expected a garishly colored minivan, but the guy at the airport desk said those were all out, so our ride was a black stretch limo someone else had just cancelled. No extra charge, he said. It was going downtown anyway.

I'd never been in a limo. The leather was exquisite.

Jason insisted on taking my suitcase for me, and I let him. Somehow he only needed one arm for two suitcases, so I insisted on taking his other arm and leaning on him a little, and he let me. Maybe he was less grossed out than we both thought. Also, when did his arms get muscles?

Ordinarily I'd have taken some serious time to admire the lobby. Light-colored woodwork, nice rugs, chandeliers, everything. It wasn't ostentatious, just elegant. Understated in a way, like it already knew it was fabulous, so it didn't have to try to impress anyone. For a girl who thought luxury was a nice Hampton Inn with a complimentary hot breakfast, it would have been a treat, if my one desire hadn't been to assume the fetal position and whimper pitifully until I put off this mortal coil.

Maybe tomorrow. If I lived.

A smartly-dressed, graying Hispanic man appeared. I half-expected the bellhop to have gold braid on his shoulders and a dorky hat, but this man was in an expensive gray suit, and I might have to get Jason a shirt in the same muted orange, if he kept being nice, with the same light gray tie. Except that the tie alone was probably worth more than my car. So, not the bellhop.

"Welcome," he said to my brother. "You must be Jason. I recognize you from the photograph. It's our great pleasure to have you here."

It was the twenty-first century, I thought, when even phone calls came with photos. Small wonder that hotel reservations did.

"Uh, thanks," Jason said. I attempted a smile. If I'd known there'd be a royal welcome, I'd have put the reservation in my name. On second thought, how was it in his name at all? He was too young.

"My assistant manager was just telling me you had cancelled, but I looked up, and there you were. I am Rafael Tenuro, the manager, and we are all at your service."

He gestured subtly to someone behind us, and a younger, lighter-skinned man appeared, wearing a blue suit that could have been a uniform but didn't have to be. Still no funny hat.

"Jorge will take your bags. How else may we serve you?"

Jason surrendered the luggage, looking bemused. No, that was wrong. Bemusement was too sophisticated for little brothers. He was just surprised and puzzled.

"We'd just like to check in, I think."

"No, no, no. There's no need for that, sir. We'll handle every-thing. May I show you and the lady to your suite?"

"Uh, sure. This is my sister."

If he'd said, "That's no lady; that's my sister," which he might have, I'd have tried to kill him where he stood. Even if it killed me.

"I see," said the manager. "A great pleasure, ma'am. Will more of your party be arriving today?"

We stepped into the elevator. The manager held a card to a sensor, then pushed the button for the top floor, the 18th. I hoped it was a fast, gentle elevator.

"Late tomorrow afternoon," Jason said.

We had all wanted to fly in tomorrow, but there weren't enough cheap fares available, so Jason and I came a day early. Mom was speaking at a professional meeting on Monday, and Dad was free, so we were spending the whole weekend in Portland. A nice family weekend, while I was home from school in New York.

The extra day for Jason and me would be fun, we'd all thought. He could help the natives Keep Portland Weird for a weekend, whatever that might mean for him, and I could check out the glitzy Apple store and spend hours and hours shopping for books at Powell's.

The best-laid plans. Portland wasn't fun yet. Not for me. I could have read a calendar and seen this coming.

"Very good, sir," said the manager.

The elevator ride was quick and relatively humane. The manager chattered the whole time, and Jason answered mostly in monosyllables. I leaned against the elevator wall, clinging to Jason's arm—which actually helped.

Across a small foyer from the elevator, the manager proudly showed us into the most luxurious hotel suite I'd ever seen. It looked as big as the house we grew up in, but much nicer.

"We're completely modern here," he said. "If you've heard of smart homes, we have smart suites. Is anyone in your party named Alexandra?"

That was random.

"Uh, no," said Jason, looking puzzled again.

"Very well. Just address the system as Alexandra, and you'll be surprised what it can do."

"What if our mother's name was Alexandra?" Jason asked.

Not *was*, doofus. *Were*. Subjunctive mood.

"We would simply change her name."

"Our mother's?" Jason deadpanned.

"No, sir, the assistant's name."

"Could you make her a man?"

"Of course, if you wish."

"Nice," said Jason. "Alexandra will be fine. How come she isn't answering when we say her name?"

Great. I was in agony, and he was geeking out, with the manager's eager help.

"She doesn't think we're talking to her." He raised his voice slightly. "Alexandra?" There was a soft, electronic *bong*. "Alexandra, which restaurants are presently open downstairs?"

Bong.

Alexandra answered in a refined British accent and a low, slightly husky voice. "The Forty-Fifth Parallel is open for lunch and dinner today, serving French and New American cuisine until 10 p.m. The Bamboo Garden, featuring a menu of fine Asian dishes, will open in 23 minutes for dinner and cocktails, and will remain open until midnight. Tony's Café is open until 1:00 a.m., serving brick oven pizza, pasta, salads, and sandwiches. Room service is available around the clock and is complimentary for guests in the penthouse suites, except for alcohol."

"Would you care to try it, sir?" asked the manager. His pride was like the lobby: obvious but understated.

"Alexandra," Jason said, "please show us the room service dinner menu."

Another soft *bong*. A large flat screen came to life, showing us a menu with pictures that looked good enough to sample.

"Alexandra, could you read us the list of entrees at the Forty-Fifth Parallel?"

Bong.

I knew what he was doing. He'd seen the menu, and now he was testing the system's French. He did it to humans working at French restaurants too. He'd studied a lot of French in high school, and he'd crushed on an exchange student from Lyon for an entire school year.

"Tonight's specials include *Bar au Beurre Blanc et Crabe*, a seared sea bass filet with crab meat in a sherry butter sauce; *Filet de Boeuf aux Morilles*, a grilled filet mignon in a morel mushroom brandy cream demiglaze; *Carre—*"

"Alexandra, stop. Thank you."

Bong.

Jason turned to the manager. "Her French is pretty good. Will she take our order?"

"Of course, sir, and as you heard, all room service is complimentary while you're here, except alcohol."

The bellhop arrived with our bags. He must have taken a slower elevator.

"Ma'am, sir," said the manager, "here are your key cards. You'll need them on the elevator as well, for this floor. Is there anything else I can do for you at this moment?"

"No, thank you," said Jason. "I think my sister just wants to rest for a while."

"Of course, sir. Please don't hesitate to alert me anytime, for your slightest whim. My direct number is by the phone, or you can ask Alexandra to connect you to the manager. She can also help you with the Wi-Fi."

"Thank you, sir," said my brother. He turned to the bellhop and slipped him a ten-dollar bill. Mom had given us both some cash for gratuities, with the admonition, "It's a nice hotel. Don't be stingy."

"It's my honor and pleasure, sir," said the manager. "Good day."

The bellhop followed him silently out the door.

Jason was right. Resting was exactly what his sister wanted. But there was something I had to tell him first. It was my duty as a sister.

"She's perfect for you," I half-said, half-gasped. The pain again. "Who is?"

"Robot Alexandra. Gorgeous accent, even does French. Waiting at your beck and call. Completely servile, with a reasonably sexy voice. And she offers you free food. Oh, wow," I said, exhaling like a woman in a childbirth class. If that wave of pain was my karmic reward for teasing him, it was almost worth it.

His eyes twinkled. "Alexandra, do you love me?" he asked. I wanted to hit him for trying to be funny while I was in torment.

Bong.

"I'm sorry, I don't know what you mean."

"That's okay," Jason said. "Wait 'til you get to know me."

Alexandra didn't reply.

"She seems like a sensible girl," I said. "But all this is a bit"—I winced in pain—"a bit over the top. Help me to the sofa, okay, jilted cyber lover boy?"

He helped me to the most comfortable sofa my body had ever encountered. The leather seat in the limo was a park bench, by comparison.

"What else can I do for you?" he asked.

I closed my eyes and took a couple of deep breaths.

"Well, if it wouldn't be too gross for you, could you sit by me for a few minutes, and I'll sort of cling to you in agony and maybe put my head on your big, brutish shoulder?"

"Yeah, sure," he said. "If you promise not to say the C-word again."

"Deal," I croaked.

Ten minutes later, or maybe thirty or more, he asked, "So is this helping at all?"

"Yeah, it is. Thanks. You know all those times I called you a loser?"

"Yeah."

"You're not a complete loser."

"Yeah, I actually knew that the whole time." He sounded amused. "I'm a great guy, when you get to know me."

"I like that you're so humble too."

"Thank you. You're a pretty good little sister once in a while."

"Thank you," I said. "Little?"

"Shorter," he said.

He deserved a slap, maybe, but all I could do right then was squeeze his hand—and I did it gratefully.

"Does talking help now?" he asked.

"Seems to. The music too. Where'd that come from?" It was a gentle string quartet, probably Haydn. "No, don't tell me. I'll guess. Alexandra is also a classical DJ?"

"Yep. And she already knows you like string quartets, because I told her."

"You really are a half-decent brother."

"Yeah, I really am. So you know all those times Dad tells us how much he misses us when he travels?"

I nodded.

"If he stays in places like this, I'm pretty sure I don't believe that anymore."

"No kidding. I've never even seen a penthouse suite before. And he's getting this free, with points or whatever?"

"Yeah, I think so."

There was a gentle knock at the door. "Room service."

"Come in, please," Jason called. To me he said, "I ordered dinner for us while you were asleep. The voice recognition stuff is pretty cool. I can talk softly, without disturbing you, and she responds just as softly."

I hadn't realized I'd dozed off, but I must have. I hadn't heard him starting the music either.

"I'm sure you two will be very happy together. Now get up and let her in. Room service, I mean." He stood and headed for the door, but it opened before he got there.

A slight but elegant young woman appeared with a silver cart. White lace covered whatever was on it.

"I have two dinners, sir. Would you like me to set your places in the dining area?" Her blonde hair was pulled back tightly into a perfect bun, and she wore an immaculate white blouse with black slacks and black rubber-soled shoes—the consummate service professional, except that she was blushing.

"Just a moment," Jason said. "Sarah?"

"Yes, sir," the woman said.

He looked at her name tag. "Oh, you're Sara too. I meant my sister, Sarah."

"I'm sorry, sir."

"No worries. Sarah, do you feel like sitting at the table, or do you want to eat right there?"

"Here, I guess."

The evidence was growing. He'd turned into a nice brother, while I was away at school. Who knew that would ever happen?

"I can set both places on the coffee table," Sara said.

"Thank you," said Jason. He turned to me. "I got a steak, medium well, and some salmon. Take what you want; I'm happy either way. The fruit's for you, and I'll share my broccoli and mashed potatoes, if you want."

Any day but today, I'd have taken the salmon. But when the cramps didn't kill my appetite, they made me crave red meat. He couldn't have known that, and he wouldn't have wanted to. But he'd ordered the steak the way he knew I liked it, not the medium he preferred, in case I picked it.

"You're so thoughtful. I'll take the steak."

He turned back to our server. "Did you hear that, Sara? Sarah says I'm thoughtful."

"Yes, sir." Her blush deepened.

A lace tablecloth appeared, and I watched her set our places. She wasn't just efficient; she was artful and precise. She lifted the lids from our plates and asked if there was anything else she could do.

"No, thank you," I said. "This is beautiful."

She nodded deferentially, and I did my best to send Jason a psychic message. *Give her a very nice tip! Give her a very nice tip!*

"For your trouble," he said, and handed her another ten, which would have been a big chunk of our dinner budget.

"My pleasure, sir. Thank you, sir."

"Thank you," he said, smiling. Kind and charming to the help, my little brother.

"Sir, may I speak freely?"

His brow wrinkled. "Of course."

She was silent for a moment, subtly biting her lower lip. A little human chink in her perfection.

"Are you allowed to sit for a moment?" Jason asked, when she didn't continue immediately.

"If that is what you wish, sir."

"Then please sit. Is there anything you're not allowed to do?"

My eyes grew wide. What was he thinking? I couldn't imagine him actually doing anything wildly inappropriate, but he wasn't above a bad joke.

"My instructions are to do whatever you wish," she said, "so long as it's not illegal, immoral, dangerous, or otherwise inappropriate." She was blushing again. Or still. I'd lost track.

"So what did you want to say?"

"Well, sir, . . ."

"Can the 'sir' already. I'm Jason."

"Thank you." She looked like she wanted to wring her hands. "Jason, sir, I know this is unprofessional, but I just want to tell you how much you've meant to my mother and me."

"Come again?"

She took a deep breath.

"My stepdad put my mother in the hospital before he left, and she was there for a while. And he hurt her . . . spirit . . . more than he hurt her body."

"That's awful," Jason said, "but how—"

"Your song helped us through those long weeks in the hospital, and the first month or two after that. It's so beautiful, so true. We can never thank you enough. We even thanked God for you. And your song."

Her face and neck were bright red.

"My song?"

"'It Was Never Your Fault,'" she said.

"I'm sorry. What was never my—"

Holy crap. "Jason, I just figured it out," I said, temporarily forgetting my discomfort. "It all makes sense now."

He looked baffled. "What?"

"Sara," I said, "do you know who we are?"

"Yes. You're his sister Sarah, and he's Jason Borland."

"Jason Borland, the pop star?"

"Yes, of course."

"Sara, no," I said. "He's not. He's Jason Brower, my little brother. He's only famous in his own mind, and he can hardly carry a tune on an iPod."

"Pardon me?"

"We're not who you think we are. There's been some mistake. So we probably shouldn't be in this gorgeous suite either."

"You're not . . . He's not . . . He looks like . . ."

"No."

She stood. "I have to speak to the manager. Please excuse me." She began to leave, but turned back. "Do you want your tip back, sir?"

"No, of course not," Jason said.

"I'm sorry for telling you my personal problems."

"No worries," he said.

I smiled for the first time in hours. "Tell you what, Sara. Just ask the manager to come see us. Don't tell him what's going on, okay? We'll do that. It'll be fun for my little brother."

"As you wish," she said.

After she left, Jason and I look at each other in wonder. Then we burst into laughter. That is, he laughed. I laughed and hurt, which made we wonder why I'd thought laughing was such a good idea.

"That's why they rolled out the red carpet," I said. "You do sort of look like him. Except he's handsome."

"I don't even know what he looks like. I hope they still have the room Dad actually reserved," he said.

"I'm sure they do. As far as they know, the Browers haven't arrived yet."

He grinned. "Look around, little sister. The Browers have arrived."

"I see what you mean."

"But I'll bet we get to pay for room service after all," he said.

"Good thing you didn't order the lobster."

"Or the caviar or the thing with shaved truffles. Maybe you shouldn't have told anyone."

"It was the right thing to do," I said. "But it would have been fun to watch. Who knows how many of the staff are adoring fans of the celebrity who isn't you? Let's eat."

I started on the fresh fruit. The strawberries were perfect. The kiwi slices were just right, not mushy or crunchy. The pineapple had a dash of cinnamon. I had to try that at home.

There was a knock at the door. "Manager."

"That was fast," Jason said. "Please come in!"

When the manager stepped into the room, Sara was a pace behind him.

"Sir, I noticed that your dinner order didn't include a beverage," he said, "so I brought you a bottle of our finest champagne. If it's not to your liking, we have some excellent wines. In any case, it's complimentary."

"Thank you," Jason said, accepting the bottle. It was probably the first time he'd ever touched a champagne bottle. As far as I knew, he'd never drunk alcohol. Neither had I, but today I might have considered it.

"Sara said you wish to speak with me. There's nothing wrong with the suite, I hope. Or our service."

"No, it's very comfortable, thank you, and Sara's a treasure."

My brother, the charming gentleman. I was . . . proud of him?

"Thank you. She's one of our best. How may we serve you?"

"We'd like to tell you something. Would you please have a seat?"

"Of course, sir, if you wish. Thank you." He sat in a wing chair, leaning forward, all concern and curiosity. Sara remained standing.

"There's been a misunderstanding," Jason began.

"I'm very sorry, sir. How can we make it right?" the manager said.

I spoke up. "It's nothing like that. You've made it far more than right already."

"I'm sorry, ma'am, I don't understand."

"First of all," Jason said, "We need you to take the champagne back. Not that we don't appreciate it."

"Is there a problem, sir?"

"Well, for starters," Jason said, "isn't the drinking age in this state twenty-one?"

"Yes, sir."

"Well, my sister Sarah is twenty."

"But surely you—"

"She's my older sister."

"I don't understand, sir. I thought—"

Smiling pleasantly, Jason explained the mix-up, while I finished my fruit. I enjoyed watching the manager's face as he began to understand. It went from worry to puzzlement to mild shock to resigned amusement.

"Thank you, sir," he said. "You didn't have to tell us. We'd never have known, at least not until you were long gone."

"Just tell us what the right room is," Jason said, "and we'll go there. And please bill our room service there."

"Would you excuse me for a moment?" the manager asked. "I'll step out and call the front desk."

Sara stayed. She smiled in a reserved, I'm-at-work sort of way.

"Sorry I'm not who you thought I was," Jason said. "But I hope things go well for you and your mom."

She smiled shyly. "Thank you. I have a good story to tell her tonight. I wish all our guests up here were as kind and . . . normal . . . as you two."

"Thanks," Jason said. "For the record, I'm the normal one. Sarah here, well . . ."

"Loser," I said, and turned to the other Sara. "He sings like a chain saw. And he snores like he sings."

She began to giggle, but stopped herself and just smiled. This time it was a genuine, human smile, not a professional one.

The manager returned. "Ma'am, sir, our famous guest really did cancel this afternoon. Would you like to enjoy this suite tonight? We'll move you into the correct rooms tomorrow, before the rest of your party arrives. That's your parents, right?"

We both nodded.

"Your dinner and whatever else you care to order while you're on this floor are still complimentary. I'm sorry for the misunderstanding, but I hope you feel welcome here anyway. We aim to treat all our guests exceptionally well."

"You've made us feel very welcome," I said. "Thank you. Tomorrow will be ideal."

"Very well. Again, my apologies for the confusion. If you'll excuse me, I'll leave you in Sara's capable hands." He slipped out.

Sara's tone was still polite, but less formal now. "I'm available for anything you need, and after my shift ends, Yolanda will be happy to take care of you. Just ask Alexandra, or pick up the phone and don't dial anything. It's a direct line to me. Anything you need will be my pleasure." She smiled, more at Jason than at me. "It really will."

"I think we'll be fine," I said. "But thank you."

She picked up the champagne bottle the manager had forgotten. "I'll take this. Are you sure there's nothing I can bring you?"

"Now that you mention it," Jason began. I was too far away to hit him.

"Yes, sir?" Sara said.

"It's Jason. My dear sister hoovered up that excellent fruit plate already. If you could maybe bring each of us one of those in an hour or two, that would be nice. Maybe we'll watch a movie or a game or something."

"I can also bring you hot, buttered popcorn, if you wish."

"Yes, definitely. Real butter?"

"Of course, sir. A large bowl?"

He nodded seriously. "Large would be best. I don't suppose you have a good bottled root beer, or maybe a ginger beer? Three or four bottles should be plenty."

"I'm sure I can come up with something."

"Thank you."

"It's my pleasure. Please excuse me."

I could have sworn she slipped through the door without opening it, but I probably just missed it when the next cramp hit.

"After dinner," I told Jason when it passed, "I'm going to explore until I find a bedroom here, and turn in early. You can bring in my fruit plate when it arrives. In exactly one hour, I'll bet. And one of the drinks, if you can spare it. Please?"

We turned our attention back to dinner. The food was still warm. The extra-thick plates seemed designed to hold their heat. It was all much too good for talking, but after a few bites of the best steak I'd ever eaten, I paused, fork in hand, and asked, "'Hoovered up'? Where did you get that?"

"Some British film at school. I've been waiting to use it on you for months. And you deserved it, after the chainsaw crack."

"You do sing like a chainsaw."

"I meant the snoring."

"Of course you did. Close your bedroom door tonight, okay?" I grinned, sort of. "You really are a loser, you know."

"I know."

"I'm proud of you, little brother. While I've been off at school, you've turned into a pretty good guy. I'm serious. You may be ready for a girlfriend."

It had just dawned on me that I would miss him, when I went back to school. I hadn't before, but now he was worth missing.

"Already have a girlfriend. But proud of me for what again, little sister?" He sounded serious, but he was fishing for compliments.

"You haven't let your worldwide fame go to your head. You're kind to the little people and your sister. You're a gentleman."

He grinned. "Yeah, I'm okay. I have to be, for my parents' sake. My sister didn't turn out so well. She's pretty much a dork."

Yeah, maybe, I thought. And you get a big, long, dorky hug when I leave next week. I might even cry a little. If I'm still alive.

"Loser," I said.

Missed You

MINDY AND HER DEAREST friend, Diana, asked the server to recommend a local wine to accompany the curry at the posh new restaurant near the waterfront. He had them taste a 2019 Bainbridge Island Siegerrebe, "one of the Puget Sound's best and most distinctive offerings." They found it spicy, fragrant, and irresistible. Ordinarily they'd each have ordered a glass, but it was Friday evening, so they ordered the bottle.

Both women found the first glass relaxing. After that, the effects diverged. The second glass turned Diana into a philosopher; some things hadn't changed since they were college roommates. Mindy's second glass depressed her; that hadn't changed either. Her cocktail at the bar before they were seated probably hadn't helped. Diana had wisely sipped a ginger ale.

"I've been thinking," Diana declared. "Men cannot possibly be the meaning of life. If they were, dumping ours would not have felt so liberating."

"I still want one," Mindy griped.

"Me too," said Diana. "A better one. Ours were not the pinnacle, the Space Needle, the Washington Monument of upright, modern manhood."

"I didn't divorce Sam to feel liberated," Mindy said. "It was because he felt so liberated. He must have shared his pinnacle with a dozen other women in the four years we were married. I was oblivious for the first three and a half." She suppressed a hiccup. "Years, not women."

Diana half-filled both their glasses with the rest of the wine. "Men suck. And we're out of wine, which also sucks. Being out of it sucks. The wine itself does not suck."

Mindy raised her glass. "Better make it last. A tiny toast: to the infinite suckitude of greater Seattle's men. But not all of them, Mindy hopes with historically unwarranted optimism."

Diana raised hers. "To the infinitude of male suckitude. And Mindy's undying optimism."

They clicked their glasses together, took a sip, and regarded each other with languid stares.

"I'm not sure *infinitude* is a word," Mindy said solemnly.

"And *suckitude* is?"

"It should be."

"You need a man who gets you," said Diana after a long silence. "Not just your face and smile and figure. Which is looking pretty good for our age. Your figure. And face."

"So do you. And yours too." Mindy raised her glass again. "Tiny toast: to our pretty good but tragically unappreciated figures. And faces."

• • • • • • • • • •

B OB SET DOWN HIS fork, wiped his lips with his cloth napkin, and took a swallow of water. "You said your friend is the chef here?" he asked.

"Yes. Is everything okay?" The VP of Engineering had declared it his personal mission to wine-and-dine Bob into accepting a job offer which, he said, was merely a formality.

"My sea bass is never this good," Bob said. "I'd love to ask him what he's doing that I'm not. Suppose he's too busy to talk on a Friday evening?" He glanced around them. The restaurant wasn't completely overrun.

"Tom's off this weekend, unfortunately," said the VP. "We should have come last night. We could have postponed that exquisite curry at your hotel until tonight. Or you'll just have to move here and ask him later. Our barbecue scene won't meet Texas standards, I'm sure, but the seafood's good."

Manners having the better part of candor, Bob did not reply that the seafood was better in San Antonio, thanks to the warmer water of the Gulf. He smiled faintly instead. "I gather you're not on the Committee for a Lesser Seattle."

The VP chuckled. "I don't think it was ever actually a committee, and I never warmed to the idea of discouraging people from coming here. But I'm impressed. Haven't heard about that in at least a decade."

"I haven't either," Bob confessed. "It's the sort of odd thing I remember."

The VP savored a bite of his steak. "So, Bob, can we agree that this is not a job interview? Just two colleagues—dare I say friends?—out for a fine dinner near the waterfront?"

"Works for me," Bob said.

"Thank you. Are you married? Any children? I can legally ask, since it's not an interview. I'll be happy to tell you about mine."

"No children. I thought I was married, but toward the end, she kind of wasn't."

"Sorry to hear that. Good riddance?"

"It was no picnic for her, being married to a workaholic engineer. She's in graphic design, by the way. She's very good. And I'm less of a workaholic now."

"A healthy evolution," declared the VP. "We heartily endorse that at Bennion Aerospace, as we discussed in your interview, which this isn't. Engineers are more productive when they work reasonable hours and have lives."

Bob smiled. "Couldn't have said it better myself."

"I think that is how you said it."

Bob raised his glass. "Verbatim."

• • • ● • ● ● • • •

"Mindy, Mindy, Mindy, Mindy, Mindy," Diana said expansively. "Who was the last man who really *got* the essential Mindy, made you happy, and didn't ruin things eventually by being himself? Don't say that weirdo from freshman year."

"With the hair?" Mindy asked.

"Right. He was gross. Don't say him."

Mindy silently reviewed her modest resume of former boyfriends, excluding her ex-husband and the weirdo with the hair.

"Well, who?" Diana demanded.

"Pretty far back," Mindy said. "What was that boy's name?"

"What boy?"

"Um, ninth grade."

Diana pursed her lips. "When you lived with your mom? You overestimate my considerable powers. We didn't meet until college, remember?"

"I know that. Myself I was asking." Mindy felt puzzled for a moment but moved on. "He had a huge crush on me. I moved back to Dad's and broke his heart."

"Yours too?"

"Not really. I wanted someone more exciting. He was nice to me though. Liked me how I was. Didn't try to change me."

"I wonder where he is now," Diana mused.

"Probably married with kids. You know, kids like us, when we were kids."

"I wonder where he is now," Diana repeated.

"Not happening, Di."

"Methinks Mindy doth protesteth too much. Tell me anyway. I need to hear about a happy relationship."

Mindy just stared.

"Seriously, Mins. What was it like?"

Mindy sighed. "He came to my junior high volleyball games, even though he was in high school. He was a year older, a sophomore. He was never condes—...con—...He never looked down on me for being in junior high, which I was back then. In junior high."

"I like him already," said Diana. "Tell me more."

. . . . • . • . . .

Tonight's restaurant was just around the corner from Bob's hotel, thank heaven. Jet lag from crossing two time zones should be gone after two days, or so he'd read. This was day three. Then again, his evenings had been filled with late, leisurely dinners, after which it was always at least two hours before he could sleep.

Bennion wanted him, and they weren't shy about it. It had begun to feel extravagant. Much as he enjoyed the forty-dollar piece of fish tonight, a ten-dollar burger—three hours ago—would have been perfect.

On his way to the hotel elevator he passed last evening's restaurant. The curry really was excellent, like the service and the ambiance. Some of tonight's patrons were still visible through the windows.

On the 18th floor an impeccably uniformed young woman from the hotel staff was raising her fist to knock on his door.

"May I help you?" he asked.

She turned to face him. "Mr. Reed?"

"Yes." He hadn't noticed the basket in her other hand, but now she presented it to him. It held a wine bottle and what looked like a selection of expensive chocolate bars.

"This is for you, sir, compliments of . . ."—she hesitated, probably remembering—"Bennion Aerospace."

"Thank you." He took it by the handle and read the card aloud. "Bob, this raspberry wine is a local treasure, made for chocolate. Thanks and best wishes from Bennion Aerospace."

He checked her nametag. "Thank you again, April." He tipped her a ten instead of a five. It felt very late, and she was the image of professionalism.

"My pleasure, sir, and thank you. Good night."

He set the basket near the oversized television in his room. He would fly home tomorrow morning. Some of the chocolate could be breakfast, and he could pack the rest, but he should probably just leave the wine for the hotel staff.

He picked up the bottle, studied the label, and changed his mind. Was there a safe way to pack a wine bottle in a checked bag? He should stop by the hotel gift shop before settling in for the night. They might have something.

• • • • • • • • •

"H E WANTED TO LEARN about volleyball," Mindy said, "to understand my games, so he took me to high school games we could watch together. Which I wanted to see them anyway."

"Get to the romance," Diana commanded. "Diana needs romance."

"We held hands a lot. A lot a lot a lot. He said I was pretty, but I didn't believe him, because braces and gangly legs and stuff. He laughed at my jokes. And listening to me talk. He was good at that. Talked not so much about himself."

"You have to go back to ninth grade for a nice guy who was that nice to you?" asked Diana. "That's so pathetically sad."

"I know, right? He kissed me once if he could ask me. No, wait." She spoke more slowly. "Asked if he could kiss me."

"And you said . . ."

"I said he didn't have to ask, just do it. He said, 'I like you, Mindy.'" She looked up at her friend. "That was my name then. Mindy. Just like now. Mindy. He asked, not to . . . because he didn't want to scare me away." Mindy sighed loudly. "It was right before Christmas. I remember he gave me a nice gift, but I don't remember what it was."

"And?"

"I gave him a movie gift card or something."

"Not my question."

"What?"

"Did he kiss you?"

Mindy nodded slowly. "My first kiss. It was nice. Then I broke his heart and came back to live with Dad. He had emergency surgery, I mean Dad, and he needed help for a while, so I went back to Mom's to get my stuff, then finished school here. I wrote to him. Not Dad. The boy. A letter. After he wrote to me. Also a letter. He wrote to me again, and I didn't, and that was all."

"You must have liked him less than he liked you."

"I wanted someone more exciting. Did I say that already? I saw him when I spent Mom with Christmas during senior year. He was home from college, and a girlfriend. We just said hi and saw when . . . when we saw each other at church."

"I wonder where he is now," Diana said.

"I already said that," Mindy said. "No, you did. Stop saying that."

"I wonder where he is now," Diana repeated.

"I wasn't the same Mindy then, even if I had the same name: Mindy."

"I wonder where he is now."

"Let it die, Di."

"I wonder . . . Okay, I get it," she said. "What can we learn from this? Where do we find men to really get us? And adore us? And lavish us with kisses, etc.?"

"Let me know if you find mine," Mindy said. "I'm closing my eyes for a minute." She sat back and slipped into a haze.

· · · · **·** · **·** · · ·

THE INFLATABLE WINE BOTTLE protector inspired confidence in Bob—as it should, since it cost half of what he guessed was the price of the bottle. He pumped it up to test it overnight for leaks. He'd pack it in the morning.

He sampled some chocolate before he brushed his teeth. It was exquisite. If the wine was equally good, it would be worth the effort.

Pausing to fold some loose receipts into his wallet, he noticed that his Visa card wasn't in its usual place. He searched his wallet, then his pockets, then everywhere he'd been in the room since returning from the gift shop.

He didn't clearly remember putting it away after paying there. He resigned himself to another trip downstairs.

. . . . **.** . **.** . . .

"**I** WISH YOU WEREN'T leaving tomorrow," Diana said.

Mindy didn't open her eyes. "I'll be back in a month. I promised Dad and Stepmom—she's not my real mom; she's a whole different person—and I'd start visiting more. Need you to escape. For me to escape. So be here, okay?"

"I'll be here." Her tone brightened. "You should stalk him on social media."

"My dad?"

"Are you drunk? The boy from ninth grade."

"I'm not on social media," Mindy said. "Like the plague I avoid. It."

"I'll stalk him for you. What's his name?"

"Bobby Reed. R–E–E–E–D, I think."

"Yeah, I'll bet." Diana tapped at her phone. "Foothills High, Class of 2006? A year ahead of you?"

"Did you find him?" Mindy asked. "I mean, already did you find? Him? Already?"

"Just gathering data. What else do you know? College? Friends? Family?"

"His sister was my grade. Sally, short for something. Not Sarah. But not short. She was taller than me."

· · · · ● · ● · · ·

Bob retrieved his card without difficulty, then basked in the relief of not having to cancel and replace it. A moment later he added the relief of not having run into a restaurant door face-first, when two giggling women threw it open and rode a seductive waft of curry out into the lobby. He'd stopped to examine last night's menu in the adjacent window, then failed to give the doors a wide enough berth as he moved away.

Had he been slightly less alert, he'd have at least a headache now, and he might have left the women with some bruises or worse. In his embarrassment he'd barely looked at them as they apologized to him, and he to them. They seemed cheerful and somewhat lubricated as they ambled away.

· · · · ● · ● · · ·

Mindy and Diana lounged quietly in the back seat of their Uber for the first few minutes.

Mindy sat upright. "Salomea."

"What?" Diana asked. "What does that mean?"

"Her . . . his sister's name. Tall for Sally. Long for Sally, I meant."

"Unusual name. Good clue."

"It means peace, I think," Mindy said.

"Peace is good," said Diana.

"If we had more wine, we should drink to peace."

· · · · ● · ● · · ·

Bob had worried too much, probably, about waking up to catch the hotel's airport shuttle to SeaTac at 6:00 a.m. It was now 4:30 a.m., and he couldn't get back to sleep.

His first-ever trip to Seattle had grown tedious. They'd offer him the job managing some pretty good engineers, but the past two days had convinced him he didn't want it. The work was interesting, but the culture was wrong. Bob's prospective new boss, just under the VP, was prone to shift blame and talk behind people's backs, among other evident vices. Perhaps that explained the vacancy.

By 5:15 a.m. he was dressed, packed, ready to check out—and still too early. He sat at the desk and opened his laptop for some work.

"I had a friend in Seattle once," his assistant had written at the end of a housekeeping e-mail from late yesterday.

So did he, but he couldn't recall who. He leaned back and closed his eyes. It took a minute, but it came to him. She'd said, "I'm going back to Seattle, Bobby." What was her name? Her leaving had ruined his Christmas break that year. January too.

Mindy Johnson.

He remembered her in her volleyball uniform. Purple kneepads. Blonde, straight, shoulder-length hair. Happy smile after a win. She moved like an athlete—a cute, smart, girl-next-door sort of athlete. She was the best player on the team, but there wasn't a vain bone in her body. He'd been head over heels. Where was she now?

She was his first heartbreak. He'd had much greater heartbreaks since. His divorce, for example. The last two years of his marriage before that.

He typed her name in the Facebook search box, knowing there would be thousands of Mindy Johnsons. None of them had mutual friends with him, but that had been a long shot. Besides, she probably wasn't Mindy Johnson anymore.

What was her mother's remarried name? It was unusual. Maybe he could find her that way. Aha. How many Maureen Schwabedissens could there be?

Facebook didn't help, and Instagram was mostly for the young. The stepdad's name was Bill, he thought, and there were some William Schwabedissens, but none with ties to the old town, and the ages were wrong. He googled obituaries to no avail.

At a free people-finding site he'd used for a class reunion, he found her mom and stepdad still alive, in their early 70s, living at the address he remembered. He coughed up a dollar for a one-time trial to get more information, but the only possible relative listed for either spouse was the other. No children at all, though he remembered a son too, not just Mindy.

What if she wasn't really a daughter? He didn't remember her looking like her mom. What if they just said that to avoid embarrassing her or someone else, but she was really a niece or something? Or a foster child? Or the daughter of a close friend? Maybe she and her little brother were in witness protection now.

It was 5:45 a.m. The investigation was over. It was getting silly anyway.

On the shuttle he checked the Southwest app. His flight was on time. He'd arranged his own travel, so they wouldn't waste money on first class. His spot in the boarding order for the Las Vegas leg was A-49. He'd get the aisle seat he wanted, probably just behind the exit rows but close to the wing, for the smoothest ride.

He was past airport security when he learned his flight had been cancelled and he'd miss his connection to San Antonio. They put him on a later flight to Denver, connecting to an even later flight home, which was fine. He wasn't hurrying home to a date or anything. They were nice enough to bump him up to the priority group, the first 15 people to board, so he wouldn't get stuck in a middle seat. They even waived the fee for that. It probably helped that he'd smiled and spoken calmly with the agent.

Grounded until mid-afternoon, he alternately worked and dozed in the main terminal until lunchtime. After some decent fish and chips from a place called Louie's, he found a seat near his gate and dove back into work.

· · · ● · ● · ● · ● · ·

M INDY'S MID-AFTERNOON FLIGHT HOME to Denver was boarding B-1 through B-30 when she reached the gate, and she was B-18. It was perfect timing, except that she'd broken an unladylike sweat getting there.

A window seat over the wing was empty. The man on the aisle lifted her carry-on into the overhead bin. She thanked him with a smile, and they settled into their seats.

She sneaked a good look as he fiddled with his seat belt. Business casual, a bit over average height, not noticeably overweight, about her age, empty ring finger, dirty blond hair that was short but not too short, and what she could see despite his mask suggested a pleasing, masculine face. She'd noticed his eyes first thing.

If the middle seat stayed empty, maybe they could chat. So far, all she'd heard was, "Sure, let me get that for you" and "My pleasure." He had a cheerful, gentle baritone.

Five minutes later, a younger man with dark hair, earrings, and a few days' growth squeezed into the middle seat. She caught him checking her out. When he tried to strike up a conversation with her, she was polite but not chatty or the least bit encouraging. By the time the flight was taxiing and the attendants began demonstrating seat belts and life vests, he'd retreated to a video on his phone.

She glanced past him. Aisle Seat Guy was watching the life vest demonstration. She guessed that flight attendants noticed and appreciated things like that. When it was over, he opened a book.

· · · · • · • · • · · ·

THEY BLAMED AIR TRAFFIC control problems in Denver, when they explained that the flight would sit on the ramp for 30 minutes or more before takeoff. They said it was okay to use cell phones, even if the aircraft door was closed. Bob settled in for a long wait.

The man in the middle seat had tried to get the woman next to him involved in conversation, but she'd had none of it. Now he hunched over his phone, watching something, and she appeared to be asleep. Bob looked just long enough to appreciate her shoulder-length blonde hair and a nice figure for a woman roughly his age.

How would she look without the mask? Maybe she'd wake up and take it off when they brought snacks and drinks.

His phone vibrated. He tapped a button and said softly, "Bob Reed."

It was the VP. "Bob, Devin Straight. I called to say we just sent an offer, so when you can, please take a look."

"Thank you, Devin. I will."

"I shouldn't tell you this, but there's room to negotiate. I know you have other offers."

Bob had one other offer, plus a good current gig.

"I appreciate that," he said. "I'm on a plane, but I'll take a look and get back to you Monday morning."

"Perfect. You know, Seattle's a great place to live."

"I get that impression. Thanks again for your hospitality. Looking forward to wine and chocolate."

"You're more than welcome. Have a good flight. Hear from you soon."

Bob allowed himself another appreciative glance at the dozing woman in the window seat. Mid-thirties, give or take. And he still liked what he could see of her figure. Realistic but plenty attractive.

After nearly an hour, the plane started to move again.

· · · • · • · • · ·

MINDY AWOKE AFTER TAKEOFF and opened her eyes just long enough to see—but there was nothing interesting to see. Not without leaning forward to see the man on the aisle. That would be too obvious, and it might encourage Middle Seat Guy. She closed her eyes.

Sometime later she heard a flight attendant taking drink orders, but she wasn't thirsty. Someone in front of her asked if they were serving wine again, after everything went away for the pandemic, but they weren't.

Wine hadn't helped Mindy last night, excellent though it was. It had only sent Diana on a silly goose chase on her behalf and prompted long-forgotten memories of that boy. What were the chances that he was still—or ever—as kind as she remembered?

She pretended to sleep until the others' drinks arrived, then noted with satisfaction that she felt genuinely sleepy again.

· · · • · • · • · ·

T HE MAN IN THE middle seat stirred. "Excuse me," he said to Bob. "Could I get out for a few minutes?"

Bob looked up. "Of course." He slipped a business card into his book to mark his place. "Going forward or aft?"

"The back."

Bob moved forward into the aisle, and the man moved stiffly toward the aft lavatories. Bob sat, replaced his seat belt, and looked for a moment, then another moment, at the sleeping form by the window. She was pretty, in the girl-next-door way he preferred.

When the younger man returned, they buckled into their seats again, and Bob reopened his book.

· • • ● • ● • • ·

M INDY AWOKE ONLY ENOUGH to note that they were descending, and a flight attendant was talking about connecting flights, which didn't apply to her. Denver was her destination. She faded back into sleep, idly wondering why it came so easily when it wasn't time to sleep.

· • • ● • ● • • ·

T HEY'D CANCELLED CONNECTING FLIGHTS to other Texas cities, and Bob worried about his. They assured him it was still on the board and running almost as late, so his connection would be fine.

A few minutes later, a flight attendant came over the PA system again. "Ladies and gentlemen, nine of you are connecting on Flight 2810 to St. Louis. That flight leaves about 15 minutes after we roll up, and the door closes ten minutes before that. So here's what we'll do. We'll ask the rest of you to keep your seats until those nine passengers have disembarked. Then we'll deboard as usual. Don't worry. You'll make your connections too. We really appreciate your help with this.

"For you nine St. Louis passengers, go immediately one gate to your right, and that's your flight. They're holding the door open just long enough for you to get there. Have your boarding pass ready. If you checked baggage, I'm afraid it will have to go on the next flight. If you have only a carry-on, you'll be fine. If any of this is a problem or you have other concerns, hit the call button and we'll figure it out. There's a later flight to St. Louis tonight, if you need it."

"Nice of them," said the other man to Bob. "That's my connection."

"Did you check bags?" Bob asked.

"Nope. Just a carry-on."

"Your lucky day," Bob said.

• • • ● • ● • • • •

M INDY AWOKE WHEN THE tires hit the runway. Once again, sleeping had made the flight seem short.

A flight attendant came over the PA system, asking everyone to let nine St. Louis passengers out first, to make their flight before it left. Mindy was pleased to discover that Middle Seat Guy was one of them. The man in the aisle seat helped him retrieve a very heavy carry-on from the overhead bin, then sat back down. A few others passed by, and then the normal deboarding process began from the front. It would take a few minutes to reach her row.

"You connecting?" she asked the man with the deep, pleasant voice and beautiful grey eyes.

"San Antonio. You?"

"This is home." She yawned behind her mask. "Pardon me."

"Home sounds really good right now," he said.

"Home to your family?" she asked.

"Home to my tropical fish tank, a TV remote that works, and my very own bed. Especially the pillow."

"I don't even have a goldfish," she said. "I had a cat for a while, but I like to be in charge when I'm home."

He chuckled musically. That and his eyes told her she would like his smile, if he weren't masked. "Did you enjoy the flight?" she asked. "I pretty much slept through it."

"Good book," he said, "but your way sounds better. I'll try it on the next leg."

She smiled under her mask. Just talking to this stranger made her happy.

Their row was next. He helped her with her carry-on again, then stood back to let her into the aisle ahead of him. "Have a good evening," he said.

"Thanks," she replied. "Have a safe flight." A thought struck, and she felt her eyes twinkle. "Pleasant dreams."

$$\cdot \cdot \cdot \bullet \cdot \bullet \cdot \cdot \cdot$$

BOB TRIED NOT TO watch the woman too much or too rudely, as he followed her up the jetway. His stomach produced a timely growl, and he let it distract him. Lunch was hours ago, and breakfast had barely happened at all.

He checked the departure monitors immediately. Boarding for San Antonio would start in 25 minutes, four gates down. There was a hamburger place on the way. He didn't know Smashburger, and it didn't sound particularly appetizing, but the line was long enough to be promising and short enough to get him to his flight in time, so he joined it.

· · · · · ● · ● · · · ·

Denver was Mindy's home airport, so she knew all about the Smashburger—and she really, really wanted one. The fancy tots too, with rosemary and olive oil. But she was a grown-up, and grown-ups have to resist sometimes. After a much-needed visit to the restroom, she gave Smashburger a wide berth. She refused even to look at it—longingly—on her way past.

She moved out of the foot traffic and stopped. There was no rush. She had no checked bags to retrieve, and a girl deserved a hearty meal after a long flight.

No, she thought, a girl deserved a healthful meal. She didn't keep her not-quite-girlish figure on burgers and Smash Tots. She resumed walking.

A message arrived from Diana. "Sorry, Mins. I give up. There are lots of Salomeas and a million Sally Reeds, but I didn't find your guy. Sorry."

It would have been fun to know, Mindy thought, but it was a fantasy anyway. She'd never see Bobby Reed again. If she did, she wouldn't recognize him. If she recognized him, she might not like him. If she liked him, he probably wouldn't be available. If he was available, he probably wouldn't want her. And there was a good chance he wasn't as nice now as she remembered.

But somewhere she needed to find a man who cared about her the way he had, when she was in ninth grade. A man who got the essential Mindy. But where to look next?

· · · · · ● · ● · · · ·

O N THE FLIGHT TO San Antonio, Bob had a row to himself. He sat back in his aisle seat, closed his eyes, and found himself envisioning the woman from his earlier flight. She was easy on the eyes, well dressed, looked professional. He would like to have seen her entire face—ideally her smile—without the mask.

It was too bad about the guy in the middle seat. At least the flight would have passed more quickly. His brief conversation with her was pleasant enough.

Where was Mindy Johnson now? What did she look like? What was her life like? Was that even her real name and her real family? Would he recognize her? Would she remember him, if they chanced to meet?

Was she still in Seattle? Not that he would be back there soon. He hadn't opened the offer yet, but he wasn't taking the job.

He smiled wryly, consciously chose distant memories from his sophomore year over present and future what-if's, and began to fade away.

Acknowledgments

There are twelve short stories and a novella in this collection. Every one of them made its way through a friendly but discerning gauntlet called Good AF Writers (AF is for American Fork), a chapter of the League of Utah Writers. More than a dozen writers there offered helpful critique of at least one of these tales; some saw most or nearly all of them over the past several years. Among them I particularly thank Tim Tarbet, Paul Warburton, Karen Felt, Gayelynn Watson, Cassandra Carlson, Sean Jones, Melissa Lundquist, Dustin Steinacker, and Rebekah Walker—not only for their thoughtful critiques of multiple stories in this collection, but also for years of friendship and encouragement.

My critique partner Silvia O'Dwyer provided valuable early feedback and encouragement for some of these tales.

The stories which were previously published each had at least one editor. Among these I especially thank Emily Wheeler. Her insightful notes on "There Might Be Another Way" went beyond commas and a few typos and pointed the way to a stronger story.

Finally, writing is not separate from life. I could scarcely measure or fully categorize the blessings of friends, neighbors, and family. A writer needs a life, and mine overflows with extraordinary souls. I thank them all.

"Utterly charming . . . clever and kind."
—2025 Utah Book Awards

a 2025 Utah Book Awards Notable Read
winner of a 2024 Bronze Quill Award

In *Poor As I Am* (a novella) two grad students meet in a story of five Christmas Eves. Will the money he doesn't have or the money she doesn't want get in the way? Or does love conquer all, especially at Christmas? Then, in eight short stories, two eleven-year-old detectives investigate a Christmas mystery, a girl in a reindeer costume craves a Christmas kiss from Santa, and more.

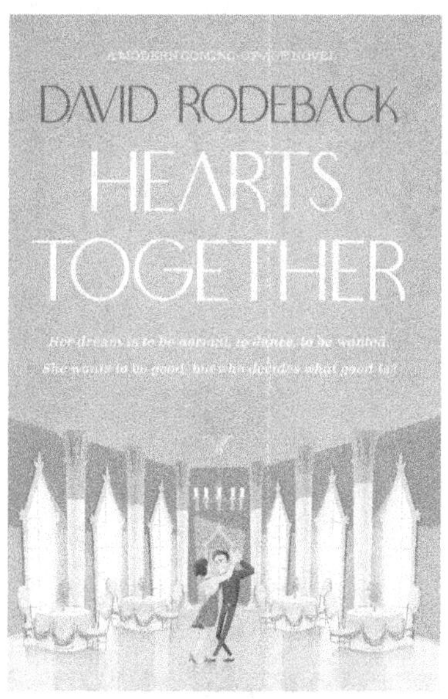

High school sophomore Jenny Miller goes to dances but doesn't dance. Sitting is safer, in case she has a seizure. When she meets a boy who likes to sit and talk with her, an unexpected but welcome adventure begins. He even persuades her to dance with him.

It's not quite the blissful romance of her dreams. He's an athlete, and he's too popular to be interested in a girl like her—according to other girls, and she fears it might be true. Then jealousy turns to bullying.

Meanwhile, these two believing Latter-day Saints are breaking a few of the many dating rules they learned at church, where some are eager to judge and to assume the worst.

Amid rumors, judgments, and bullying that turns breathtakingly cruel, can they face another day? Is fitting in at school or church worth the price? Is love? And which of the many things they hear at church does God actually expect them to obey?

A long novel for teen and adult readers who enjoy long novels.

About the Author

David Rodeback had eleven Christmases in Boulder, Colorado, then nine in rural Southeast Idaho. Santa has since found him in Pennsylvania, Idaho again, upstate New York, and lately in Utah.

He served a two-year mission in western Pennsylvania and New York for the Church of Jesus Christ of Latter-day Saints, then completed degrees at Brigham Young University and Cornell University. He is Chief Marketing Technology Officer at a Utah manufacturing company.

He has worked as a speech writer, editor, translator, and writing instructor; has won a Telly Award as a writer for commercial video; has managed and advised political campaigns; has spent more than 30 years in lay leadership in his church (but prefers to teach); has blogged off and on for two decades on topics from politics to faith; and has seen exactly 66 words of his writing carved in stone. Since beginning to write fiction almost a decade ago, he has won a handful of prizes for short fiction.

He and his wife have four children and two grandchildren.

Let's Connect!

David is easy to find on Facebook (authorDavidRodeback), and at Medium, Simily, Goodreads, and Amazon, or you can connect more directly here:

Author website: DavidRodeback.com
Blog: BendableLight.com
E-mail: author@davidrodeback.com

Want to bring David to your classroom, writing group, or other venue, in person or virtually? Inquire at the e-mail address above.

Sign up for David's quarterly e-mail **newsletter** with this QR code. (It points to DavidRodeback.com.)